NICARAGUAN HELL

NICARAGUAN HELL

BY

DORAN INGRHAM

BOOK # 4

IN THE

MARK INGRAM SAGA

Cover by Ken Farmer

THE AUTHOR

Doran W. Ingrham — Inactive US Marine — Vietnam Veteran. Retired Risk Management/Close Security Specialist (call sign 'Zorro'). Extensive global experience dealing with terrorist threats, drug cartels and despot leaders of third world countries.

He has a vast working knowledge of weapons, explosives, urban, jungle and desert survival skills as well as intel gathering used for covert (Black Ops) actions and Executive Protection. International Combat Pistol and Sniper competitor. He also has numerous appearances in film, television series and commercials. Doran now lives with his wife, Maria Mae...exact location undisclosed.

DEDICATION

This novel is dedicated to all the men, women and MWD K-9s who stand in harm's way to defend and protect the United States of America, especially our wounded warriors. I am forever grateful for your sacrifice. In addition, I dedicate this book to the Risk Management Specialists I worked with around the globe providing security for our clients. In your memory and honor I will keep the tales of our work as close to the truth as allowed by law and common sense. I promise never to divulge your true identity.

ACKNOWLEDGMENTS

First, and always, I thank my wife, Maria Mae, for her endless support and encouragement. Second, I must give a nod to Buck Stienke and Ken Farmer. I would not be a published author today without their invitation to coauthor "Black Eagle Force: Blood Ivory". Their advice and guidance is invaluable while writing each and every novel in the Mark Ingram Adventure series. Last, but not least, I appreciate all the readers and fans who keep the fire burning to write another story based on the years working as a Risk Management Specialist.

ISBN-13: - **978-0-9962483-0-3** - Paper
ISBN-10: - **0996248307**
ISBN-13: - **978-0-9962483-1-0** - E
ISBN-10: - **0996248315**

Timber Creek Press
Imprint of Timber Creek Productions, LLC
312 N. Commerce St.
Gainesville, Texas

Contact Us:
Published by: Timber Creek Press
timbercreekpresss@yahoo.com
www.timbercreekpress.net
Twitter: @pagact
Facebook Book Page:
www.facebook.com/TimberCreekPress

First printing - 3 April, 2015

This novel is a work of fiction...except the parts that aren't. Names, characters, places and incidents are either the products of the author's imaginations or are used fictitiously...and sometimes not. Any resemblance to actual persons, living or dead, business establishments, events or locales is entirely coincidental...except where they aren't.

BLACK EAGLE FORCE: FOURTH REICH (Book #5)
By Buck Stienke and Ken Farmer
www.tinyurl.com/befreich
BLOOD BROTHERS - Doran Ingrham, Buck Stienke
and Ken Farmer
www.tinyurl.com/bloodbrothers1
DARK SECRET - Doran Ingrham
http://tinyurl.com/darksecret-2
BLACK STAR BAY by T.C. Miller
Http://amzn.to/1oYSFO6

HISTORICAL FICTION WESTERN

THE NATIONS by Ken Farmer and Buck Stienke
Www.tinyurl.com/the-nations-Bass
Audio version: www.tinyurl.com/NationsAudio
HAUNTED FALLS by Ken Farmer and Buck Stienke
Www.tinyurl.com/haunted-falls-Bass
Audio version: www.tinyurl.com/HauntedFallsAudio
HELL HOLE by Ken Farmer
Www.tinyurl.com/hell-hole-Bass3
Audio version: www.tinyurl.com/HellHoleAudio
ACROSS the RED by Ken Farmer and Buck Stienke
Www.tinyurl.com/AcrossRed
DEVIL'S CANYON by Buck Stienke
Www.tinyurl.com/devils-canyon-B

SYFY

LEGEND of AURORA by Ken Farmer and Buck Stienke
www.tinyurl.com/LegendAurora-E
AURORA: INVASION by Ken Farmer and Buck Stienke
www.tinyurl.com/AuroraInvasion

Coming Soon

MILITARY ACTION/TECHNO
BLACK EAGLE FORCE: ISIS by Buck Stienke and Ken Farmer
BLACK STAR MOUNTAIN by T.C. Miller
EL ZORRO PLATA by Doran Ingrham

HISTORICAL FICTION WESTERN
BASS and the LADY by Ken Farmer & Buck Stienke
Book five of the Bass Reeves Saga

COMMENTS

Packing enough heat, heroics, and danger at every turn, readers who enjoy action-filled stories wrought with mercenaries and military types ridding the world of evil one bullet and one bad guy at a time, will devour this third book in the Mark Ingram adventure series, Nicaraguan Hell. In dialogue laced with irreverent humor and authentic jargon straight from the author's life as a young Marine in Vietnam and later as a "risk management specialist," Doran Ingrham reels you in with a protagonist who is charming but doesn't suffer fools lightly. With each turn of the page, you will swear you're deep in the jungles of Nicaragua, and once you take care of the bad guys, all you want to do is get out alive. - Kathleen M. Rodgers, award-winning author of The Final Salute

"The Mark Ingram Adventure novels by Doran Ingrham are guaranteed to raise your heart rate with authentic adrenaline-pumping, nonstop action. Consult a cardiologist before reading. The brutally realistic action races from page one to conclusion as you march side-by-side with one of the best action heroes today in the underbelly of international intrigue." - T.c. Thomas ~ Retired Military, Hakkorya Jutitsu Martial Artist, Best selling Author of the Black Star action adventure series: Black Star Bay and Black Star Bomber

"I know first hand about the world Doran Ingrham writes. I worked twenty-five years as a Risk Management Specialist. As he points out so well, it is not glamorous or sexy. It is a dark, ugly, dangerous world. I am certain he lived the life he writes about. Only someone who has could portray the business as he does. I am always looking forward to his next book. - Robert 'Slash' Thompson ~ Former Navy SEAL, Retired Risk Management Specialist

"The Mark Ingram Adventures series might have been ripped straight from the real life of the author, who worked for years in "risk management." His own lifetime of adventures translate to page after page of exhilarating excitement for the reader. Doran Ingrham's books make one feel that they are not only watching the action, but are right in the middle of it." - Fred L. Funk, Fred L. Funk, award winning author: Ministry and Moonshine.

TIMBER CREEK PRESS

CHAPTER ONE

AMERRISQUE MOUNTAINS
Nicaragua
December 14, 2004

"Range…550…wind one quarter factor…right," DeLeon, muscular former Colombian DEA sergeant and spotter for Mark Ingram said quietly.

"Target?"

"Fifth rider…Grey horse…Range 525…"

Mark—wearing a ghillee suit—lay on his poncho under the cover of a low dog seed tree branch. His M14 National Match rifle—lovingly referred to as Betsy—was resting on his hydration pack aimed at the advancing column of men. He made an adjustment to his Nightforce Scope. Satisfied with the doping, he slowed his breathing, let a breath out half-way and squeezed the trigger.

Colonel Alfredo Hernandez Sacasa never heard the sound of the shot—due to the titanium suppressor. The .308 round impacted his chest just below the neck throwing his lifeless body onto the rump of his mount. The animal felt his rider shift on his back causing it to bolt forward as the dead man slid off hitting the rocky ground and tumbled down the mountainside.

The men under the Colonel's command scrambled for cover and began to fire wildly—without any clue as to where the shot came from.

"We go now?"

"Yup…only getting paid for El Bastardo Negro…Got no quarrel with the others."

Both men eased back from the shooting position and began packing their equipment. A single round impacted the tree above them causing both to hug the ground.

"You think they know where we are, Zorro?"

"Nope…if they did there'd be more than one round. Let's get the hell out of here before they figure it out."

With their weapons and equipment collected they scrambled down the backside of the mountain to the three tough mountain mules they had tied to a picket line.

In a matter of minutes the they rode off with DeLeon leading the pack animal.

"Who hired us to kill the scourge of Nicaragua?" DeLeon asked.

"Hal took the contract…"

"No, I mean who hired Hal."

"Hell…no idea. Don't care," Mark said before taking a swallow from his CamelBak drinking tube.

"He had a family. I saw them on the news…"

"Don't care."

ORO del CHRISTI MINE
Nicaragua
JUNE 11, 2014

Three black SUV vehicles and a US military surplus six ton truck drove in the damaged gate and stopped in the center of the compound. Crank—a 6'2", former Navy SEAL with blonde hair—the team leader, Rhino—retired South African Commando at 6'4" with black hair—and a team of well-armed international operatives jumped out, setting up a defensive perimeter immediately. The only thing that had changed since the assault and destruction by Nortino's rebel force on the mine previously was a new mass grave for the dead.

The equipment and demolished buildings remained as they did when the rebel forces withdrew. Structures were burned and partially destroyed. Huge earth moving equipment and rock crushers as well, showed evidence of explosive charges rendering them useless.

"Striker…high ground," Crank ordered, pointing at the demolished guard shack on a small rise. "Katana…sweep the buildings."

Without responding Striker and his spotter sprinted from cover to cover, working their way up the steep mound of tailings near the center of the main compound. Katana used hand signals to direct his three man team to what had been the workers barracks before trotting off in the lead.

"Yahbo…You're a natural bro" Rhino said in his thick Afrikaner accent—his Galil R4 South African manufactured rifle at the ready sweeping the area.

"Cheyenne…Badger…Malakhi…run the jungle. Weapon teams download the heavies. Set up in a triangle there…there…and…on top of that building." Crank pointed out the positions he preferred.

Men scrambled to unload the Browning .50 caliber machine guns and ammo from the cargo truck before moving to the locations ordered.

"Commo?" Rhino asked as he shouldered the main radio on his massive back.

Crank answered with a look to his number two. "That small building…it'll do. Let's get this place battened down! A Tsunami's coming our way…let's fuck 'em up…fuck 'em down…fuck 'em all around," he yelled to everyone as they spread out following his orders.

"Ja…we gonna have some fun tonight," Rhino said as he carried the communications gear to the shack.

An hour later Crank held the first field meeting. "Bad guys are bound to know we've landed. Katana, you take three men…set the claymores and trip flares as soon as it's dark. Striker, pick a hide...take Poncho with you as a spotter."

"Good to go where I am," the former French Legionnaire sniper replied.

"Bunker down...harden your position with what ever you find. Rhino...Splinter...on me with the commo. Get us linked in with the Honduras Army...Shit gets real, I want gunships headed our way, ASAP."

"What about *comeda*?" Poncho, the small ex-Honduras Army sergeant asked.

"Eat 'em cold," Crank replied as he marched off like a big cat on the hunt toward the burned-out building housing the field radio with a SAW on his shoulder.

"Surfer dude seems to like his new role, he does," Rhino said with a smile and a silly British style palm open salute to the others before following him.

Night had fallen two hours prior. The men waited in darkness for an attack they felt certain would come before dawn.

"Splinter...pass the word. Rotate the heavies fifty yards clock wise, one at a time," Crank ordered.

The slender black-haired former Army Ranger from Georgia slipped out of the building without a word and belly-crawled through the rubble to the closest machine gun team.

"Sweet," Rhino whispered.

"If the assholes have been watching, they fixed our positions since we set up. Based on the damage here...they have RPGs at least. Maybe mortars. No sense in giving 'em any advantage."

"Roger that mate. I'm going to give another jingle to the girls in uniform. Make sure someone is still on the line." Rhino picked up the handset of the Falcon II 150.

"When you're done we move...get under that big hunk of burned out machinery." He pointed to a huge rock crusher...

SANTA BARBARA, BRAZIL
Highway

Mark pulled over on the shoulder of the paved two-lane road and gazed down on the valley below. The tree covered hillsides and ravines gave way to open grass meadows that stretched as far as the eye could see. *Ain't Texas...but it'll do.*

A Park Ranger vehicle passed, then slowed and stopped. The driver stepped out and started back to Mark. *"Olá Senhor Carson. Muito bom te ver de novo."*

"Ola Sergio. Work with me...my Portuguese is pretty rusty. How are you?"

"I am good. You are good?"

"Very good. Nearly home."

"Yes...you have been gone a long time now. How long you stay this time?"

"Not sure yet. Good to see you again. I should get back on the road. Want to arrive before sundown." Mark looked back down the way he came.

"Yes...yes of course. You call on me if you need some things. By the way...how is my English?"

"Very good. You have studied hard since I last saw you."

"It is necessary. So many American tourist come now for vacation. Drive safe my friend."

"Sergio…Any Chinese tourists?"

"No. Not that I know of. Why do you ask?"

"They seem to be buying up land every where these days. Just wondered if they had made it here yet."

Mark turned onto a gravel road that led to his gate an hour before sun down. He entered a numerical code, and then placed his finger tips on the recognition pad. As he waited for the slow moving gate to open, a familiar voice came over the intercom.

"What is the password?"

"Zorro," he answered knowing full well his old friend could see him on the security camera feed.

"I fire up the grill, *mi amigo*."

CHOLUTECA, HONDURAS
Batt Energy Technology Office

Malcom Winslow stood studying a geological survey map of Choluteca Province laid out on a large wooden table. The ceiling fan turned lazily above him stirring the hot humid air. He used a red highlighter to mark locations of the most interest to his employer—John Batt. Using the latest technology, including satellite imaging, the fifty year old engineer painstakingly worked on what his employer was gambling to be the next big find for his company.

BOOM!

An explosion rocked the building, rattling the glass and causing several items on the long table near the open windows to topple to the floor. Winslow dropped to his knees, crawled under the table, curled up in a ball covering his head.

The electricity flickered, and then the lights went off. *Damn! I can't wait to be out of this third world shit hole. This is the second rebel attack in four days.*

CHOLUTECA, HONDURAS
El Blanco Gato Apartments

Reynoldo Bolanos watched the cloud of smoke and dust rising over the city skyline before walking back into the one bedroom hideout with a smile. In his hand he held a cheap throw away cell phone that he had used to trigger the bomb at the electric power station two blocks away. As he detached the battery and crushed the phone under his heel, he spoke to his associate in Spanish, "That will keep them busy, la Rata."

"Si, Reynoldo. We go now?" Cisco asked. His small frame bent due to spina bifida. His pockmarked facial features were sharp and gaunt. All of that and the fact his two upper front teeth protruded significantly, garnered him the nickname, la Rata—the rat. Yet, no one questioned his skills with explosives.

"We wait. The police and military will be stopping and questioning everyone for hours. Open the bottle of tequila. We will have a celebratory toast to your good work."

Cisco moved to the cupboard, opened the grime-stained sagging door with his left hand—missing the first two fingers and thumb—as he spoke, "As you wish, Reynoldo. I am anxious to get out of the city and back to the countryside. I feel trapped...suffocating in this mass of..."

"Tomorrow my friend...or...the next day. If we are apprehended by the authorities we will never get back to our families. Patience. Each blow we strike here in the city delays the imperialist foreigners three fold in their efforts to exploit our resources and...our people."

TEGUCIGALPA, HONDURAS
ZETA Compound

Oscar Puto relaxed on recliner covered with a dark red woven cloth bearing ornate designs indicative of the long gone Mayan culture. A pair of young blonde amply endowed American girls—wearing Brazilian bikinis—played pool on the ornate table.

His residence was located south of the capital city and consisted of several hundred acres. The colonial style buildings—stone covered in white plaster with red tile roofs—were laid out in a square covering five acres with connecting eight foot walls. Like many high ranking cartel members, he lived an opulent life style—exotic foreign automobiles, a private Gulf Stream G650 Jet as well as AugustaWestland AW101 helicopter and a stable of expensive race horses. His appetite for pleasure required a steady turnover of beautiful women.

He took a sip of fine cognac, dipped the butt of his Cuban cigar in the fiery liquid before drawing in and exhaling a blue cloud of smoke. A dozen flat screen televisions covered the wall in front of him. He was obsessed with the news and, though not relying on mainstream media for his intelligence gathering, he reveled in the broadcasts that involved his illicit business.

He used a remote to increase the volume from the screen playing the TeleProgreso Honduras National TV station. A middle-aged male reporter stood in front of the carnage inflicted on the city.

"Today in central Tegucigalpa a suspected terrorist attack on the main electric switching station has resulted in massive outages for the inhabitants of our capital city. Though no terrorist group has yet claimed responsibility for the act, one of our inside sources told us it has all the signs of being la Rata and El Fantasma Revolución de Honduras."

Photographs of Cisco and several other known members of the EFRH flashed onto the screen as the announcer continued, "It is well known the rebel group wants the latest National Congress of Honduras trade and concessions agreements with foreigners revoked. Off the record, a member of Congress said that attempts to reconcile disagreements with the rebel forces are presently at a standstill. President-elect Juan Orlando Alvarado commented that once he officially takes office, the dispute will be one of his first concerns to resolve."

NICARAGUAN HELL

Oscar muted the sound and turned to the screen with ongoing international stock market reports. *Nice...my investments are up again today in Asia...and holding well in Europe.*

MARK'S HACIENDA

Mark stepped out of the rental SUV and surveyed the grounds. There were a dozen trees within the five foot high rock perimeter fence—topped with a three foot ornate Spanish style wrought iron grill—providing ample shade and respite from the blazing sun. The late afternoon shown on lush green pastures with a golden light. The landscape was dotted with an occasional Cerrado tree.

The stable had a bank of solar collection panels on the roof and several squirrel cage electric wind generators revealed alternative power sources. A ten foot diameter water generating Aero windmill rotated atop a thirty foot tall steel tower just to the south outside the enclosure.

To the casual observer the residence appeared to be a classic Brazilian hacienda—with a few high tech modern additions—situated on a small rise. To the eye of a trained observer it looked like a hard target.

A dozen red and white longhorn cattle grazed in the distance—gifts from Hal McCambell for a satisfactory resolution to a difficult contract in Malasia several years earlier. Three Manga Larga Marchador horses—a breed originating in

Brazil with a accelerated four beat gait that made the ride very smooth and comfortable—cropped on the tender grass.

Mark gave a trio of shrill whistles and watched with admiration as the three horses looked up, their long ears and slender defined heads giving them a regal appearance. He gave a loud Lakota Souix call, *"Yee-U-Ha"*.

The wiry animals turned and loped toward him—picking up speed as they ran. *Been gone over two years and still they come a runnin'. Probably think I have a carrot or two up my sleeve.*

As the equines neared, tossing their heads, bucking, farting and playfully kicking at one another, DeLeon said. "They remember you pretty good."

Mark turned to see the former Colombian DEA sergeant coming through the gate. Right behind him was Stranger—a black German Shepard missing her left front leg—making a beeline for the Texan.

Woof, Woof, Woof!

Mark knelt down and reached out for the jubilant canine as she barreled toward him. He expected her to stop before she ran over him—he was wrong. The retired DEA drug sniffer leapt into his arms at full speed—knocking him onto his back like a hundred and five pound rocket.

"Ohhh…Shit!"

The joy-crazed dog began licking his face while tap dancing on his chest. The long separation now over was a time of celebration.

"Easy, big girl…easy," he said as he rolled over and sat up.

"Didn't see that coming did you, Plata?" DeLeon laughed. "Haven't seen her this happy since your last visit."

The interior was cool though not air-conditioned. The double cinder block walls—filled with sand and covered with plaster—provided excellent insulation. The ceiling fans and screened windows provided a pleasant breeze—enhanced by two large attic fans that sucked in air and expelled it through roof vents. Mark noted that everything seemed in its place even after an extended absence.

A dark mahogany bookcase filled with hardback books and a few trophies involving equestrian or international shooting events covered the wall on both sides of the fire place. Above the hearth, a large framed photo—printed on canvas giving it the look of an old hand-painted portrait—of his father, grandfather and brother on a ranch in the Big Bend.

The boys were twelve and fourteen years old and dressed like any respectable west Texas cowboy would be—tall worn dirty boots, spurs, faded denim jeans, large bandanas and snap button western shirts. The final touch was the dusty felt cowboy hats. *Long ago and far away now,* he thought.

ORO del CHRISTI MINE
Nicaragua

The first night had passed without an assault and the men had spent the following day fortifying their positions. The second night, only intensified the feeling of foreboding that the hammer was about to fall.

Striker and Poncho were the first to recognize movement in the tree line. "Crank...tangos...twelve o'clock," he whispered over his mic.

Pantera, a black stocky retired Marine Gunnery Sergeant, manning the number two .50 cal reported, "Tangos...nine o'clock." He and his assistant moved quietly while rotating it to cover the approaching threat.

"Mangos...seven o'clock," Jackal, ex-German Kommando Spezialkrafte sergeant and ever the joker, called in a thick guttural accent. He and his gunner's mate also positioned themselves and their heavy weapon to engage the enemy.

"Easy...Fire when our flares go," Crank replied.

"Oro del Christi calling Honduras Army fire support one," Rhino called over the radio. Nothing but static answered. "Oro del Christi calling HA fire support one."

Static was again the only response. Crank and Rhino shared a look—their faces smeared with black and green camo grease. Both men checked their weapons one last time.

"Fuckin' beaners...probably jacking off in the head," Crank said softly.

A single flare rose above the compound followed by a fulsaide of small arms fire from the tree-line.

"Hold boys...they're looking for our positions," Crank said through his throat mic.

The gunfire ended as the flare dimmed and faded out. A second flare flew skyward and began to float slowly to the ground, washing the landscape with an eerie ghostlike illumination. The barrage returned.

"Striker…you have a fix on flare thrower?"

"10-4."

"Shut him down."

"Roger."

The defenders hugged the ground or made small against whatever cover they had chosen. Dirt and other debris flew skyward across the mine yard. Waiting for the signal to fire was more worrisome than the incoming as each man had lived through fire fights multiple times.

As the third flare went up, Striker fired. His suppressed Sako TRG—with a ATN day-night scope—made little sound, but it's effect was deadly.

Nortino dove to the ground as the .338 caliber round sliced through the foliage nearby. It struck the man launching the flares in the stomach.

"Uggnhh!" He groaned the massive thump followed by an intense burn in his belly. He flew backward, landing on his back like a sack of rocks.

A trio of RPG rounds joined the small arms fire and impacted on or close to the original heavy machine gun positions.

"Shit…Surfer called that one right," Malakhi said to his assistant. "Owe that crazy man a beer for sure."

Striker fired on the closest RPG shooter—laying a trio shots into the position. One hit a grenade round as the man attempted

15

to reload. It exploded in his hand killing him and the two men next to him.

Nortino belly-crawled behind a boulder and peered over it as his grenadier died. Unable to cancel his initial order for attack without proper com gear, he watched in horror as his force charged from the jungle and assaulted the compound.

"Wait for the claymores...then give 'em hell!" Crank ordered, seeing the trip flares rise as the enemy advanced.

The defenders opened fire when multiple antipersonnel mines exploded, sending tens of thousands steel projectiles into the advancing force. The withering interlocking .50 caliber fire coupled with rifle and SAW accompaniment made quick work of the survivors.

Arms and legs flew free from the bodies of the attackers as the hot steel shredded them. Those who were not cut down immediately, dove to the ground seeking respite from the ruthless barrage. They did not find it.

Adom and Ido—Nigerian mercenaries for hire—dispensed firing their M16s and began lobbing 40mm grenades from their launchers.

The screams of the dying was obscured by the roar of gunfire and explosions. A few—very few—managed to crawl back into the trees and escape the killing field.

Nortino watched—seething with anger—unable to save his men and women. When the firing stopped, he saw the carnage before the last flare faded. Those still alive called out screaming in pain for their mothers, lovers or God.

The defeated rebel leader reluctantly crawled into the forest. When he felt he was far enough away, he ran to his frightened mule, mounted and rode off as if El Diablo himself was behind him.

"Cease fire! Hold your positions." Crank scanned the field with night vision goggles. When confident there was no further threat, he turned to Rhino. "Oh, hell yeah!"

"Well done, bro," he replied as they bumped fists.

A voice came over the radio, "Fire support one calling Oro del Christi…Come in Oro del…"

"Turn out the lights, girls…the party's over," Crank sang into the handset, imitating Dandy Don Meridith.

The two blood brothers started laughing. The tension of waiting, the intense battle and abrupt ending to the fire-fight left both men relieved and giddy.

When he gathered himself, Crank called to his team, "Report. Anyone down?"

Every man called back affirming they were uninjured.

"Bakgut, Zorro's gonna love this one," Rhino said. "I don't think the whole braking dance took more than five minutes…Some sort of friggin' record."

SHENYANG, CHINA
Dadong District

Zhi Peng Wu sat reading a coded message from his number one enforcer, Feng. The room reeked of incense, stale cigarette and hashish smoke.

Trail goes cold. All associates go to heavenly rest. I wait San Jose. New associates arrive go Panama.

He wadded the paper up and tossed it angrily into the trash can. He reached over and pressed down forcefully on the intercom button. "Pon. Come here."

The slender bespeckled assistant entered hesitantly. He had read the message and knew Zhi would not be pleased. "Yes, Grand Dragon."

"Call the men in Cebu. Tell them tickets await at the airport for Costa Rica. Purchase them…one way."

"Yes, Grand Dragon." He bowed and exited the room quickly.

Zhi loaded his yellowed ivory pipe with a blonde chunk of hashish then placed a series of opium oil drops in as he considered the latest turn of events. *Feng is not performing as he has in the past. How is it one Yakuza woman can evade him…and eliminate five brothers? How did the American Steve McCallister disappear? I must call Chia…have him roll the bones again.*

CIA HEADQUARTERS
Quantico, Virginia

Director Emerson Walsh sat at the head of a long oval conference table in a secure room as the clock neared midnight. Ten of his highest ranking subordinates sat listening to his orders.

"Shelby, I want a complete security system scan. Reboot everything with a new password." Walsh handed his head of IT a note with the word…'Godzilla', hand written on it.

"Yes, sir."

"Montgomery, there is renewed activity by the EFRH in Nicaragua. Get a line on the bastards and submit a plan to eliminate the threat."

"Yes, sir."

"Remington, there's intel a new alliance between the ZETA and Triad is forming. Full report by Friday."

"On it, sir."

"Willoby, Taylor and Smith…an operative formerly known as Zorro turned up in Bangkok. He went completely off reservation some years ago. I want to bring him in for debriefing. Whatever it takes…find him."

"I remember him. Did quiet cleanups. I think…his last known employer was Hal McCambell," Willoby said.

A scowl crossed Emerson's face. "Great…The crazy Scotsman."

"How did we learn about Bangkok?" asked Taylor.

"Patrick Mallory, Deputy Minister at the US Embassy ran a check on him…But he's gone now. Present location unknown."

"I'll run his passport…"

"Waste of time. McCambell has them printed like the Federal Reserve prints twenty dollar bills. Get cracking on the facial recognition data out of Thailand…That's it gentlemen." Walsh got up and left the room.

"Who is this Zorro?" Smith shuffled papers into his brief case.

"A ghost…a real ghost," Willoby answered.

***

CHAPTER TWO

MARK'S HACIENDA
BRAZIL

Having finished his daily Zen meditation and self-defense three steps, Mark walked back into the hacienda from the rock patio.

He moved several books on the shelves to the left of the fireplace then tapped a cover for what looked like an electrical outlet. The covering snapped free and he swung it clockwise to expose a keypad. Entering a series of numbers, he stepped back as the book case began to swing open—revealing a storage space filled with firearms.

He lifted an elegant black powder rifle off its rack and held it for a moment—looking at his name stamped on the barrel—before bringing it to his shoulder. He aimed out the open doorway to the patio just as DeLeon walked in.

"I surrender," the Colombian said in Spanish with a smile as he held his hands up.

"Ain't loaded...see you've been keepin' the gardenin' tools maintained," Mark replied in Spanish.

DeLeon closed the screen door after Stranger had entered. "Once a month. Inspect and clean every one. You hungry yet?"

"Had some left over steak and a couple of eggs already...They just don't make rifles like they use to," he said as he admired the slim well-balanced handmade underhammer rifle with a highly polished curly maple stock, brass trigger guard and patch box.

"I need to go into town this afternoon. Out of feed for guineas and chickens...gonna need oats for the horses by the weekend," DeLeon said as he passed through to the kitchen.

"I'll hold down the fort 'til you get back. Did you talk to your sister yet?"

"I did. She is driving out this weekend to deliver your friend. Said the kids want to go horseback riding before you leave again."

Mark replaced the long rifle and removed Betsy. He slapped the bolt rearward with a knife hand and latched it open with his thumb. Seating the buttstock into his shoulder he aimed out the open door again—first looking down the iron sights then using the NightForce scope. He scanned the tree line until he found a four inch wooden post with a yellow flag fluttering in the wind.

"Any of the posts need new wind flags?"

"Possibly. We ride fence tomorrow...find out. Be good to put couple of hours on the mounts before the kids get here."

SAU PALO, BRAZIL
Sao Palo Zoo

Marta Maria had just concluded an early morning staff meeting and was walking across the lush landscape grounds to her office accompanied by Chikako—a former Yakuza assassin. The Asian woman was using a walking cane due to her injury in Costa Rica three weeks earlier while evading a Triad hit team.

"We will leave Saturday morning…usually takes four hours to get to Mark's place."

"I can not thank you enough for all you have done, Marta. I hope I can…"

"Don't be silly. I'm happy to help. It's the least I can do for one of Marks friends. I don't think you ever told me how you two met."

"We…ah…met at an elephant sanctuary in Kenya. I was visiting and he…ah…showed me the sights."

"Mark's like that. He has spent many hours here at the zoo. Just falls in and helps the staff with anything around the animals…especially the elephants. I often tell him he should have been a zoo keeper."

"That would be…different." A sly smile passed over Chikako's face. *Zorro a zoo keeper? I'd pay to see that.*

"After we pickup Angelica and Alejandro we should stop for sushi. I know this little place…the owners are Japanese. He and his wife are really sweet people."

"Sushi would be good. I'm surprised at all the Japanese people I've seen."

"Manufacturing and high tech businesses seem to bring them in."

Umm...hope there are not any Yakuza lurking about Chikako mused.

"I know what," Marta said as she pulled her cell phone from her purse and dialed. A familiar voice answered.

"Zorro."

"I have someone here you should talk to," she said before passing the phone.

The Yakuza held the cell to her ear and paused for a long moment before speaking. "Hello..."

CIA SAFE HOUSE
Managua, Nicaragua

Alan Matthews, head of CIA operations in country—a balding mid-thirties Caucasian—waited for his secretary to depart before answering the phone. He noted the call was from an old buddy stationed in Washington, DC

"How you doing Jerry?"

"Good as it gets. There's more tail in DC than I can ever tap. How's it going down in the arm pit of Central America?"

"It's hotter than a ten dollar whore in Tiajuana...I'm dying here. What's up?"

"I was having a few beers last night with some locals. I overheard a former secret service agent bragging to his buddies that he was headed to Honduras…"

"The point…other than rubbing it in my face you're living high and I'm in the land of Latino goat shit."

"I was just getting to that…this guy was bragging he just finished a security contract in Thailand…with Zorro?"

"As in…our, Zorro?"

"Sure sounded like it to me…said he was using the name Steve McCallister. Rubber lips said they were working for Hal McCambell."

"I'd give my left nut to get my hands on that son-of-a-bitch."

"That's the really good part Alan…this guy's going to Honduras to work a new contract with Zorro. You'd be neighbors down there in the land of beans and yucca."

"When?"

"Next month."

"You hear anything else…you let me know. That bastard owes me," Alan said while looking at his left hand—missing the last two fingers.

SAN PEDRO SULA
Honduras

Carlos Pineda—gang lord of the local MS-13—rode in the back seat of a nineteen ninety-one black Lincoln continental low rider. His driver and number one enforcer sat in the front.

Behind and in front two other vehicles carried an armed force of his soldiers providing additional security.

"I do not care about the excuses. Tell Soto he has until noon tomorrow to deliver," Carlos said using his cell phone.

"Soto has enlisted members of the Honduras army to protect him..."

"As have we. Remind him...I know where his family lives. If I do not have the product by noon I will declare a blood vendetta."

"Yes, Carlos..."

A barrage of small arms fire erupted and a hail of bullets impacted all three vehicles. The first car swerved to the left and crashed into a parked bus—the driver shot through the head. Three men staggered out and returned fire on the attackers on the roof tops, in windows and doorways surrounding them.

The Lincoln roared forward—running over a woman and her child crossing the street—crushing the mother underneath the vehicle and throwing the infant onto the hood before impacting the windshield and flying over the moving car to land hard on the dirty street. The bulletproof hardened vehicle deflected round after round without injury to the men inside.

The third car raced after their boss with the men inside firing wildly out the windows at anyone and everyone regardless of involvement in the gunfight. An old woman ran from the sidewalk to the lifeless baby. As she picked it up the car hit her and continued without pausing.

"What is going on?"

Carlos spoke calmly, "I think Soto has sent his answer to my request. Have Zapata visit his home."

As the two vehicles raced from the danger zone, the men in the first car were slain one by one.

NICARAGUAN NATIONAL ARMY HQ

General Duvan Robelo Sacasa—mid-sixties, sculptured white hair and mustache—busied himself painting a small mounted Napolianic war cavalry piece. On a 4 by 8 table behind him was a topo layout of the battle of Waterloo. Several hundred additional miniature pieces were laid out in formations reflecting historical correctness.

His aid entered with a small white envelope and laid it on the table next to him and left without speaking. He knew better than to disturb the second in command of all the Nicaraguan Army forces.

Setting the freshly painted piece down, the General meticulously cleaned his brushes before opening the envelope.

He stood up abruptly and moved to an ornate hand-carved desk where he picked up his cell phone.

"Alan Matthews."

"This is General Sacasa."

"What can I do for you General?"

"I was just informed an operative of yours…code name Zorro, is coming to Honduras."

"How would you know that?"

"The USA is not the only country in the world with intelligence measures…"

"Of course I didn't mean to suggest your country is without sources. First, let me qualify…the gentleman you refer to is no longer working for us. Hasn't for several years…"

"Then what would be your interest in him?"

Alan was taken back realizing his phone conversation on what he considered a secure link had been tapped. *Damn…what else has Sacasa been privy to.* "He owes me on a gambling debt. The bastard has stiffed me for five years."

"I would be very grateful to have an interview with this…Zorro. I invite you to come by my office tomorrow…1100 hours so we may discuss it."

TEGUCIGALPA, HONDURAS
ZETA Compound

Oscar Puto walked into a shipping container located at the back of his equestrian center—one of many used for storage of equine supplies such as bales of hay and grain. This one was empty except for a few wooden crates.

As he entered, a burly heavily tattooed Hispanic male moved a crate and lifted a trap door exposing a well-lit staircase. The cartel boss walked down into a underground interrogation room.

"Ahhh…no…please. I told you all I know," a slight of build Latino cried—his face bloodied and bruised, his bare upper body bleeding from multiple wounds.

"Enough," Oscar said, quietly dismissing the interrogator.

An enforcer moved an elegant purple cushioned chair in front of the battered man and Puto sat down. He carefully cut the end off a Cuban cigar and lit it—all the while ignoring the tortured man.

"All this…business…," he said as he waved his hand at the man's wounds. "…disgusts me…tell me what you know…and it will end."

"I know nothing…nothing."

"You and your brother steal from me…this I know. And yet you know nothing of it?"

"Si…nothing. We are good soldiers."

"Then how do you and your family live so well? New cars, new houses and…you have a beautiful young mistress."

The battered man looked up at Oscar with a deeper look of terror in his eyes. "I do not have…"

"Bring her," Oscar ordered. As he waited he studied the tip of his cigar—gently blowing on it to increase the glow.

A bodyguard returned with a bound young Nicaraguan woman. She was attractive, her black hair streaked blonde in the fashion of the day and dressed in designer clothing well beyond her means.

"Riki, what…Aeee!" The handler jerked her head back by the hair.

"Delores…If you harm her I swear I will…"

"You will what? Kill me?" Oscar said with a smirk on his lips. "I think not. Now…tell me where your brother and my cocaine is…or Delores will not be so pretty."

"Riki, please…Ahhh!" she screamed as she was pushed to her knees beside Puto—scraping her bare knees on the coarse concrete floor.

Oscar took a long draw in his cigar as he gently moved the woman's hair from her face, raised one eye brow as he looked to Riki, then turned and placed the smoldering cigar tip on the young woman's cheek just below her right eye.

"Aee!" she wailed as she writhed in agony.

"Okay. Okay…stop. I tell you."

"All these unpleasentries. So unnecessary, Riki. Now, tell me…everything."

Puto's cigar was short when he walked out of the container and looked at the night sky. He listened to the sound of his horses snorting in the pasture to his right and started toward the white rail fence.

"What do you want done with them?" his enforcer asked from inside the steel container.

"Feed Riki to the wood chipper…then the pigs. As for the girl? Give her to the men. Let them enjoy her…then dispose of her as well."

"As you wish, Don Puto."

CIA SAFE HOUSE
Managua, Nicaragua

Alan Matthews slipped his Browning 9 mm into a concealed carry holster in the small of his back and flipped his loose fitting floral patterned cotton short sleeve shirt over it. He placed a white straw hat with a small brim on his balding head, picked up his attaché case and walked out the side door of the three story stucco building into the alley.

He entered the back seat of a dark green nineteen ninety-seven Chevrolet sedan which drove off as he closed the door. At the end of the alley the vehicle paused as a one horse cart passed hauling sweet potatoes to the market place.

"What is so important we could not..."

"Shut up, Daniels. Just drive."

The driver looked back at the CIA chief in the rearview mirror. "Where to?"

"The city square."

When the sedan entered the square, Alan tapped his driver on the shoulder and pointed to a quaint coffee shop. Once the vehicle parked, both me got out and walked to the large three tier fountain in the center of the square.

"Our security has been hacked. General Sacasa has been intercepting our communications..."

"How is some third world monkey going to do that?" Daniels asked as he laughed.

"No idea but he has. You ever hear of an operative...code name, Zorro?"

"No. Not that I can think of...should I?"

"He's been off grid for a couple of years. Did some quiet contracts. Just learned from Jerry Dillard back in the states he's headed to Honduras..."

31

"What's the history lesson have to do with our commo being hacked?"

"General Sacasa called and wants to meet Zorro."

"Is there a reason in all this?"

"Connect the dots. I just had a conversation informing me the man is coming. Now the general wants a chitchat."

"I'll get the IT guys on it immediately."

"Take them off property to discuss it. The whole house could be bugged…Sweep it."

MARK'S HACIENDA

A light blue Toyota 4 Runner pulled up to the front gate. Marta Maria, her children and Chikako—leaning on her cane—stepped out into the midday heat to the greeting of Stranger barking viscously. Once the children started calling out to the German Shepherd, she switched her defensive attitude to one of excitment—whinning and wagging her tail excitedly.

DeLeon came around the house and waved. "Hola!"

"So good to see you," Marta replied in Spanish.

"Let Stranger out," Alejandro said, joined by his sister, Angelica in a similar request.

"I'm coming…hold on," DeLeon replied.

"Where is Mark?" Marta she looked around the grounds and at the house.

"We did not expect you so early. He takes a ride. He should be back soon."

"Chikako, meet my brother DeLeon. Deleon…Chikako," Marta said in English as she opened the wrought iron gate.

Stranger rushed out and into the arms of the two children—who immediately began lavishing affection on her.

"Hello, I am not good with Spanish."

"Is okay…we speak English so not to exclude you," DeLeon responded. "You are the famous one."

"Famous?" Chikako answered.

"Zorro say to me you are."

"I see…okay then, I guess."

"Is all good. You make an impression on him."

Chikako looked away to hide her embarrassment and pleasure at the news. Across the pasture she saw Mark riding a dun horse toward them at an hand lope—its black mane and tail flying in the breeze. "He rides well."

Marta Maria and DeLeon looked in the direction Chikako was viewing. The Texan looked like he was born on a horse—in truth not far from it as he had been on a saddle with his grandfather at the age of two—moving in perfect sync with the animal like a dance.

"He is quite good, isn't he?" Marta commented. "He really loves his horses…Doesn't he, DeLeon?"

"Very much. That dun is his favorite. He name him…Lakota Two Moons. Something to do with Indian heritage, he say…Do you ride, Chikako?"

"A little. Nothing like that though," she replied as she admired the union between horse and rider.

"Whoa," Mark commanded softly as shifted his weight backward and stepped from the saddle. Lakota stopped on a dime and slid to a halt, drawing perfect elevens as Zorro dismounted and walked toward the new arrivals in one fluid movement.

He removed his wide-brimmed palm leaf hat and held it in front of him—his Smith and Wesson .44 special revolver worn cross-draw. "Howdy! Welcome to outlaw's hideout."

Alejandro and Angelica ran and wrapped their arms around him as Stranger jumped up placing her single front paw on his chest.

"Tio, Mark! I love you," Angelica said excitedly.

"I want to ride your horse," Alejandro said before racing off to the standing steed. "Can I? Can I ride him?"

"Later…I need to change the saddle for you. Marta Maria, wonderful to see you again," he said as he scooped Angelic up and carried her to her mother.

"You still have your beautiful pony tail, Tio," the little girl said with a giggle as she gave his long gray hair a pull—then waved it up and down.

Marta wrapped her arms around him, kissed him on both cheeks. "If it is so wonderful why has it been over two years?"

"Work. But hey…I'm here now."

Chikako stood quietly watching the interplay between the others and Mark. A sly smile crossed her face. *Not such a tough guy today are you?*

Mark—behind his chrome aviator sun glasses—had his eyes on the Asian woman the whole while he conversed with Marta and the children. As the greetings concluded he spoke to her, "How do you like the place?"

"It's nice. Very remote. Very…quiet."

"You look good with a cane." He a smiled. "Let's get ya'll settled in before it's time to fire up the grill. DeLeon…help me with the luggage."

"Si, patron."

Mark turned and spoke to the waiting horse. "Lakota…barn."

The animal nodded its head then turned and started walking around the rock fence toward the back of the compound. He knew the saddle was coming off, a refreshing shower and some plain whole oats awaited him on arrival.

HAL McCAMBELL'S OFFICE
Dallas, Texas

Roger 'Blaster' Mantle and Mike 'Dog' Sloan sat in the reception area waiting on a meeting with their employer. It was a sparsely furnished room—giving little clue to the vast financial empire Hal had built over the years. A few framed prints of the NFL Cowboy greats—all with Hal—and several imitation plants in wicker baskets served as decoration. The furniture, modest but sturdy, showed signs of extended use.

"You get the memo about the annual bonus party?" Roger asked.

"Yeah. Never been to Miami," Mike replied.

"There are some hot women down there, let me…"

The electronic dead-bolt clicked and Maggie entered the room and held the steel bulletproof door open. "Hal will see you now."

As the two entered the office, Hal was concluding a phone call. Both men stopped in front of his desk and waited.

"Don't care if your schedule changed, Batt. We have a contract that clearly states date and time. If you go early...you go in naked. I'll have to call you back." Hal hung up without waiting for a response. He eyed the two agents for a moment. "Looks like you two survived the first contract."

"Yes, sir," the two men responded in unison.

"Sit." The old Scotsman indicated two chairs covered in rich dark leather. "Debrief...Blaster you first."

Both men shifted slightly as it was their first time to lay out a completed operation for the owner.

"We arrived and followed Zorro's instructions to the best of our abilities. There were...a couple of things...ah, that came up we weren't expecting."

"Really?" Hal smiled slyly. "Like what?" *Unexpected? Zorro? Imagine that...*

"Well...McCallister got involved in a hostage retrieval in Bangkok, for one."

"And?"

Mike glanced at Roger, "He ended up in a fire fight with an Islamic terrorist group on the island of Mindanao..."

"You two were there?"

"No, sir," they responded.

"So you're passing down what? If you weren't there...you have no idea what really happened. I want to know what you two did. Don't tip toe through the tulips with hearsay." Hal got up and moved to his wall of fame.

"I have my journal. Do you want me to read from that?" Mike asked.

Hal picked up a photo of himself, Mark and five other heavily-armed hard men dressed in jungle fatigues. As he returned to his desk, he handed it to Roger. "See anyone you recognize?"

Mike and Roger studied the photo for a moment before Blaster handed it back to Hal.

"You and Zorro," he said.

"When was that taken?" Dog asked.

"Long time ago. That was the last field op I pulled." Hal looked at the photo. "We went into the Congo to extract some Catholic missionaries. Zorro and I...we're the only two on the team to make it out."

"He never said any thing about it," Roger said.

"My point exactly, bonehead. I put a shadow on you since you got back." He replaced the photo on the credenza and lifted another photo of himself, five of his grandchildren and Mark on a deep-sea fishing trip.

Mike and Roger shared a look.

"You two flapped your lips in a DC bar. Bragged about the contract you worked in Bangkok."

Both men stiffened.

"The reason Zorro never mentioned it is…" Hal paused then fixed his gaze on the two men. "…it's against McCambell policy to talk about any work we do. This was covered in your orientation. That's strike one. You two plan going to the annual bonus event in Miami?"

"Yes, sir."

"You were looking at a 10 K bump for Bangkok…Now, you're not. I know you guys talk to each other…but outside the company?…This is the last time I'll hear of it…Is that clear?"

"Yes, sir."

"Zorro tells me you two could make a couple of hands in a year or two…or three. With that in mind I'm still scheduling you two pups to work with him in Honduras. Bangkok was anglefood. Whole lotta bad guys in Hondo…Turn your journals over to Maggie before you leave." Hal picked up a folder on his desk and opened it. A long moment passed before he looked up.

"Why the hell are you still in my office?"

Roger and Mike jumped up and bumped into each other getting out the door. Hal smiled watching their hasty departure.

CHOLUTECA, HONDURAS

Reynoldo Bolanos and Cisco 'La Rata' walked into the Tica bus station and purchased two tickets. The terminal was crowded with locals taking the only transportation they could afford. The two insurgents operated separately and remained so until they boarded the bus. Honduras Army soldiers checked everyone's papers before they were allowed to enter the bus headed for

Zambrano. Once it left the city the two men moved to adjoining seats.

"The new identification papers worked well. Soon you will be with your family," Reynoldo said softly.

"Si...soon."

"We give the imperialist much to think about while we were in Choluteca."

"My wife's sister is getting married next week. I want to attend the wedding," La Rata said.

"Fine. We give a little time before we strike again. I have a shipment of syntex coming in next week. Two...three weeks...then we hit them. I am considering Soto Cano."

"The US air base? How would we gain access?" Rata asked nervously.

"We will have assistance. I can say no more about it."

PANAMA CITY, PANAMA

Feng and his new team wandered separately through the oriental section of town showing a photo of Chikako. Though located in central America, the atmosphere was decidedly Asian. The answer was always the same. No one had seen her.

Late in the day the men assembled at the edge of the community.

"Anyone see her?" Feng asked in Mandarin.

The men responded in unison or shook their heads indicating there had been no success.

"We start again in the morning. She must have been here. Tomorrow we check the bus stations, airports and the docks."

As the men entered three different cabs—each with a local Chinese driver—Feng made a call.

"Zhi Peng Wu's office."

"Inform the Master it is Feng."

A moment passed before the Dragon Wu came on the line. "Do you have her?"

"We canvassed the Asian district all day. No one claims to have seen her. Tomorrow we…"

"I had Chia roll the bones. He tells me she was close to a transportation waterway. Big boats. Heavy traffic, but now she is in the countryside."

"Which countryside?"

"Further south. He said there are many Japanese near by."

"What does this mean?"

"Sao Palo. Sao Palo has the largest population of Japanese in the world…other than Japan itself. Tickets wait you tomorrow morning."

"Yes, Master."

"Feng…I grow weary of the wait."

The Triad hit man felt a chill run down his spine. Dragon Master Wu was not know for rewarding those who failed.

"I will find her."

***

CHAPTER THREE

MARK'S HACIENDA

Mark, Chikako and DeLeon sat on heavy wooden benches on the patio—all hand-crafted from large tree trunks. A pleasant breeze blew out of the east and rustled the leaves of the trees as the moonlight filtered down. Marta joined them with a bottle of tequila, a porcelain bowl of sliced limes and a wooden bowl of salt.

"The children are asleep. All the excitement wore them out," the Colombian woman said as she set the items on a table.

"Alejandro could be a good rider one day," Mark remarked.

"I go and check the horses." DeLeon walked off.

"How's the leg by the way?" Mark asked.

"Better. Maybe another week…or two."

"You never did tell me how it happened," Marta asked.

"A tree thorn," Chikako replied giving Zorro a look. "I…fell in Costa Rica. It swelled up like a soccer ball."

"Ouch. Well…I'm going to bed. I'm sure you two have some catching up to do," Marta remarked as she moved to Mark and kissed him on the cheek. "We leave after lunch so get the children on a horse again early…please."

"Done deal. Hey…how about you bring your parents out next weekend? We'll celebrate."

"Celebrate what?" asked Marta.

"My birthday," Mark replied.

"How old will you be?" inquired Chikako.

"A hundred and six."

Both women laughed as Mark poured two shots of tequila and handed one to Chikako.

"Well, it feels like a hundred and six."

Marta departed leaving the two alone on the patio. They sat under the stars entranced with the tranquility. Neither spoke for some time.

Finally, Chikako broke the silence, "Marta told me how she got to Brazil."

"Hell of an adventure."

"You have a history of helping damsels in distress it seems."

"Based on what?"

"Well…there's Marta and Dame Daphnie…me…"

"I don't think you qualify as a damsel in distress. A friend in need…maybe, but damsel in distress? Don't see it."

She sat studying him for a few moments. "You ever get tired of it?"

"What?"

"Endlessly looking over your shoulder."

"A guy has to make a living."

"Ha...you made enough for three lives in Hong Kong. Unless you already spent it all."

"Nope. I paid off this place. Set up a trust for Marta's kids. Bumped a couple of life insurance policy pay offs in the Philippines..."

"What happened there?"

"Moro National Liberation Front happened."

"Still...doesn't sound like you would be broke."

"I made a couple of donations to wildlife foundations and paid a computer guru for his services in Bangkok. All in all down about five mil. So no...I ain't broke."

Mark stretched his arms out on the back of the bench, leaned his head back and stared at the night sky. A Rusty-barred owl—commonly known as the Brazilian owl—began to hoot.

"You never told me how old you will be," Chikako said as she poured another pair of shots.

"Old enough to know better."

The two sat in silence absorbing the solitude. Mark stood up and stretched his back. "Long time no ride...I need a bath."

Chikako flexed her injured leg. "Nice comfort room. Like the overhead brass shower head."

Mark looked to her with a smile. "Care to try it out?"

"What about Marta and the kids?"

"Other end of the hacienda." Mark moved to her, took her in his arms and smelled the scent of her neck. "I'm glad you're…safe."

"Ummm…is that a gun in your pocket or are you happy to see me?" she said in a good Mae West imitation.

Mark pulled back and kissed her softly. "Pistol's in the small of my back…But you knew that."

"Happy is good." She returned his kiss passionately.

NICARAGUAN NATIONAL ARMY HQ

A Captain entered Sacasa's office with a communication and laid it on the General's desk as he snapped his heels together smartly and waited at attention for his orders. Duvan set his cup of coffee down, put on a pair of glasses and picked up the single sheet of paper.

Report from security group at the Christi del Oro mine indicate fierce battle early this morning. Heavy rebel force casualties. Request for military to verify and assistance to clear the dead.

Await orders.

Colonel Hector Julio Hernandez

Sacasa laid the communication down and wrote a reply which he handed to the Captain. "I want to see this for myself. Have my car brought around in thirty minutes. I have an important meeting to attend to before I leave…Impress on Colonel Hernandez he is to wait for my arrival before departing."

"Yes, my General."

Sacasa moved miniature Napolianic soldiers to a new position on the game board as Alan Matthews entered his expansive office. He continued to do so as he spoke to the CIA agent. "Did you study the Napoleonic wars?"

"No, can't say that I did. Impressive layout."

"Each piece is historically correct. I paint them myself."

"Un-huh. Looks like a lot of effort. So…what did you want to discuss, General?"

"Hitler was not the first to underestimate the cruelty of the Russian winters. Bonapart fell because of the severity as well. Of course we don't have that difficulty here in Nicaragua."

"That's an understatement." Alan pulled a white linen handkerchief from his hip pocket, removed his straw hat and wiped his forehead. "I have some matters waiting. What did you want?"

Sacasa picked up one foot soldier and used a magnifying glass to study it. "This man, Zorro," he said before tossing the figure into a small woven palm basket with a dozen others.

"What about him?"

Taking the collected pieces to a small electric smelter in the corner the officer unceremoniously dumped them in. A cloud of blue and red smoke drifted off the pieces as the paint burned.

"I would like to interview him."

"In regards to what?"

"He may have some knowledge of my brother, Colonel Alfredo Hernandez Sacasa's untimely death."

"What makes you think he would know about it?"

Duvan fixed his eyes on Matthews as he returned to the game board. "There is a rumor...It would allow my family some sense of closure if we knew more about the circumstances."

Damn...Wouldn't surprise me if he tapped the Colonel. "I wouldn't know. I just want him to pay his gambling debt."

"Then we could work together for our mutual benefits."

Alan watched as the pieces on the game board were moved about. "When is he suppose to be here?"

Sacasa looked up with a smile. "Come now Matthews. He is going to be in Honduras...according to my intelligence report. I thought you might arrange a meeting to collect your debit then I would collect mine."

"That's way off book..."

"I would be deeply in your debt if this was to happen."

Hell...why not? Excellent payback for the sack of shit. "When did you say he would be in Honduras?"

"Soon...next month. With your intelligence resources it should be easy for you to find out when and where...By the way your woman, Carmen, I think is most attractive. It would be a shame if anything were to happen to her. By accident of course."

Alan stood starring at the General with a new look of understanding as to what he was being told to do. He had no real feelings for the woman other than she warmed his bed nicely, but the thought of her being used in this fashion rubbed him the wrong way. "Yes it would. Anything else?"

"No. I look forward to your...success."

NICARAGUAN HELL

SAN PEDRO SULA
Honduras

Carlos Pineda addressed his gang in a small courtyard from a second story balcony. His mood was darker than the men had ever seen before.

"If it is war they want? It is war they shall have...I want the heads of every man, every woman, every child in the Tarzanes on a spike...In this yard before we are done."

"Carlos, we are outnumbered..."

"To hell with numbers! We will strike swiftly...without mercy. We are Mara Salvatrucha!"

"What is your plan?" a gang member asked.

"First...we kidnap an American. Not just any American, a wealthy capitalist pig. Pincho, I want you to set up a stakeout at the airport...Find me someone to be our bait."

"That is it? We kidnap..."

"Enough! I will reveal the rest of my plan when the time is right. Just find me a capitalist pig."

"What do the rest of us do?"

"Drive by some of the Tarzanes places of business. Bloody them. It will lead them to our trap when we are ready."

As the gang members departed, Carlos sat down in a brown wicker chair. A dark-haired full-figured woman in her early thirties came out the door and began to rub his neck and shoulders. He closed his eyes and relaxed briefly, and then made a phone call.

47

"What do you want now?"

"A list of wealthy Americans in or coming to Honduras."

"Why?"

"You want to continue our working relationship...no?"

"Why an American?"

"Think of it this way...you rescue the kidnapped American and become a hero."

"I don't follow..."

"The abduction is blamed on the Tarzanes. The government of Honduras, eager to win favor with the US destroys them. I give you the American. A win-win for both of us."

"Your brilliance impresses me, Pineda...How soon does this need to happen?"

"Quickly. The Tarzanes interfere with my business. This delays your next payment. So...the sooner the better."

"I have someone in mind. You will have to eliminate his security force..."

"That is a specialty of mine, Matthews."

MARK'S HACIENDA

Mark and Chikako rode in a battered green Land Rover across the property following a pair of dirt tracks.

"That's the windmill I need to repair up ahead. DeLeon would usually takes care of it, but like I said earlier...he decided to ride back to Sau Palo with Marta and the kids."

"Sorry I missed saying good-bye."

"He'll be back before my next contract."

The truck slowly bumped along the roadway climbing the low hill—at the top sat the windmill and an old stone tank.

Hoards of bright green and yellow grasshoppers flew up in front of the truck and scattered or landed on it. Nearby a group of Brazilian rosewood trees provided the only source of shade. Mark parked under them and they climbed out.

"Beautiful view." Chikako scanned the area.

"Yeah…I considered building the hacienda up here originally. Let's eat before we deal with the windmill." Mark lifted a cooler and a wicker basket out of the back of the Rover.

"Working great now. This is the first well I had drilled after I bought the place. Hit water at eighty feet, but I had 'em take it on down to a hundred and twenty."

The fan blades spun in the breeze and the sucker rods made a rhythmic clicking sound as they moved up and down drawing the water from below.

"What's that for?" Chikako asked seeing Mark pull a bundle of surveyor plastic flags from the back of the truck.

"Laying out a five acre plot…A gift to DeLeon. He deserves his own place."

"What would merit such a generous gift?"

"Long list. Gauging by the water level in the tank, I think the swimming hole will be open tomorrow afternoon about this time. You bring a swim suit?"

"No. In fact I don't have much to wear at all. What I did, stayed in Costa Rica when I made a run for it."

"Well…neither do I. Tell you what…tomorrow mornin' we go into Campinas and pick up a few things for you."

Chikako moved a loose strand of hair from her eyes as she watched Mark laying out the boundaries. "That would be great…The contract in Honduras. What is it? If you don't mind telling me."

"Wet nurse some mining engineers."

"You have a team already?"

Mark paused from pacing off the distance to where he intended to plant the next flag, turned and studied her for a moment. "Not completely…Interested?"

"Maybe. But I'm used to defeating teams like yours."

"Could be an asset. If you know how to hit the client…then you would know our weakness."

The two stood sharing a look. "I have a role I've been considering for a long time now. I call it the *Trailer*. Someone who's always…around the team and clients, but never a recognizable member. Someone with your skill sets would be a perfect fit. We could figure it out together."

"An Asian woman always close by? I would stand out like a blonde Polish whore…don't you think?"

"One word…disguise."

A trio of white egrets flew overhead and slowly turned in a long circle before landing near a low stone trough—fed by the overflow from the cistern.

"We'll finish this tomorrow. Lots of critters coming in for a drink soon." Mark headed for the truck. *Chikako on six? Wonder how her long gun skills are…*

NICARAGUAN HELL

NAIROBI, KENYA

Lutto, a 6' black woman—President Mobutto's long time secretary and closest confidant—relaxed on the patio of her tenth story apartment. She wore a long flowing floral-print dress as was the custom of her tribe. The view of the city at night stretched out below and faint sounds of the street wafted up. A pleasant breeze gently stirred the tropical plants growing in large containers.

After the attempt by rogue military units to overthrow his presidency—thwarted by Mark, Rhino and Crank—Mobutto had rewarded her with the luxurious and secure residence for her perceived loyalty.

She answered a call on her secure cell phone—used only to communicate with her business associates in China. "Hello."

"Good day, Madam X. I hope you are well."

"I will be better when your money arrives."

"It is in the box today. Your information proved very valuable."

"Did you find him?"

"No. Not as yet. But we will. Do you have another shipment prepared? The Dragon Master wishes to fill new ivory orders in the west…America specifically."

"It departs Mombassa on Saturday. I will place the needed documents for Hong Kong in the box when I pick up the money."

"Excellent, Madam X…excellent. One more thing…"

51

"The answer is no."

"But you did not allow me to finish."

"I have no interest in your other business deals. Ivory and horn fulfill my needs. Good-bye."

"We would pay a generous sum if the man we seek were to return to Kenya and you informed us in a timely fashion."

"How generous?"

"One hundred thousand pounds."

"You must want Mark Ingram very badly."

"We were informed his name was Steve McCallister. Who is Mark Ingram?"

"A man of many names it seems. I will inform you."

CAMPINAS, BRAZIL

Built on vast stretches of grass fields—hence its name—the city of a over one million people sat a little over 2,000 feet above sea level. This elevation made for perfect coffee production and once the railroad to Sao Palo—ninety-six kilometers to the southeast—was completed in 1867, the industry boomed.

Mark had chosen the area to build his hacienda due to the mild temperatures—average highs in the mid eighties and average lows in the low forties.

Mark and Chikako walked out of the Iguatemi Campinas mall into the pleasant seventy-five degree weather with several shopping bags between them.

"Enough clothing. Let's go see an old friend. Get you some sensible shoes," Mark said.

"You are no fun to go shopping with. Rush…rush…rush." Chikako smiled. "I still need a swim suit."

"What for?"

"You want to swim nude?"

"Works for me. Besides…the suits here in Brazil are not much more than bandaids. Ah…here it is. These guys make some great footwear." Mark opened the door to a small family owned shoe shop.

Half a day's shopping was packed in the back of the Ranger and three miles out of town Mark brought up the subject of Honduras. "I'll be working with two of Hal's newbies. Did…okay in Bangkok, but nothing like it'll be in Hondo."

"Only three of you?"

"Four, if you take on the role of trailer…Here's what I've been thinking. A member of the team floats around always ready to insure there's a back door for us and the clients…How are your long gun skills?"

"Never spent much time on them. Pistol, knives, sword…long bow."

"Umm…maybe have DeLeon handle the rifle then…"

"He's going?"

"Worked with me before. Has great instincts and better than most with a rifle. I'm thinking you cover us in close and he covers you and us from further out. Man…I love it when a plan comes together."

Chikako watched Mark as they traveled and discussed the new concept. *He's like a kid making up a game with this. An interesting...dangerous game.* "I need to start working out. Make sure the knee is a hundred percent."

"Tonight after the swim...You know what? We could do some blade work when you're ready. I haven't had anyone to spar with in a long time."

"You have the swords?"

"Several. Including the one you saw in Rhino's Nairobi vault...But I'm thinkin' wooden Katanas. I've seen you in action and I'm not interested in getting carved up."

"Ha...you dueled Akihiko in Kenya and won? I don't think you have much to worry about."

"Yeah, well...better lucky than dead. And I have a scar to prove it...Wooden Katanas for us."

Mark's satellite cell rang. He recognized the tone. "Crank...how goes it?"

"Excellent so far. We're at the mine. Got hit the second night. Good guys thirty...Bad guys zero."

"Sweet...What can I do you for?"

"How soon you headed to Honduras?"

"Couple of weeks. Why?"

"Just wanted to know how soon we'd be neighbors. Once we get this show running smooth I want to come visit."

Mark looked at her watching the passing landscape. "Yeah, sure. I'll call you if you need me..."

"Oh, I got this one, Zorro. Me and Rhino got it tied down tight. Hey...Chopper coming in. Some Nicaraguan General wants to inspect last night's fandango."

"Play nice. You may need a friend in high places before you're done. Keep in mind...they ain't never showin' up 'til the dance is over." Mark hung up.

"Business?"

"Crank's on a contract in Nicaragua. Wants to come visit after we get to Hondo."

"Un-huh. I'd like to miss that. I don't want to..."

"No problem. I'm a big fan of the crazy surfer, but not everyone is."

"No...no, don't get me wrong. I think he's great, but...Maybe later. I think he may have gotten the wrong impression in Singapore."

"You mean the big ol' sloppy kiss at the airport?"

Chikako glanced over to see him smiling at her. She blushed. "I was...I don't know what I was..."

"Yeah you do." He chuckled. "You were taggin' your options."

She reached over and punched him in the shoulder. "Shut up! Are you always this direct?"

"Makes life easier. Pussyfooting around gives me a headache."

ORO del CHRISTI MINE

A Russian Hind Mi-24 helicopter and two Hind Mi-17 transport attack helicopters—sold to Nicaragua by Libya—approached from the west as Crank and Rhino finished a meal of MREs and hot coffee. The aircrafts circled in a defensive formation before the Mi-24 descended and set down in the compound.

"Where the hell were these guys when we needed them?" Crank asked.

"Listening to umpapa tuba music and pressing their uniforms," Rhino replied.

"Did not know the Nics were flying Russian choppers."

"Wicked sons-a-bitches. Dealt with the braks in Angola."

"Zorro said to let you handle the politics what with your presidential experience in Kenya. So…you're on point."

"Moffie said that? Well, well, wonders never cease. My Spanish sucks, so translate if need be."

"No problema *mi amigo*. Get us some PDQ response in the future. Bad boys won't be so sloppy next time."

"Roger that."

General Sacasa stepped from the chopper, straightened his jacket, adjusted his polished pistol belt and holster. He settled his ornate hat and walked toward the waiting contractors with his riding crop under his left arm. Two field grade officers followed him—both wearing immaculately pressed uniforms. Six well-armed enlisted soldiers dismounted and fanned out.

"Who is in command here?" Sacasa asked in fluent English.

"I am," Rhino replied. "Appreciate you stopping by, General."

A sergeant ran up holding a ball cap with EFRH printed in faded letters on it. "General…Nortino's rebel group."

"How many dead?" Sacasa responded in Spanish.

"There are twenty-nine bodies, sir."

Sacasa turned to Rhino and returned to English. "How many men did you lose?"

"None."

A surprised and quizzical look crossed the General's face as he tapped his riding crop on the side his knee-high boot. "None?"

"Zero, zip…nada," Crank answered.

"And who are you?" the General asked.

"My number two. We are here to provide security for this mining operation and would be grateful for some assistance. If I'm right, those boys and girls will be back…and probably more of them next time."

"Very likely." Duvan studied the two men in front of him for a moment. "What is your name and who is your employer?"

"Rheinhart Fabian. We work for the Oro del Christi mining corporation. Now, about the assistance. I am authorized to offer a small incentive…"

Sacasa turned to his men. "Search the dead for intelligence. Send the gunships. Sweep the surrounding area out to five miles."

The men hurried off to follow his orders leaving him alone with Rhino and Crank.

After the officers departed, the General pulled a silver case from his coat pocket, removed an expensive Davidoff cigarette and lit it with a engraved silver lighter bearing the rank and emblem of his command. "How small?"

"Fifty thousand dollars for a combat platoon…twenty-four seven and quick response attack choppers on stand by."

"That is…very small."

"Seventy-five thousand. Direct deposit to the bank account of your choosing…"

"One hundred thousand…Cash. Used bills…tens and twenties delivered by courier. A hundred thousand will be…a deposit of good faith. Thereafter, another ten thousand a month to continue."

"Done. I'll have the funds available within the week."

"I look forward doing business with you Mister Fabian. Your predecessors were not so wise. Do you have any immediate needs?"

"Not at this time."

"I only see five men. Where is the rest of your force?" the General asked as he scanned the mine's grounds.

"This is it. I'll have more men on the ground shortly."

"Five men? You wish me to believe…only five men did this?" he said sarcastically as he waved his crop at the bodies scattered across the ground outside the compound.

"A small band of determined men can do what armies deem impossible…You've heard of Thermopylae?" Rhino smiled.

"Yes…yes I have. Very well, as soon as your courier arrives, I will have my best platoon sent to join you." The General turned and marched back to his helicopter.

"Dude, that was slicker than snot on a doorknob," Crank said.

"Learned it from the wise one. He pulled the same negotiation in Chile couple of years ago," the South African replied. He used his throat mic and spoke to the team members dispersed in the surrounding forest. "Stay low till the Federales are gone."

One by one the men positioned in the jungle to cover those in the compound responded acknowledgment.

CIA HEADQUARTERS
Langley, Virginia

Sam Willoby in his early sixties—Caucasian, crewcut hair—knocked on the door of Director Emerson Walsh's office.

"Come in."

Willoby moved to the desk and laid a folder on it marked *Steve McCallister/Inactive*. "The file you requested. I've been informed by Jerry Dillard this man may be in Honduras next month."

"How solid is this intel?" Walsh asked as he opened the folder and flipped through the pages.

"Remains to be seen, sir. Dillard overheard a former Secret Service agent claim he would be working with McCallister down there. Some sort of private security contract for an engineering firm."

"Smells like more of Hal McCambell's kind of business. Have our station director alerted..."

"Sir, Agent Thomas was transported to the Bethesda last week with dengue fever. A new director has not been assigned as yet..."

"Have Alan Matthews take over there until the new man is in position. He's more than capable of handling both Nicaragua and Honduras." Walsh paused as he viewed a page buried in the documents. "Hmmm, looks like he already knows this McCallister...worked together in Colombia and Peru."

"I'll contact Agent Matthews immediately."

"Communicate with him on a drop phone."

"I'll do that, sir."

Walsh closed the folder and placed it in a desk drawer before looking up. "You seem to have some knowledge of the man yourself."

"I do. Worked with him on the Silent Night operations."

"As I recall they were very successful."

"Yes, sir."

"How many did this Zorro participate in?"

"All of them. He was our go-to man. He only missed on the El Cobra mission."

"I'm not familar with that particular assignment."

"Cobra was the code name of a high ranking cartel enforcer in Columbia. He had been a member of the Colombian DEA but turned and did considerable damage before he disappeared."

"Ah...I remember now. Killed his own stepbrother right? Also, a member of the DEA down there."

"Uh huh...He vowed to eliminate his entire family as well. McCallister deviated from his orders and facilitated the escape of Captain Lopez's family. By the time he was back in the game, El Cobra had vanished."

"We should find this Lopez family?"

"Already set the ball in motion. You'll find photos of his wife…Marta Maria Lopez, her children, parents and brother DeLeon in the back of the folder."

"Is Bianca Toro still working in Panama?"

"I believe so. Why?"

"Transfer her to Honduras. Sometimes it takes a hunter to find a hunter."

***

CHAPTER FOUR

MARK'S HACIENDA

Chikako watched as Mark opened the gun vault on the left side of the fireplace. He took Betsy and a magazine bag out and leaned the rifle against the rock mantle—hanging the bag on the gas chamber. He also removed two antique Katanas—one in a dark purple scabbard the other in royal blue—before closing and securing the door.

"You mind?" she asked as she reached out for the swords. "Nice…very nice. How did you get these?"

"The Masamune is a gift from my instructor in Morioka. This one…was Akihiko's, it's a Gassan Sadatoshi."

"Masamune, the finest sword maker of all time. And your instructor gave it to you?"

"Left it to me in his will. His daughter delivered it, said her father never forgot…never mind. Not important."

She glanced at him. *Another damsel in distress?*

He closed the vault door and latched it before moving to the right of the fireplace and repeated the process to open a second one—filled with handguns and machine pistols.

"Take your pick. Except for the Mac 10 or 11s."

Chikako moved to the vault and studied the numerous weapons. "What's so special about them?"

"Gordan Ingram's a relative. I have one from each of the manufacturing plants…collector items, so to speak."

"I'm a fan of .45s. Don't care about shootin' a bad guy more than once," she said as she checked the chamber.

"Rule sixteen: If all you have is a handgun, make sure the caliber starts in four…Try this one." He handed her a KRISS Super V—a new weapon chambered in .45 ACP. "Not readily available yet but…I called in a favor."

"Interesting."

Mark admired her handling of the weapon. "You can fire with one hand…joke you not. After we finish laying out the five acre boundry, we'll pop some caps."

"Before or after the swim?" she said, inspecting the weapon closely with a sly smile.

"Before…Save the best for last." He removed a Combat NCO grade 1911 A2 and closed the vault.

Stranger lay on the floor—head on her paw watching the two with eager eyes—while the weapons selection occurred. As soon as Mark picked up the M14 and started for the back door, she jumped up and raced to go with them.

"Wanna go, girl? Do you?"

"She is not afraid of gunfire?"

"Nope…even after being shot…"

"Shot?"

"Stranger's a retired sniffer dog. Took two 12 gauge rounds on a slash and burn operation. Lost her leg and half of her left lung."

"How did you end up with her?" She knelt down and rubbed the excited dog's head.

"Captain Lopez…Marta's husband called me. Said they were going to put her down. I ponied up for the vet bill." He opened the door.

Stranger bolted out and headed straight for the covered parking and the faded green Ranger. She danced around excitedly while she waited for Mark and Chikako to join her.

"You…are a conundrum."

"How's that? Just because a warrior is damaged ain't no reason to leave 'em behind." He opened the tail gate.

The three-legged dog jumped inside and sat down with her tail banging on the back seat and side wall.

SAO PALO, BRAZIL

Feng and his new team sat on the balcony of an exclusive home in the Morumbi neighborhood. With three bedrooms, a private pool and jacuzzi, as well as an elevator, the home was a reasonable R$32,000 a month—not that price was a concern for the number one Triad in the state. Chu Li read a communication from Grand Master Wu. When he finished he folded the single sheet of paper, and then used a candle on the table to ignite it. When certain it was burning, he laid it on the soil of a planter next to him.

"I missed her in Costa Rica. Suspected she fled to Panama. I was there when Master Wu sent us here."

"I am having her photos sent by e-mail to all our members in Brazil. I am also having fliers printed to distribute throughout the Asian community."

"What if she sees them?"

"I worded the flier to indicate her family is worried for her. Suggesting they suspect she has been kidnapped…"

"Chikako is an orphan."

"No matter. The goal is to blanket the Asian sector. Someone will have seen her."

"What arrangements for our housing have you prepared?"

"There is a tenant building I own in the center of China Town. I ordered my manager to prepare two apartments for you and your men."

"I am anxious to begin. When will the fliers be posted?"

"Tonight. Take your rest until tomorrow. I will have meals delivered to you…and other comforts if you desire."

Feng looked at his men and noted their interest in the offer. "Send comforters for the others…I do not require one."

Chu looked to the three women sunbathing nude on the balcony for a moment. "I think Natal might change your mind." He picked up a small brass bell and rang it.

The three women looked over. The Triad boss motioned for the Italian beauty to join them. She was tall, slender with enhanced breasts and moved gracefully to join them as she pulled on a light blue silk robe—doing nothing to hide her physical attributes.

"Yes, master," she said with a Italian accent.

Chu looked to Feng and smiled as he cocked his head.

"Send her," Feng said without smiling as he put on his dark sunglasses. *Tomorrow will come soon enough...I deserve a little recreation.*

PANAMA CITY, PANAMA

Bianca Toro—Colombian, medium height, voluptuous hard body—relaxed in one of the cities many WiFi coffee shops checking her e-mail. She opened one marked: Transfer Details. Effective immediately. Tegucegapi, Honduras. Contact Alan Matthews upon arrival.

She sat back in her chair and closed her iPad. *Interesting. What could be of any importance in Hondo?*

Walking out the door, she noticed three men who looked out of place. *What are camel jockeys doing here?*

Hailing a cab, she also noted they followed in a battered, rusty, yellow VW bus.

"Take a right at the next intersection," she ordered the driver.

The bus turned as well. "Take me back to the coffee shop. I think I left something there."

The driver made a u-turn without speaking. Bianca glanced back to see the yellow vehicle did so as well. *Honduras may be a good thing.*

When the cab stopped, she handed the driver the fare plus a ten dollar American bill. "Wait for me. I'll be right back.

She moved through the shop and exited out the back into a narrow alley. To her left was a rusted blue ladder attached to the wall. She scrambled up and knelt on the black tar roof behind an eighteen inch stucco wall as she attached a suppressor to her H&K .45. When the Middle Eastern men entered the alley, she shot the first two in the head and the third in the shoulder, and then the left leg.

The wounded man attempted to pull a pistol—she shot him in the hand.

Assured he could not defend himself, she moved down the ladder, kicked his pistol out of reach, but continued to keep hers pointed at his face. "Who are you? What do you want?" she hissed.

He answered painfully in Arabic—a language she could not understand. She checked his pockets and those of the dead men and found nothing other than a few bills of Panamanian money. "One more time. Who are you...and what do you want?" Bianca jabbed her gun under his chin, forcefully.

Hearing only Arabic, she pulled the trigger, sending the bullet into his brain—ending his agony, but leaving her without answers. *Damn his breath smelled like...a goat's ass.*

Back in the cab, she gave the driver an address two blocks from one of the CIA safe houses.

Once inside, Bianca moved a dresser and pulled a loose board from the floor. She lifted a metal ammo can out and removed her pocket litter. Inspecting the various passports, she settled on two and put them in her purse—the others in her roller bag. She next removed a pair of drops—cheap throw away cell phones bought with cash having no contract or means of being traced.

Bianca made a call and while waiting for an answer began to toss her clothing into the blue suitcase.

"Zorro."

"Bianca."

"*Hola mi Corazon*...Long time no hear."

"Same. You in the Americas?"

"Maybe. What's up?"

"Any line on Middle Eastern goat fuckers operating in central America?" she asked as she packed her personal items in a large shoulder bag.

"Not a whisper. You?"

"Just had three tail me. Left them in an alley waiting for the seventy-two virgin bus."

"My sat phone is secure. If you're on a drop, where are you?"

"Panama City, but I am being transferred to Hondo."

"Interesting…I have a contract coming up there next month. Contact Taco Muerez. He hangs at the Red Parrot in the art district…He'll take care of you till I arrive."

"I'll do that. Dumping this phone. Call you once I get to the land of beans and yucca. Gotta go." Bianca disconnected from the call, removed the battery, crushed the cell and flushed it down the toilet. With one last look around the shabby room, she picked up her bags and walked out.

MARK'S HACIENDA

"Business?" Chikako asked as she loaded a fresh magazine into the submachine gun.

"Former undercover DEA headed to Honduras."

"Do you trust him?"

"Her…Bianca Toro and yes. Long story short…she saved my white ass twice before I took a contract with DeBeers in Africa."

Chikako pulled her hearing protection into place and fired a series of short bursts at the targets scattered across the pasture in front of them. She finished and removed the protection. "Part of the team in Honduras?"

Mark picked up on the question behind the question. *Umm…Asian woman smells Latina woman.* "Nope. The team is set as far as I'm concerned. Besides, she has her own gig and doing well at it, I hear."

"What's that?" She loaded ammo into a empty magazine.

"Cleaner for hire. Went out on her own after Marta's husband was killed."

"Colombian?"

"To the bone. Let's run another couple of mags and get out of the sun. Have some of the left over ribs…kick back 'til it's time for a swim." Mark started a string of fire with the NCO pistol.

After a dozen rounds to adjust for distance, a solid ring floated back from the eighteen inch steel plate at four hundred yards. "Damn. Performs as advertised. Too bad the .45 is done by the time it gets there. Probably leave a hell of a bruise though."

Chikako did not respond, but continued loading a mag.

"For the record, Bianca's also an orphan."

"Look forward to meeting her," she answered before ripping off a full magazine, dropping it and doing the same with a second one.

Stranger looked to Mark, then trotted off to the Land Rover parked under the mahogany trees.

Yeah girl…I got the same vibes.

TEGUCIGALPA, HONDURAS

Alan Matthews and Bianca rode from the airport to the safe house. Daniels drove and listened to the two in the back discuss her assignment.

"…and that's it in a nut shell," he concluded.

"I don't get it. He's clean. Why does the agency need to bring him in?" She looked out the window—hiding her dislike for the instructions.

"Not ours to question. Just be a good soldier. Find him when he arrives...deliver him to me."

"What's the pay?"

"Alive $20,000. Dead...nothing."

"I'll be honest, bringing Zorro in if he doesn't want to come...is impossible."

"Come on now. Don't sell yourself short. A woman with your skills..." he looked over at the attractive woman. "...I'm sure you can manage it. I hear you have a certain effect on men."

"What if..."

Alan turned slightly on the seat and looked directly at her. "Not a good option. If you fail, I'll be forced to take...other actions."

Bianca rode in silence until the vehicle pulled into the alley beside the safe house. She got out, took her roller and shoulder bag from the trunk and walked back to the street. The two men watched her leave.

Daniels spoke first, "I didn't get the impression she was too keen on the deal."

"I didn't either...Have plan B ready. He's coming in, like it or not."

ORO del CHRISTI MINE

"Need a chopper, Hal. The road from Tegucigalpa to the mine is impossible to control. Hell…after they hit the mine the first time, they overran an Army outpost a few clicks from here. Killed every one both places…"

"Understood. I'll run it by the del Christi corporate suits. What else you need?"

"A chow wagon…and a cook. The MREs are about gone and the boys are bitchin' for some decent food."

"Give me a day. I have to go. Couple of Senators want to play a round of golf this afternoon. By the way, damn fine job so far. I'm not surprised…you've been running in Zorro's shadow far too long. Finish this assignment and I'll have something…"

"Thanks, gotta go. Cheyenne's coming in from a scout. Oh…schedule a resupply on ammo. One more rodeo, we'll be throwing rocks."

"Can't have that. I'll have the resupply dropped on you with the mess hall."

Crank, Rhino and the team reviewed a topographical map as Cheyenne laid out the search results.

"I followed their tracks to the river…about here. They left four mules…so they had to have had boats. Blood on three mules with pack saddles. No idea if they went up or down…"

"Had to be up would be my hunch." Rhino used a short stick to point at the area without road access. "Too much civilization down river."

"That's where I'd go," Crank said. "No way of telling how many men at their main base…Better for us to wait for them to come at us again."

"I calculate enough munitions for one more assault. Hal, give any indication when we will be resupplied?" Badger asked.

"Twenty-four hours and a honey wagon for hot meals," Crank replied.

"Finally some good news," Striker said, voicing the mood of the men.

"There's a suit from Tegucigalpa suppose to arrive this afternoon to assess damages…"

"That'll be easy. Have to start from scratch. I took a close look at the equipment this morning. Not even any parts to use," Jackal added.

"What about the money for the Army girls?" Rhino asked.

"Shit…I knew I'd forget something. I'll call him back when we're finished."

"We're finished, bro. Get the Scotsman on the line and get the money rolling this way. I'd bet your dick the rebels come back with a lot more firepower…and soon."

PUNTA GORDA RIVER BASIN
Nueva Guinea, Honduras

Nortino had four men under his camouflage net giving them orders. "I want every man and boy who can carry a gun here in two days. Go!"

The men left to collect their gear and those who had a camp woman said their good-byes.

"We lost some of our best soldiers," Jorge remarked.

"We will have to make new best soldiers. I want the Oro del Christi mine force destroyed," the angry Captain replied. "We will have members of Collin's fighters with us..."

"He is crazy, El Capitan, remember what he did..."

"Crazy will be perfect. He can lead the assualt himself. If he dies, we will inherit his men. It has been my dream to combine our forces for a long time."

"We should get the mortars hidden at the old mission."

"Take four of our best men with you. You can be back before we attack the mine."

After his number one departed, Nortino pulled the envelope he discovered at the Army outpost his force had over run and opened it. A smile came to his face as he read the handwritten note mixed in with the military dispatches:

Captain Rios. General Sacasa has a new mistress. Lucia Mendoza. Resides #11 Marsellas Circle. Residencial Las Hadas. Visits 09:00 every Tuesday. He has requested you take over as head of security. Expect transfer soon.

Nortino replaced the message in the envelope. *Lucia has succeeded. Beauty, brains and a true patriot. I feel certain she will gain information that would benefit our cause.*

MARK'S HACIENDA

Chikako moaned, and then collapsed on Mark's chest. The two lay on a blanket—on a wooden deck on the east side of the stone cistern—wrapped in one another's arms.

"I'm…"

"Shhh…" Mark whispered. "Relax…be still."

He ran his hands up and down her bare back as he kissed her on the neck and shoulders. She gasped then squirmed at his tender caress.

The sun sank below the tree line and the sounds of the day birds stilled leaving only the wind and the creaking of the windmill disturbing the silence.

Finally she rolled off of him and settled with one arm under his neck and the other resting on his chest. "We could buy a ship…maybe a Mason 43 or 44…just sail around the world."

"Then what?"

She slapped him on the chest. "Sail around it again, you ass. The point is…" She traced a scar on his neck with one finger. "…you've outlived your nine lives."

"I've already committed to Hal for…"

"To hell with him. He will always have one more. You and I…we're the same. Living on borrowed time."

Mark rolled onto his side and looked into her dark eyes. He gently brushed a strand of hair from her face. "I…I need to tell you something." His eyes moistened. "I was married. I had a son…"

She reached up and wiped a tear from his cheek, but did not speak—waiting quietly for him to finish the story Crank had shared on a flight to Hong Kong.

"They were murdered. They were alone and I was…was in fucking Afghanistan half a world away unable to do a damn thing."

"You were not there for a reason…"

"It was a drive-by shooting. They were just collateral damage. If I had been there…"

"If you were there, you could have died as well."

"I can't stop thinking I could have made a difference." His voice broke as he tried to hold back the pain.

"Stop beating yourself up. You will never get over the loss…but don't keep holding it in."

"I should have been there."

"You were not there. You can not undo the past…Let it go."

Mark buried his face in her neck and began to cry. The anger, pain and guilt flowed from his body as she held him close.

"Let it out…let it go." She stroked the back of his neck.

When he had finished, he felt as if a huge burden had been lifted. Not gone, but less heavy on his heart. "I'm sorry. I didn't mean to…"

"It's okay. I am happy you shared with me. We are the same. We are damaged goods...I had thoughts of you after we separated in Singapore. Feelings I'd never had before."

Mark did not move as she spoke until she revealed that she had felt something for him. He lifted himself up on one elbow and again gazed into her eyes. "So did I...think about you. When you called me in the Philippines I realized how helpless I felt that I could not be with you...Protect you..."

Chikako placed her fingers on his lips and stared into his blue eyes for several moments. "I never knew what a family meant. The orphanage where the Triad found me...I built a wall. A thick one to protect myself from life...of being bought and sold like a piece of property. Remember when we first met?...I told you I wanted out."

"No one should be subjected to that."

"Alone in Costa Rica...I had time to think...really think. You treated me with respect..."

"You deserve respect...I don't care a damn about your past. I...I love you for who you are now. As long as I'm alive, no one will ever harm you again...No one."

She reached up and pulled him down close and searched his eyes. The moment seemed eternal. He kissed her softly on the cheek, and then her lips—they let the kiss linger.

No idea what I did to deserve this but I'll take it...take it 'til hell freezes over.

McCAMBELL'S OFFICE

Hal was on the phone discussing a contract with a client when Maggie came in a placed a note on his desk: Emerson Walsh. Line two.

She departed without waiting for his response.

"I have to go. I'll have Maggie fax you the contract." Hal hung up without waiting for a reply. He tapped his pen on the desk for a moment. *Wonder what the Director of the CIA wants now?*

"Walsh, what's on your mind?"

"Hello to you too, McCambell. How are you?"

"Skip the bullshit. What do you want?"

"Need a word with Steve McCallister..."

"Never heard of him." The veins on his neck began to bulge and his face turned red.

"...went by the call sign Zorro. Where is he?"

"No idea who you're talking about."

"I understand your attitude, what with the outcome in the Congo..."

"Really? Is that right?" Hal continued to tap the pen. He turned his chair and looked at the faded photograph of the team prior to jumping into the Congo. His blood pressure continued to rise.

"I was just following orders. The call to cancel the extract came from up the ladder..."

"Five good men died, Walsh...you chicken-shit ass kissing..."

Walsh's voice hardened, "If you want to keep the shipping contracts going with the Shop, you will tell me where...."

"DOD contracts are way above you, dickwad. As for McCallister...never heard of him. So go fuck yourself." Hal slammed the receiver down. *What the hell has Zorro gotten himself into now? Jesus Christ...has the Triad looking for him. Wait a minute...Triad...CIA...fuck me runnin' sideways.*

"Maggie, get Zorro on the line," he bellowed so loud his wife and the waiting businessmen in the outer office could hear his anger clearly.

Two minutes later, she entered the office. "I left a message for him and sent a text as well. When he calls, do you want me to put him through..."

"Use the phone in the conference room. Tell him Emerson Walsh is looking for him and tell him to take my damn call when I get through with these lace panty-wearing ass-wipes and call him back."

"All right, dear...Now calm down. Take your blood pressure medication...I'll have the clients come in when you let me know you're relaxed."

"Yeah...okay. Five minutes."

Maggie paused at the door. "Any idea why Mister Walsh wants to talk to Mark?"

"Whatever it is...is shit on a stick. Those squirrels in the CIA are never looking to help anyone but themselves."

***

CHAPTER FIVE

SAO PALO, BRAZIL
Oriental Market Place

Feng waited in the shade at a street side cafe for his men to report. The heat and humidity had him sweating profusely, soaking his shirt and waistband. He sipped a chilled Chinese herbal tea when his cell vibrated—alerting him to a text message from Zhi Wu:

Add the name Mark Ingram to the list for the white-haired Caucasian we seek. Report your progress.

He returned the phone to its holder on his belt just as one of his men arrived.

"An old woman in the fish market says she saw the Yakuza several days ago. She was with another female and two children."

"Where are they now?"

"She had never seen them before and they have not returned."

Feng sat quietly for several moments. "Was the other woman Japanese?"

"No, she was Hispanic. So were the children."

"So...our lost dove may not be in the Asian district after all. Go to the cab stands. Show her picture. See if any driver recognizes her."

CLUB SABA
Dallas, Texas

Roger, Mike and Chris Klien—another McCambell agent—sat watching the dancers move to the Salsa music. It was only mid-afternoon, but several working girls were in the club.

The ambiance was typical of a dance house in Brazil—flashing lights on the dance floor, large planters and urns with tropical foliage, exotic birds in cages and a live band. More women than men were on the floor and the three operatives were taking in the view with more than a good measure of interest.

"You ever worked with Zorro?" Mike asked.

"Couple times. Chile...Java, before he went contract," Chris answered.

"How'd it go?" asked Roger.

"In Chile, the friggin' Tupac made a play for the clients. Had to jump and run to the airport with the bastards right on our ass. One operative bought the farm. I took one in the butt."

"That the worst one?" Blaster asked with eyes on a slender Latina who kept smiling at him while dancing with a pair of other women.

"Oh, no…the jihad assholes in Java were worse."

"How come?" Dog questioned as the waitress delivered another round of cold beers in icy mugs.

Chris waited until the woman was gone before answering, "Towel-head freaks were all hopped up on drugs, man. Hell…had to shoot some of them four or five times before they went down."

"What were you carrying?"

"Nine mil. I upgraded to a .45 soon as we got out."

Roger and Mike exchanged a look. Both men contemplating the change in caliber themselves.

"What's the skinny? He didn't tell us much in Bangkok," Mike asked.

"Well…His wife and kid were killed in a drug related drive-by in San Antonio years ago."

"No shit?"

"What I heard at a bonus party couple years ago. Rumor has it he twisted off and fucking invaded Mexico looking for the gangbangers that did it."

"Really? All by himself?" asked Mike with a peaked sense of interest.

"That's how I heard it. Whole lotta Mexicans got fucked up. The guy telling me about it...Crank, said the body count hit fifty."

"Crank? The surfer dude?"

"There's only one Crank...Other than that, all I can say is I'd take any contract with Zorro. Knows his shit and seems to have some sort of sixth sense. Man, it's freakin' spooky how he knows hell is coming before it gets in range."

"You two have fun sitting on your ass. I'm going to dance with the sweet thing that's been eyeing me," Roger said as he got up and walked onto the dance floor.

"She's hot," Chris agreed.

"Blaster likes the little spinners...You sure you don't have any other intel on Zorro?" Mike asked.

"Well...Hal has an annual shoot at a private range north of Dallas. Zorro has taken the pistol competition six years in a row."

"I believe that. We saw him cut down some loony with a knife in Cebu last month. Crazy bastard was running right at the client and McCallister tapped him out before we could clear our holsters."

"That's Zorro. One other thing...don't get in a sword fight with him. The son-of-a-bitch dueled a Yakuza Katana master in Kenya. Cut his head clean off," Chris added as he stroked his first finger across his neck.

Mike sat starring with a look of disbelief. "Swords? Jesus, is there any way he can't..."

"I doubt it. You notice the scar on the left side of his neck? Some FARC hit man in Colombia managed to stick him with a broken beer bottle. Crank says Zorro broke the guy's neck before he collapsed himself. Would have bled out except for the surfer's medic skills. Zipped the wound up with Super Glue."

"Give me a break...no friggin' way," Sloan said completely enthralled with the story. "You know? I did see a scar."

"Crank and the rest of the team stole a plane and flew him to Costa Rica. Took him to one of Hal's under-the-table medical guys. He sewed him up nice and clean...said another millimeter and it would have sliced the carotid."

"Man, you're jerking my chain...aren't you?"

"Hey...you asked. I'm just telling you what I heard. He has some sort of code. Reads the *Art of War* all the time. He's an inactive combat Marine That right there proves he's one seriously crazy mutha. Oh, that reminds me...you hear about the hero shit he pulled in Afghanistan?"

RED PARROT
Teguciagola, Honduras

Taco Muerez—forty year old former Honduras State Police Captain—waited at his regular table near the back of the club. He wore a khaki long-sleeve shirt rolled up above the elbows and a pair of dark green cargo shorts. His palm leaf hat lay on a chair beside him and a pistol between his legs—ready for what ever may come.

Bianca stepped into the cool dark room from the intense midday sun. The light behind her outlined her voluptuous figure through the light yellow cotton skirt and white blouse. She moved to the bar and paused to let her eyes adjust and recognized Taco when he lifted his beer bottle in a salute before taking a drink.

As she moved through the crowd several men made comments to her—which she ignored. One man reached out to grab her waist as she passed. She gripped his thumb and twisted it back causing him to tumble from his chair to the floor. Without speaking, she moved on with the patrons hoorahing the fallen male.

"Taco?"

"Zorro did not lie when he said you are beautiful. Have a seat. Would you like a refreshment?"

"Shot of tequila and a cold beer." Bianca moved a wooden chair to the wall and sat down beside Muerez.

He waved a waitress over and ordered her drink and another for himself. "You here to work with Zorro?"

"Not sure yet. When is he going to arrive?"

"Soon. Where are you staying?"

"Somewhere quiet."

"I'm sorry…I did not mean to pry into your affairs. I just thought you might need someplace."

"I'm good. Who supplies the toys here?"

"I do. What are your needs?"

"Couple hundred .45…a twelve gauge pump with ammo."

"Concealable?"

85

"Definitely."

"Anything else?"

"Where do the young men go to find a woman?"

Taco was taken back a bit and turned to look at the stunning woman next to him. "Where ever you go I would think."

"Last time I was here it was El Pluto, but I drove by it on the way…looks deserted now."

"It was bombed about six months ago. The owners never reopened. The hot spot now is the Nieve Negro in the Hyatt Regency hotel."

Bianca downed the tequila shot and chased it with a long pull on the cold beer. As she stood up, she handed a small slip of paper to Taco. "Thanks. Here's the number to reach me. Call when you have the items I need."

"I will call tomorrow. Be careful…the state police are not to be trusted."

"Where are the police to be trusted?"

He watched her walk out. *If only I was younger…and richer.*

McCAMBELL SAFE HOUSE
Dallas, Texas

Mike woke up to the sound of his cell phone. *Oh, man…not going drinking with Blaster ever again.* He fumbled to open it without looking to see who it was. "Hel…lo."

"Get your ass up and moving. I'm sending you and Roger down in advance of Zorro."

"Yes, sir. When?"

"Have a jet leaving in three hours for Nicaragua. It will drop you on the way."

"Does Roger know?"

"That's your job. He left the club with a Hispanic slut last night. Track him down and be at the Addison airport before the plane takes off. Hanger F."

Mike stared at the phone for a moment after Hal hung up. *How did he know Blaster?...Still got a tail on us. Duh.* He sat up, then fell back on the bed. *Oh...my head.*

Easing to a sitting position, he dialed Mantle's number and left a message when he did not answer. *Hope he picks this up in time.* As he moved to the shower his phone rang.

"Sloan here."

"Hey dog...it's Blaster. What's up?"

"Addison airport. Three hours. Hanger F. Hal's sending us down ahead of the contract."

MARTA'S HOME
Sao Palo, Brazil

DeLeon answered the door to find Pablo—a driver for a local cab company—standing with his hat in his hands.

"Hello, Pablo. Come in."

"No...I am working and must pick up a fare. I just wanted to tell you the manager posted a photo of the Asian woman staying with Marta."

"What? Why?"

"Don't know…but the poster says there is a four thousand Brazilian reward for the person who finds her," he said before walking back to his cab.

DeLeon stood in the backyard under a cabana next to the small swimming pool and made a call. He watched the house anxiously as he waited for Mark to answer.

"Zorro."

"Problem. Pablo…you know him, drives a cab? Tells me there is a reward poster at the cab company with your friend's photo on it."

"Any idea who posted it?"

"No, but…"

"Where is Marta?"

"She's at work. The children are with their grandparents."

"Call Marta. Tell her there's an emergency. Tell her I'm…injured, fell off a horse, whatever. Use your own judgment. Go get the kids and grandparents. Leave as soon as you can."

"I will do this."

"You got a weapon?"

"My pistol."

"Go in the garage. Pull the wooden panels off the wall in the back east corner. There's a MP5 and ammo in a waterproof container."

"Your friend is in trouble?"

"No time for details. Just be on the lookout for any Asians with tattoos. Call me when you're thirty minutes out."

MARK'S HACIENDA

Chikako slept in a hammock with Stranger laying underneath when Mark walked onto the patio. He sat down on one of the benches and watched her. The black dog lifted her head, looked at him, yawned, then lay back down, stretched and sighed.

This shit with the Triad has to end...even if I have to go into China to do it. He stood watching the sleeping woman and dog for a long minute.

Mark had several weapons laid out on the heavy wooden coffee table and leaning against the fireplace mantle when she came in from her nap.

"Expecting war?" she asked with a smile.

"My Black Eagle Force friends have a motto: Semper Paro Bellum."

"Meaning?"

"Always prepare for war."

Seeing the intense look on his face as he put a field-stripped M-16 back together the smile faded. "What is it?"

"DeLeon called while you were asleep. There's a reward poster with your photo on it in Sao Palo."

She sank onto the couch facing Mark. "I should go."

"You should stay. This is the best place to deal with whoever is looking for..."

"Has to be the Triad. Has to be..."

"Yup. We have about three hours before DeLeon and the family get here. Load some mags for the .556 and then the H&Ks. We'll stash 'em around the compound in case we're forced to vacate."

She picked up a magazine and began loading it.

HIGHWAY 364
Brazil

DeLeon drove Marta's 4 Runner. The grandparents and Angelic rode in the rear passenger seat while Alejandro lay on luggage in the cargo area. Marta talked on her cell with her employer.

"It's a family emergency. My brother has been in a car wreck. I'll call you when I know more." She hung up and put a hand to her forehead.

"How did it go?" DeLeon asked.

"Fine. I have two weeks vacation coming. It will be fine. Sit still, Chico," she said reprimanding the family Chihuahua.

"How much longer?" Angelica asked.

"An hour at most. You will love the time in the country," Marta answered.

"Zorro doesn't have WiFi. Our iPads do not work there," Alejandro moaned.

DeLeon looked in the rearview mirror as he passed the turn onto SP-215. He pulled to the shoulder and waited for several minutes watching the traffic flow by.

"Why are we stopping here? That was the turn to Tio Mark's back there?" Alejandro questioned.

"I was thinking of something and missed it. As soon as an opening comes I will turn around," DeLeon answered with a look to Marta.

After a five minute pause to insure no one was following, he made a U-turn and immediately turned right onto the two lane road. As the sun slipped below the horizon, the sky was brilliantly lit in orange, red and pink to the west.

An hour later the they pulled under the covered parking at the back of the hacienda. The kids jumped out and began calling Stranger. Mark and Chikako came out to greet the weary travelers wearing sidearms.

"What you doing with the guns?" Alejandro asked as he rubbed the dog briskly on the shoulders.

"We were out shooting today. Just haven't put them away yet," Mark answered. "Let's get everyone inside. Dinner is on the table."

Once the family was seated, Mark and DeLeon excused themselves claiming they needed to feed the livestock.

"I called Boar and Bama...they'll be here soon. 'Til then, it's just the three of us," Mark said as they crossed the patio.

"So what's the deal?" DeLeon asked.

"Chikako and I hit a Triad boss in Hong Kong. They have no expiration date on revenge. I'm pretty sure that's who's looking for her...and me, for that matter. Any sign you were being followed?"

"None. Doubled back several times. Made the sitting pass before turning onto the 215."

"Well done, *mi amigo*. We loaded the corner stash boxes around the fence, moved some firepower to all the usual locations. All we can do now is wait."

"I think we are clear, Zorro. Only Pablo knows anything about your friend and he would never tell."

"Hope it doesn't come to that. The slant eyes can be very persuasive."

"How did you get tangled up with them?"

"Ivory…the contract in Kenya led to the Triad. I thought I'd stopped it, but I didn't. So I went after the head of the snake."

"How did your friend get involved?"

"She was a Yakuza hitman…hit woman, hired to eliminate me in Nairobi. It's complicated. Trust me…trust her. She's on the run and is one badass bitch in a fight. We'll be glad she's here if the slants show up."

"You're the boss. Unless there's anything else I'm going to eat and get some sleep."

"You're good. We'll stand duty tonight. Just stay weapons ready. Oh…I put a M-16 in your closet and a six mag pouch.

McCAMBELL'S OFFICE

Hal was reading the Dallas Morning News when Maggie walked in with two operatives. Kevin Maldinado, inactive US Marine and Leo Hernandez, former Green Beret, came in to discuss their next contract.

"Have a seat. Cigar?" Hal motioned to the two chairs in front of his desk and opened his desktop humador.

Both men accepted his offer and set about preparing their smokes with a cigar clipper.

"How soon do we get started in Borneo?" Hernandez asked.

"Change of plans. I need you in Honduras."

"Honduras? What's going on in that shit hole?" Kevin responded.

"I want you on a cover assignment. I have a team going in to baby-sit a new client. You will baby-sit the team. Covertly...and report directly to me."

"Who's the number one?" Leo questioned as he exhaled his first taste of the expensive Nicaraguan cigar.

"Zorro."

Kevin coughed up smoke and looked to Hernandez before speaking. "Zorro? Is this some sort of joke?"

"The CIA is looking to have a chitchat with him. Got a call from the Director himself. You boys will make sure that never happens."

The two men sat in silence for several moments as the disposition of their assignment sank in.

CHOLUTECA, HONDURAS
Batt Energy Technology Office

Malcom Winslow worked on a geological survey map pinned to the wall when Roger Mantle and Mike Sloan walked in. He turned and looked over his glasses with apprehension at first, but seeing they were Caucasian, he relaxed.

"We're looking for Malcom Winslow," Mantle said.

"I'm him."

"Hal McCambell sent us down early to get the lay of the land, so to speak. When's your boss coming in?" Sloan asked.

"Next week. When did you arrive? I wasn't informed you were coming."

"An hour ago. How about running us out to the digs so we can get cleaned up?" Roger asked as he looked around the office then out the window at the street below.

"Of course. Give me a minute."

Roger nodded and Mike noted his partner's glance and slight tilt of his head toward the office window. He moved closer and checked out the street as well. On the corner was a black Mazda with two men standing beside it. Both were looking up at the office.

"Zorro's rule fourteen. Somebody is always looking for you," Mike said with a grin.

"Come again?" Winslow asked as he gathered up his briefcase and coat.

"Nothing. There a back way out of here?" Roger asked.

"Why yes…yes there is. Is there a problem?" Malcom asked nervously as he moved toward the window.

"Ever seen those two before?" Roger pointed.

"No, I don't think so. Who are they?"

"You have a driver?"

"Yes, that's my car over there. Next to the cafe."

"Call the driver. Have him pull over to the front."

Winslow did as he was instructed and as the vehicle moved
to the front door of the building, the two men on the street got in
their car.

"Tell the driver to wait for ten minutes."

"Okay, what is going on?" he asked anxiously.

"Let's go. Mike, you first. Mister Winslow you next. I'll
bring up the rear."

The three men exited the building onto a narrow street, quickly
crossed it and entered a bakery. Moments later they exited out
the back into an alley and walked east to a busy street where
they hailed a cab.

"This is very unusual. Why all sneaking around?" asked
Malcom as he held his briefcase across his chest.

"Just got here. No idea who those guys on the street were,
but they seemed too interested. Call your driver again and tell
him he's dismissed for the day."

SAN PEDRO SULA
Honduras

Carlos Pineda lay on a table getting a tattoo on his bald head
when his cell rang. "What?"

"The engineer's car has left, but he did not come down. He
is still inside. Earlier two men with luggage entered the
building. We saw them through his office window."

"Remain on your post. Call me when they leave.
Wait...what did the two men look like?"

"Anglos…maybe Americans."

"More engineers?"

"They looked like soldiers."

"Umm, I see. Keep me posted."

Pineda hung up and made a call. "Winslow has visitors. Call me when they arrive at his residence. I want photos of the two new men with him."

"Yes, boss."

Why would the mouse have soldiers?

MARK'S HACIENDA

A brown Nissan SUV pulled up to the front of the house and Boar—Israeli, now retired due to the loss of one eye—and Bama—big black man retired due to age—stepped out.

Mark and Chikako met them at the gate. Stranger barked aggressively. "Down girl…Thanks for coming. Pull your vehicle around back…park under the covering. We'll meet you there."

As the two men entered their car and pulled off, Chikako commented, "That makes five."

"For now. You and I have to be in Honduras day after tomorrow."

"I thought you said…"

"Message from Hal this morning. The new guys are down already. We need to be there ahead of the client as well."

"What about Marta? The children?"

"They'll be safe here. DeLeon will monitor activities back in Sao Palo. When all is clear they can go home."

Mark and Chikako sparred with wooden Katanas on the lawn—both sweating profusely in the blistering sun—while Alejandro, Boar and Bama looked on.

Though smaller, she was quick and aggressive in her attacks. Mark had to back up repeatedly while defending himself from her slashing blows. Not only was she the aggressor, she was cunning.

"Dang dog, dat gurl has you on da run," Bama said with a laugh. His rich thick southern accent—a product of his rural upbringing masked his college education—carried above the sound of the bukkens impacting with solid cracks.

After an attack starting with a kirioshi—straight downward—followed by a pair of mayoko giri—side cuts—in succession, she spun and performed a tsoki—a straight thrust that impacted Mark in the rib cage just below the heart.

"Unnhh!" he moaned.

"Stop leading with you gut," Boar chided.

Before he could recover, she returned to a Nukitsuke position with her weapon held upward—her hands beside her head—and smiled. "You are slow today."

He caught his breath with his weapon down—tip touching the ground—and eyed her for a moment. "Today?"

"You reportedly dispatched Akihiko in Kenya. Reportedly the second best swordsman in all the Yakuza."

"I told you...it was luck. And what do you mean reportedly?"

"You are stalling for time, but I'll humor you...Actually he was third."

"And you know this how?" He stepped back, straightened up, cocked his head left and right—popping his neck—and assumed a starting position as well.

"I was not allowed to compete with the men. If I had been...I would have been first," she said before rushing forward delivering another rapid series of Tabi-gata strokes at his feet followed by a spinning Yako horizontal blow—the final one resulting in her weapon resting beside his neck. She smiled as she drew it back slowly in a slicing move that would have severed his head if the blade had been steel.

"You da headless horseman now." Bama chuckled.

"She got you, Zorro!" Alejando yelled with glee.

"She sure did. I'd be decapitated for sure if these were real swords." Mark rubbed his neck. "This is why I said...wooden," he continued with a look to his adversary.

"That's three for me...zero for you," she said as she assumed a Nukitsuke stance to continue.

"Enough. It's time to prepare our meal," Marta interjected with a laugh as she walked out the back door holding a large pan of steaks and potatoes wrapped in aluminum foil. "You two can continue another time."

"Saved by the cavalry," Mark responded.

Chikako lowered her weapon and started to bow. Mark quickly tapped her firmly on the head.

"Ouch! No fair…"

"You're the last person to call foul." Mark moved back.

"Hey…you cheated, Zorro," Alejandro exclaimed.

"Pay back's a bitch," Chikako said with a gleam in her eyes.

"Alejandro…your turn," Mark said as he quickly tossed his bukken to the boy.

"Wow! Cool. Show me how you sliced him the last time."

The woman looked to Mark with a smile before turning to the boy. "Okay. First…put your feet like this…"

***

CHAPTER SIX

ORO del CHRISTIE MINE
Nicaragua

Cheyenne and Pantera lay on a small hill above the large river. Crank detailed them to record the traffic and act as early warning for any future assault by the rebel forces.

"I had a vision last night," Cheyenne said softly.

"What about?"

"Two warriors. A man and woman who rode white horses," he replied after taking a swallow of tepid water from his hydration bag.

"Uh-huh...Was she hot?"

The Indian turned and smiled. "Yeah...and she was carrying a sword."

"What? I didn't know you Indians used swords."

"She wasn't Indian. The man carried one too."

"You should write a book about your visions. Get some artist to illustrate them. Comic books are big business. Look at all the movies being made from graphic novels."

A long skiff turned toward the bank below them. Five men and two women appeared to be fishing—long bamboo poles with line trailing in the wake of the boat.

"That's weird. Those guys are moving too fast to catch any fish," Pantera said.

When the vessel neared the bank two of the men jumped out into the knee deep brown water and pulled it to the shore. The occupants had dropped their poles and picked up an assortment of small arms. They formed a quick perimeter position before trotting away on a foot path. One man remained with the boat.

Cheyenne picked up a combat radio and made a call. "Oro del Christie…incoming."

Immediately a voice came back. "Strength?"

"Six tangos. Moving your direction at the double time."

"Ten-four."

Several moments passed before Crank's voice came over the radio. "Scout one come in."

"Scout one…go ahead," Cheyenne answered.

"Only one boat?"

"Affirmative."

"Any guard detail?"

"One."

"Take him out. Set the boat adrift."

"Done. Man, these new radios are the boss."

"McCambell always provides the best. His fingers are in everything it seems," Pantera replied.

The day was nearly done and the shadows long on the river when the rebels—minus two men—returned to find their transportation and compadre gone. They milled about for several moments before moving off upriver on foot.

"Didn't see that coming," Pantera whispered.

"Stay here. I'm going to trail them for a while." Cheyenne slipped out of their hide and moved to the riverbank.

CHOLUTECA, HONDURAS
Batt Energy Residence

Roger and Mike swept the house in tandem with Winslow close behind them.

"There have not been any disturbances here since I arrived," the meek, slender engineer said.

"Good to know. How long have you been in country?" Mike asked.

"Two months and I'm ready to go home. There is one terrorist attack after another."

"You have a gun?" Roger asked.

"Heavens no. I'm an engineer."

"Who leased this place?" Mantle asked.

"Mister Batt leased it himself."

"Let's see the upstairs. Dog…you lead."

"Did you notice the car parked down the street when we arrived?" Mike asked as he started up the stairs.

"Yeah. Have you seen it before, Winslow?"

"No, I mean...I don't think so. Why?"

"People like you are the reason people like us have a job. Bad guys will scope you out for a week, maybe a month then...boom, grab your happy ass up and demand a ransom."

"Why? I don't have any money?"

"More than most folks living here. You have a driver, a car, live in this place. Easy picking's for the bad boys" Roger followed Mike up the stairs.

MARK'S HACIENDA

Mark and the team sat on the patio under a moonless night sky. The light from the hacienda windows offered the only illumination, but the group had collected in the shadows.

"Chikako and I leave day after tomorrow. I need you three to stay here 'til this is sorted out."

"I thought you were going to stay another two weeks," DeLeon said.

"Lest you forget...Everything changes by the heartbeat. Hal sent two newbies into Hondo in advance of the client. I should be there."

"How do we handle this?" Boar asked.

"DeLeon's number one. He knows this place better than I do. Fall in and do what you do best. Eliminate anyone who shows up. Use the backhoe to bury 'em."

"How longs we gonna be here?" Bama asked.

"As long as it takes. I made a call to an associate in Sao Palo earlier. Could be the solution. And Hans is creating some smoke and mirrors for the Triad to follow to Nigeria. Once there, the trail will go cold. Any luck at all...they'll head back to China."

"If not?" DeLeon asked.

"Not sure yet. DeLeon set the rotation for guard tonight. Man the tree house. Eight hour shifts."

Everyone glanced up at what appeared to be a child's play house—which it was, but actually hardened to .30 caliber safe—sitting in one of the huge trees beside the patio.

"Tomorrow we'll do a full sweep of the property. Go over the fall back positions...fine tune any other details needed," Mark continued. "Get some sleep...weapons ready."

"Any lucks at all, dis will become a full time gig. Dis place of yours be awesome," Bama remarked with a smile as he stood up. "I'll takes da first watch."

ORO del CHRISTI MINE

A Merdedes-Benz Unimog command vehicle and two US M35 two and a half ton cargo trucks pulled into the compound. Crank and Rhino met them.

"Welcome to del Christi," Crank said.

"I am Captain Mendez. General Sacasa ordered us here to provide security for your operation," the immaculately uniformed officer replied.

"I'm Crank...this is my number two...Rhino. Have your men set up over by that old barracks building. Chow at 1700."

Mendez shook hands with both men before marching off to get his troops in order.

"Nice uniforms. Got enough bling to sink an oil tanker," Crank said with a sly smile.

"We shall call him...shiney boots," Rhino replied.

Crank could not help but laugh. "Let's hold a short weapons course after they get settled in. Find out who the shooters are. Hey...M-29 mortars. Sweet. Gotta get those 81mm bad boys set up." He and Rhino exchanged looks of surprise. "I need to go see what intel Jackal has from our new guests."

Crank entered a bombed-out building—joining Jackal, Adom, Ibo and the two captured rebels. Both the Nicaraguan men were stripped naked and tied to steel bed frames leaning against the wall. Neither man was injured, but there was fear in their eyes.

"How's it coming?"

"Oh, they pretty much told me everything, once these two showed up with their knives," Jackal replied with a nod to the two Nigerians. "I see mortars?"

"Yeah, three of them. Details."

"The group is led by a former Contra named Nortino. Used to be a sergeant with Commander Zero...big boss back in the Contra days. Promoted himself to Captain. There are about a hundred of 'em, with more on the way..."

"On the way where?" asked Crank as he peeled the wrapper off a stick of mango-flavored gum.

"Here…but for now headed for Nortino's camp."

"ETA?"

"These two were part of a team sent to scout our positions. They have no idea when the next assault is coming…Soon though."

"Time to go offense…With twenty uniforms and their toys, we can get out in front of these dickheads this time," Crank said as he turned to leave.

"What about these two?"

"Dig holes. Bury 'em up to their neck…Pick a spot where they can watch the show."

TEGUCIGALPA, HONDURAS

Bianca walked through Plaza Morazan. Seeing a bench on the edge of the city square, she sat down and watched the crowd. Flocks of pigeons flew up, scattered, regrouped and landed again as the people walked by. The fountain attracted many of the local residents—especially the young lovers who threw coins in the pool as they made a wish.

How do I warn Zorro? Damn, girl…skip the politics. Just give it to him straight up. She pulled her phone from her shoulder bag and dialed. A pair of pigeons began to walk carefully towards her—bobbing their heads as they watched for any bit of food she might throw them.

"Zorro."

"Bianca…this is the number to reach me. When will you be in Honduras?"

"Sooner than expected. You there now?"

"Yes. I met with your ICC yesterday. Tools expected today."

"I didn't catch why you are in Hondo?"

"You remember Alan Matthews?"

A long pause ensued.

"Zorro?"

"Yeah…I remember that sack of shit."

"He's the number one in Honduras and Nicaragua. He wants a meet with you."

"Uh-huh. Any idea why?"

"No. Told it was strictly need to know."

"How do you fit into this?"

"I'm suppose to deliver you…"

SAO PALO, BRAZIL

No one had discovered any useful information concerning Chikako and Feng began to have thoughts that she may have departed the city. His cell rang.

"Hello."

"I am looking at a reward poster. Are you the person who had it distributed?"

The Triad hit man sat up with anticipation. "What information do you have?"

"Bring the money to the Paroquia Sao Domingos…164 Perdizes street. Tonight…eight o'clock."

"How will I know you?"

"I will be out front, wearing a red baseball cap."

"I will be there." Feng leapt from his chair and entered the apartment. *This could be it. The lead that will bring the bitch into my grasp.*

MARK'S HACIENDA

"Thanks Pablo. I owe you one."

"It is I who owe you. The moneys you gave for my son's medical bills was a gift I can never repay."

"It's now paid in full. Don't be caught alone with these men."

"It will be right before evening mass. There will be a crowd, I am certain."

Mark hung up and started to the house and the team.

DeLeon met him at the gate. "He will do it?"

"Already has. If they take the bait, they'll be in the hole tonight."

"If not?"

"Plan B." Mark's cell rang. "I need to take this."

After moving out of earshot of the others, he answered, "Captain Silva, appreciate you calling me back."

"Great to hear from you my friend. It has been a long time."

"I've been working out of the country. There's a situation I think you should be made aware of in Sao Palo."

"What might that be?"

"Tonight at 2000 a group of Triad members will be meeting with an associate…"

"Triad? They are very bad fellows you know."

"Yes…yes they are, but tonight at Paroquia Sao Domingos four, five…maybe more are going…"

"Tell me, for I am more than curious. How do you know of this?"

"It's a long story, Silva. The short of it is…they're hunting a woman and have put out reward posters for information about her. I learned of it from a cab driver."

"What is your interest in this woman?"

"She's a friend. What would it take for you to organize a meet and greet with them?"

"This is very short notice, you know? Shall we say…fifty thousand?"

"I'm thinking a hundred, including acquisition of some drugs from the evidence room."

"My friend…such evidence could lead to a long stay in one of our prisons."

"Longer the better."

"I am certain for a hundred thousand…life there, if one could call it that, could be arranged."

Mark smiled. "Done. Succeed and I'll make sure a Christmas gift arrives for you and your family…How are your wife and children?"

"They are good. Very good, thank you for asking. I should go now. There is much to do before tonight."

After hanging up, Mark grinned. "Yes!"

The others looked over, hearing his excited outburst.

"What's up?" DeLeon asked.

"Problem solved."

Mark entered the house to find Chikako, Marta and her parents playing a game of checkers on the kitchen table.

"All over soon. The Chinese boys are going to meet some of Sao Palo's finest tonight."

"Dear lord, I pray you are right," Marta's mom said with relief as she crossed herself.

"I'm going to hit the hay...Long day tomorrow." Mark headed to his bedroom.

Marta put her hand on top of Chikako's. "You see...I told you he would fix it. He always does."

"It may be over here...but there will be others. Their vengeance knows no expiration date." She stood up. "I'm going to bed as well. Thanks for a wonderful evening."

Mark had removed his shirt and shoes before turning on the shower. He turned to see her standing in the doorway.

"Are you certain. Marta's family will be safe?"

"Whoever is following you will be doing life in a Brazilian prison...Nicest thing said about any of 'em is they define hell on earth."

"More will come."

"I know a computer genius, sent him an encrypted message today including a couple of our photos and some video. He's going to create a trail for us...starts in Sao Palo ends in Nigeria...Ever consider visiting China again?"

"Hell no! Are you out of your mind?...Wait a minute...what pictures and video?"

"I pulled several off the security feed here at the hacienda. Just grainy enough to pass for airport security cameras...Trust me. Hans can do this in his sleep."

AYSEN REGION, CHILE
Hans Schoepke's Ranch

The late sixties white-haired computer guru sat staring at one of the many screens in his work room. His finger hovered over the send key as he reviewed his work.

"Hans, dear are you coming to bed?" Francisca called.

"Yes...give me one moment." He hit the send key. *Not a bad piece of work...certainly easy enough hacking the airport security systems. Wonder who is looking for her? Umm...need to leave a back door in case something like this comes up again.*

NICARAGUAN NATIONAL ARMY HQ

Sacasa read a communiqué from Captain Mendez while he enjoyed a cup of Cuban coffee. His incessant need to be an elitist caused him to scorn the finer Nicaraguan blends in favor of the more expensive one. *Collins joining forces with Nortino...splendid turn of events.*

"Major Corrales, come in here."

When the officer stood in front of his desk, the General handed him the message. "I want an attack squadron readied.

111

When our longtime enemies attack, we will support the Oro del Christi mine in force."

"Yes, my General. I will see to it immediately."

Sacasa moved to the window, still drinking his coffee—he gazed out on the base with a smile. *With General Diaz retiring next year this could be the very thing I need to insure I replace him as supreme commander.*

CIA SAFE HOUSE
Honduras

Matthews reviewed a file and paused on a photograph of Mark. His cell vibrated for a new text: When will the American arrive? Need to progress is urgent. Marketing disruptions becoming excessive.

Alan sent a reply: Patience. Expect arrival within forty-eight to seventy-two hours. Will advise. Must not be implicated.

As soon as the reply was sent, he deleted both messages from his phone.

Daniels walked in and saw the photo. "So that's him? Doesn't look like much...Hell, looks like a hippy with gray hair."

"Premature...He was the best cleaner we ever had."

"Then how is Bianca going to catch him?"

"History. They worked together in Colombia. If anyone can get close to him...she can."

MARK'S HACIENDA

"Well done Silva. Damn well done. Let me know when they are inside for good."

"I will do so for sure. If I can be of assistance in the future, do not hesitate to call."

"I will," Mark said before hanging up.

Chikako paused her martial arts practice. "We clear now?"

"Yup…damn straight, skippy. Three down permanently and three locked up."

"And your friend, the cab driver?"

"Safe and sound. Now that the initial threat is eliminated and Hans has spread the bread crumbs to Nigeria…we can go to Honduras without concern for Marta and her family. That's a weight off," he said with a smile that did not go away.

"Time for another sparring session?" She had gleam in her eye.

"Oh, hell no. I'm so sore from yesterday I couldn't take another."

"You mind if I take one of your wakizashi along?"

"Good idea…I'll take one as well. The mofos in Central America love their machetes…They'd be no match for a Japanese wakizashi."

Mark's cell rang. "It's Hans." He answered, "Zorro."

"The path is laid. You and your friend are now in Nigeria, figuratively speaking of course."

"Excellent. What would it cost to have one of your vehicle bomb detectors and a trio of room sweepers delivered to Choluteca, Honduras?"

"The three of the latest model sweepers and a new...and improved...detector would run you eleven thousand...plus shipping, tax included." He chuckled.

"I'll text you an address. Thanks for the misdirection. I'd love to be a fly on the wall when the Triad show up in Nigeria."

"I could arrange that...if you have the money."

"I was joking Hans. But...you could do that?" He watched Chikako inspect the Samurai short swords. *Must have died and gone to heaven. Beautiful, smart and some skills that overshadow my own,* he mused as he rotated his left arm to ease the ache from her repeated bukken blows.

"Most assuredly. Would you require such a service in Honduras? It would take me twenty-four hours to set it up..."

"Do it. Start with the address for shipping the electronics. What do I need on my end to view it?"

"Any of the new smart phones, if you wish to be mobile. I could also link to your fixed position security system...I suggest both."

"How hard would it be for any bad guys to hack us?"

"Surely you jest, Zorro...No one hacks my work."

"Yeah...yeah...and don't call me Shirley. I'm a computer caveman, so I leave the gizmos to you. Give Francesca my regards."

"She said the same to you."

SHENYANG, CHINA
Dadong District

Zing Wu focused on a document detailing the orders from Europe for his stolen ivory. He smiled noting the huge volume of reorders as he calculated the profits. A knock at the door broke his attention. "Enter."

Pon shuffled in with his head bowed. "There are difficulties in Brazil, Master."

The Dragon Master slammed his fist down on the desk as he stood up. The assistant trembled, knowing the news would only darken his bosses mood further.

"What?"

"Feng is on the line. He is in jail."

"Son of a whore," he cursed in Chinese.

Pon bowed even deeper, recognizing the deepth of Wu's anger. "What are your instructions, Master?" His voice shook.

"Leave him there! Do not take any further calls from him. Let his reward for failing me be forever in their prison."

The assistant backed out of the office, still in the bowed position. As he closed the door behind him he replied, "As you desire, Master."

Wu stormed around his office in a violent rage. He swept priceless artifacts off their pedestals, shattering them on the floor.

"I am Zing Peng Wu…Grand Master of the Big Circle! Why am I denied this one pleasure?"

Pon and three other men listened from behind the closed door and looked to one another uneasily.

"I have never heard him this angry," Pon whispered to the others. They all flinched when a large object impacted the door.

An hour after the last sound of breaking antiques, Pon answered the phone on his desk. "Hello."

"Great news, Pon. The woman and the man Master Wu seeks departed Sau Palo, Brazil bound for Nigeria."

"You are certain of this? It is not a good time to disappoint Master Wu."

"Positive. We intercepted visual evidence from the airport security cameras. I confirmed the tickets were bought and the passengers boarded the flight."

"Send me all you have immediately! This is just what the Dragon Master needs to quell his rage." Pon leaned back in his chair and breathed a sign of relief.

MARK'S HACIENDA

Chikako playfully sparred with Alejandro in a shaded area on the stone patio. Mark and the men reviewed a topographical map of the ranch and surrounding area.

"Your friend is good with children," Marta remarked as she delivered a fresh round of ice tea.

Mark looked up to the Colombian woman then to the two dancing around with the bukkens. "Yeah…seems to be. Just for safety sake, I want you and your family to stay here for a week or so after we leave."

"Whatever you say. The kids will love the time with the horses and swimming in the stone tank."

"A child's summer paradise."

"You are breaking one of your ironclad rules…never get involved," DeLeon said.

Without taking his eyes off the two sparring Mark replied, "I know." He smiled.

"Be careful my friend. Keep your head in the game in Honduras."

He looked at his longtime friend and former spotter. "What? You don't like her?"

"No, I like her, plenty. I mean…no disrespect, but she's hot. Smart. A wizard with a sword and she's…smoking hot…What's not to like?"

"Exactly my sentiments. Back to business…You need to brief Bama on the daily routine here. When Marta and the family go home I want you and Boar to stay with them until you are certain the Triad are permanent guests of the state."

"I will. Have you arranged transportation yet?" DeLeon asked.

"Leased a private jet. Better than owning one…Planes are like boats. A hole in the water to throw money in."

The others laughed at his reference.

"Same damn thing fer swimmin' pools," Bama added.

"Lunch is ready. Do you want to eat on the patio or inside?" Marta's mother called out the screen door.

"Inside, momma. Get the cordite washed off your hands and let's chow down. You guys have a full afternoon inspecting the ranch."

Mark and Marta lingered after the others departed. A breeze washed across the landscape rustling the leaves in the trees above them.

"You did good," she said.

Mark turned to her—wrapping his arm around her shoulders. "You think?"

"Yes…yes I do. How did you two meet?"

"A wildlife sanctuary in Kenya."

"That's what she said," Marta said with a sly smile.

"It's the truth. I never expected it to evolve…"

"Whatever, Zorro…Live…Love. Enjoy your new friend…You deserve some happiness."

"Deserve it or not…I'm gonna to do just that."

ORO del CHRISTI MINE

The team and Nicaraguan troops watched as a private contract Kazan Mi-171A2 helicopter landed in the middle of the compound.

"Well the Scotsman is aces, if nothing else," Rhino said as he shielded his eyes from the dust.

"I gotta get me one of those bitches," Crank replied. "Take over on the offload. I'm going to chat up the pilot, see if I can get a fly over."

As the blades spooled down, members of the team rushed forward and began unloading the crates of supplies. Originally intended to fly personnel, this particular craft had been modified to haul supplies for the highest bidder by a former US Marine helicopter pilot, Chuck 'Sundance' Watts.

As he stepped out of the pilot's door and climbed to the ground Crank was amazed to see a carbon copy of himself. The blond-haired blue eyed Sundance was a babe magnet wherever he went. "Hell of a bird, dude! What's the engine?"

"It's a Kazan VK-2500PS Turboshaft. You fly?" Chuck answered with a distinctive Texas accent.

"Dang right bro. So…it's a Ruskie. What's the range on this beauty?"

"Four hundred thirty-two nautical, according to the manufacturer, but this one's been modified a bit and I've made over five hundred before…What do you fly?"

"Long list, but this one ain't on it. How about a spin around the block when we finish offloadin'?"

"No problem. Only run I have today and I got some time before I meet a pair of honeys tonight."

Thirty minutes later Sundance and Crank lifted off and began a series of ever widening circles.

"You ex-military?"

"SEALs. How about a little run upriver?"

"Your camp looked like a war zone."

"Rebels wiped out the whole thing not long ago. Hit us the second night we arrived…You served?"

"Semper Fi. Four tours. Iraq and Afghanistan. This beats the hell outta getting shot at...I can tell you that. How long you going to be here?"

"Year contract. I may see it all. May take something else once we get this one nailed down. Hal contract you long term?

"Just this one drop for now."

"Give me a number where I can reach you. May need a medivac if the insurgents make another run on us."

"Will do. Recognized Captain Mendez...he's General Sacasa's go-to guy. A real buzz saw when it comes to grindin' the enemy."

"Good to know. Any chance I could take the stick?"

"Sure why not...don't look for any fancy maneuvers, though...This ain't any SeaCobra or Viper gun ship."

An hour later, Watts lifted off again leaving Crank with his team. Both men saluted one another as day light faded.

"Have fun bro?" Rhino asked.

"A little. I got his number...We get hit again, may have some that need critical care."

"That's what the cash to Sacasa is for..."

"Last thing Zorro said was, don't expect the uniforms to show up 'til the party's over. Don't want anyone bleeding out on my watch."

"The boys got the kitchen going while you were playing Sky King...Steaks and beer gonna be served soon."

"Hal's the eighth wonder of the world, he is. So friggin' tight he has the first two pennies he ever made framed in his office, but still understands…an army moves on its stomach."

***

CHAPTER SEVEN

ZETA COMPOUND, HONDURAS

Oscar Puto rode a black Thoroughbred with four white stockings out of the soft sand arena and loped across a manicured lawn to the wooded area at the back of his property.

Three late model Humvees were parked near a path that led into the trees. As he rode onto the narrow lane, he slowed to a walk and enjoyed the sounds and sights of the forest. *It is good to be king.*

The sounds of men calling for mercy floated on the breeze as he neared a small clearing. They grew louder as he joined his heavily armed ZETA soldiers surrounding four men bound and kneeling.

"Don Puto…we are innocent. We are loyal to you always," the youngest man cried upon seeing the mounted rider approach.

"Yes…we are innocent," the others repeated.

"According to Riki…you are thieves. All that is left is to tell me where my cocaine is and this business will be over." Oscar smiled.

"I was not involved. I am innocent…"

"You are Riki's cousin. One bad seed means others," Puto said with a snarl.

"Please…give us another chance…"

"Tires," the king ordered. He removed a small cigar from his vest pocket and lit it as he waited.

The soldiers began to slide old worn tires over prisoners—stacking them until only their heads were visible.

"Have you ever watched the documentaries on the show *Crimes Against Humanity*?" He allowed a slow curl of smoke to rise lazily from his lips. "It is fascinating and…enlightening to learn what other cultures consider proper punishment for certain indescreations," Puto said as he circled the men.

His horse began to prance at his command—his neck arched, head and fore quarters slightly turned to the bound men. Oscar sat a good seat and appeared to be in perfect harmony with his mount. Enjoying the moment he dropped the reins on the horses neck and crossed his arms in front of his chest—guiding the animal with only cues from his knees.

"For instance just the other night I watched an episode about Somalia. Men who deserted the army were…"

"Don Puto I beg you my family needs…"

123

"Oh do not fear…I will attend to your families soon. But first…we must conclude our business…The deserters were kneeling and tires were placed around bodies…much as you are now. I ask you one last time…Where is my cocaine?"

Oscar again cued his horse and the animal began to lope. His men started to laugh and taunt the prisoners.

"On a boat…" one of the men said.

"Which boat? Which coast?"

The ZETA drug lord nodded to his enforcers. They began to pour gasoline on the four prisoners and the tires.

"El Dulce Nombre," one man yelled.

Another added, "La Union port."

"Remember me always as you enter the gates of hell. Your sons will be mutilated and hung in public. Your women? Passed around by my men until they tire of them."

Puto spurred his horse into a gallop and raced around the men as a lit match was thrown into each of the fuel soaked tires.

The blood curdling screams of the burning men lasted but a short time—all the while the head of the Honduras ZETA circled. A black plume of smoke and the rancid odor of burning rubber and flesh filled the air.

When the flames began to subside he picked up the reins, turned his mount and rode directly at them leaping over the smoldering remains before riding off toward his hacienda.

NICARAGUAN HELL

SHENYANG, CHINA
Dadong District

Fifi—a thirty year old enforcer, his head shaved except for a long braided strand of hair that ran down his back to his waist—stood in front of Zing Wu's desk. He wore a traditional red jacket with large gold thread cuffs that reached to his knees. His face was stoic but his eyes were alight with a fierce gleam.

"Feng has failed. You will not mention his name again in my presence," Wu said in a rasping voice.

"Yes, Grand Dragon."

"Pon has a folder for you. It is all you need to know about the Yakuza and the American. They have fled to Nigeria in hopes of eluding us." Wu paused then stood up and walked to a small shrine where he lit two incense sticks before turning to Fifi.

"Feng grew complacent in his role as my number one. He will rot in a Brazilian prison for it." Zing returned to his ornate chair and sat down. He picked up his yellowed ivory pipe and began to load it with tobacco. "I considered having my second replace him but...your success in England has given me pause."

Fifi bowed slightly. "I live to serve the brotherhood, Master."

Wu smiled as he lit the pipe. "Then go to Nigeria. Find Chikako and this man who has many names. Bring them to me alive. If you succeed, you will be promoted to my number one."

"I will not fail you. When do I go? Who goes with me?"

"As I said Pon has everything you need. You may choose your own men. Five will be enough."

"As you command me so shall I do, but I wish to take one computer technician with me. May I have six associates?"

Wu eyed the young man for a moment before answering, "A computer expert?"

"Yes, only one. Someone who is gifted at hacking."

Wu smiled. "So it shall be. Go."

PUERTO CABEZAS AIRPORT
Honduras

The Cessna Citation Encore taxied to a stop at the designated space the ground crew attendant indicated.

The flight had been interrupted only by a refueling stop in Colombia. Mark and Chikako deplaned to find Alfonso Cardenal—local ICC and former Honduran army major—waiting for them next to a gray Ford Explorer.

"Zorro, wonderful to see you again. I hope your flight was a pleasant one." Alfonso extended his hand. "I see you have a beautiful companion, my old friend."

"Good to see you as well. Let me introduce Mika," Mark said.

Cardenal took her hand and lightly kissed the back of it. "Enchanted, I'm sure."

She looked to Zorro with a quizzical expression. "Nice to meet you."

Chikako had on a short black wig—cut in a straight line barely touching her shoulders and distinct straight bangs. Her pinstripe suit shouted professional business woman as did her low heeled shoes. All had been purchased in Rio prior to departing Brazil—as well as five other wigs and other items useful for changing her appearance.

"We have luggage and hardware. Can we pull the vehicle closer to the plane?"

"Yes of course. Oh...here comes the customs inspector. I hope you have the funds readily available," the ICC said looking to an overweight Honduran waddling towards them—his green uniform soaked in sweat and stretching at the seams—smoking a rank smelling black cigarillo.

Mark handed a black briefcase to Alfonso. "Ten thousand American."

"Excellent. Officer Quscal...so good to see you again. These are the two business associates I was telling you about. I believe you will find their papers in order." The ICC handed the case over.

Quscal laid it on the hood of the SUV and opened it. On top were a dozen documents—all created by Hans—giving false identities for Mark and Chikako as well as forged entry permits. Below the papers, stacks of one hundred dollar bills filled the case. He flipped through the money to ensure it was all real, looked to the new arrivals, and then closed the case and latched it.

"Everything seems to be in order. Have a pleasant stay in our country." He stamped their passports. Without further conversation, he returned to the air conditioned comfort of his office.

"You have our lodging taken care of?" Mark asked.

"Most certainly. I have rented a small resort in its entirety. There are only five bungalows and they have air conditioning. My sister's cousin is the manager."

EL CHICO DELFIN RESORT

Alfonso drove in the gates of the modest resort. A pair of faded blue dolphin statues were mounted on either side of the gate. The staff stood under a green awning in front of the main building—dressed in white shirts or blouses and green shorts.

"Hello, and welcome to the little dolphin resort," a Honduran man in his late fifties said as they exited.

"Hola...please inform your staff we will take care of our own luggage," Mark replied seeing some of the young men starting towards the back of the truck.

"Manny, let me introduce Steve Wilson and his secretary, Mika," Alfonso said.

"Very nice to meet you both. Why not get settled in your quarters...then come by the front desk and check in? Alfonso has already paid for your stay."

"Thanks. We just landed and need a few minutes to relax. What time is dinner served?" Mark asked.

"I will have a plate of cold fruits and sandwiches delivered to your bungalow immediately. Any requests for beverages?"

"Your best beer and a pitcher of ice water."

Mark and Chikako had changed out of their travel attire—he was wearing a pair of loose-fitting blue cotton exercise pants and a red tank top while she had on red shorts and a yellow tank top—were sitting on the patio facing the ocean when the refreshments arrived. Both had their bare feet resting on the bamboo railing. The young woman smiled and placed the tray on the table—breeze off the ocean was pleasant and the ceiling fan added further relief from the heat.

"Is there anything else?" she asked in only fair English.

"Not at this time." Mark handed her a five dollar bill.

Her eyes widened as she accepted the generous tip. "Thank you so very much. My name is Cecilia. Please let the front desk know if you want me to deliver anything else."

After she left, Chikako removed her wig and shook out her long black hair—running her fingers through it and massaging her scalp. "Never wore a wig before. Really makes your head itch."

"Yup...Havin' a cold one then I'm going to shower and stretch out."

She stuck a wedge of lime in a bottle of Corona and handed it to him. Grabbed one for herself and took a long drink. "Is bathing one of a secretary's duties?"

"Not usually, but since you offered...absolutely."

Mark had opened his Sun Mountain hard case golf bag and was removing his Benelli sawed-off shotgun when Chikako came out of the bathroom. She finished drying her hair with a thin

129

white towel, applied a liberal amount of coconut oil to her hands and ran them through her long black strands. She cleaned her hands with the damp towel and began brushing to untangle her silky hair.

Mark looked over and drew a deep breath seeing her lithe figure wrapped in a damp towel. *Lord have mercy.*

"I'm not looking forward to putting that wig back on."

"Only need to for dinner."

"I want one of those." She eyeing the shotgun.

"We'll make it happen once we get to Choluteca."

"When we get there, how do we stay connected?"

"Cell phones and you'll have a Motorola…"

"Not that…this." She moved to him and wrapped her arms around him.

BATT ENERGY TECH OFFICE

Sloan stood outside the office—his hands crossed in front of him—watching and listening to the sounds coming up the stairwell. Mantle and Winslow were inside. Roger stood in the shadows using the window as an observation point for the street and kept a close eye on the black vehicle.

Malcolm continued his work on a map.

"I heard from Mister Batt. He will be coming in tomorrow or the next day…depending on his schedule."

Roger never looked up. "Good to know. McCambell said he would have two other executives with him."

"Yes, but he said he plans on bringing his son as well."

"Son? How old is he?"

"Fifteen…maybe sixteen."

"I'll be right back." Roger moved to the door.

Inside the hallway, he shared the news with Sloan. "The client's son may be coming as well as the executives. Call Hal. Find out if he wants to send another man."

"Better than a daughter." Sloan dialed the McCambell office.

"McCambell Import/Export…this is Maggie. How may I help you?"

"It's Mike Sloan. Is big dog there?"

"Not right now. He's playing golf with the governor."

"Let him know that the client is bringing a teenage son down here. Changes the whole dynamics of our coverage."

"I'll let him know immediately. Are you having any difficulties? Is Zorro there?"

"Nothing we can't handle so far and no, he hasn't arrived yet."

"He landed today. You still have his number?"

"Yes, ma'am. I'll call him."

EL CHICO DELFIN RESORT

Mark and Chikako sat waiting for dinner to be served. Festive candles on the tables and a half dozen lights with a variety of colored bulbs illuminated the outdoor patio.

A pair of battered sedans pulled in the gate, parked at the office building and six heavily-tattooed Hispanic males entered after a brief glance at the patio.

"Don't like the looks of that," Mark said.

A loud crashing sound followed by a woman screaming came from the office.

"Shit," Mark said as he got up.

"I'll take the back." Chikako moved toward the rear of the cantina.

As Mark approached, he began to walk with a slight swish and held his left hand in front of his body with a limp wrist while looking at his finger nails. One of the men—his head and neck heavily tattooed—stepped out and crossed his arms barring his entry.

"Well, hello big boy. My what big arms you have," Zorro said with a lisp. "I just want to see the management about staying another day."

A solid series of blows could be heard from inside the office, followed by a body falling and hitting the floor. Mark shifted and craned his neck to look past the gang member.

"Oh, my…what was that? I'll just come back later," Mark continued the lisp and started to turn away. Instead he rotated his upper body swiftly and drove the first two clenched fingers of his right hand into the man's larynx.

The goon dropped to his knees holding his throat, gasping for breath. Mark grabbed his head and twisted it violently. A crisp cracking sound assured him the neck was broken.

Entering the office, he found the manager on the floor balled up trying to protect himself from the kicks of the Hispanic males. His wife cowered in the corner crying.

"You must pay the full amount each month!" the largest man yelled.

"I give you all I have…ugghh!" the manager said as a blow landed to the small of his back.

"Who the fuck are you?" one of the men asked once he realized Mark was in the room.

Continuing the lisp, Mark answered, "I'm in number five. Could you please stop. Violence makes me…nervous."

The leader smiled. "Go back to your bungalow before we cut you, sweetie."

A distinct change in tone occurred. "Look, lizard head, you're bothering me…"

A rage crossed the leader's face. "Who are you calling lizard head, old man?"

"I was talking with you, but it pretty much applies to your little group. The ink looks like amateur prison work."

Two of the men charged him—one from either side. Mark stepped back and grabbing each man by the back of the head and introduced their foreheads. The impact stunned them and they dropped to their knees.

Cocking both arms to his side and swiftly squatting down, he slammed forward, opening his hands just before landing a palm smash to the side of each man's head. They fell violently sideways with ruptured eardrums.

"Let me start over, *puntas*…"

Another man pulled a switchblade, clicking the release to expose a six inch blade. "I cut you good, *gringo*," he said as he moved in slashing back and forth.

Mark stood relaxed—hands down. As the knife welder closed the distance, he picked up a chair and swung it into the attacker's face. Blood spurted from his nose and an ugly gash on his forehead as he dropped to his knees groaning in agony. A swift front snap kick to the face broke his jaw and sent him sprawling unconscious.

The leader pulled a pistol from under his shirt and growled, "You one stupid *gringo*…"

A twenty-five pound porcelain vase struck the man on the back of the head and shattered—he fell like a ripe watermelon face first, breaking his nose on impact with the cement floor.

The remaining two men turned to see Chikako picking up a broom and come around the front desk—so fast she was on them before they could react. She laid into them with a viscous series of strikes to every part of their body ending with a solid blow to the groins, and then front kick to one and a upward palm smash to the other.

"Ahhhhh," they groaned as their eyes crossed and they collapsed to the floor—one man vomiting, the other defecating.

"Looks like you've done this before," Mark said to her as he kicked the knife to the side.

He grabbed the two men he had palm smashed by the hair and jerked them to their knees—slaming their faces together repeatedly. "Don't know who sent you…Don't care…gather up your slack ass brothers and go tell your boss the scam is over and to never come back. *Comprende?*...And I'm not accustomed to repeating myself...and that Zorro said so. He doesn't want me to come looking for him...trust me," Mark hissed.

"*Si...si comprende*," one managed to mumble through broken teeth.

Mark and the manager stood watching as the vehicles departed.

"I'm thinking we might hang around a few days in case the *patron* doesn't comprehend the message."

"Yes, but you should know they are part of the MS-13. They showed up about a year ago and now everybody must pay them protection money."

"Figured that by the tattoos. Get your family and staff out of here. Give Chi...Mika your cell number, but I don't think they'll be back."

Mark, Chikako and Alfonso waited in the dark for the return of the gang. Each had a position allowing for interlocking fire. The half moon dimly lit the landscape and the sound of the waves on the beach belied the coming storm.

Mark and Chikako wore black pants and long sleeve shirts and had black and dark green camo face paint smeared to eliminate any shine. Both wore body armor as well.

A GMC suburban followed by a sedan and a dual cab Chevy pickup roared in just past midnight. After the vehicles cleared, Alfonso lowered the security pole gate. He then moved back behind the stone fence and leveled Mark's Remington 870 at the truck.

The vehicles slid to a stop throwing gravel off the drive into the lawn. Before the men could exit, a withering storm of lead riddled the vehicles from suppressed weapons. The sound of bullets impacting glass and whang of striking metal was louder than the firearm reports.

Four men in the bed of the truck fell before they could dismount. Three men attempted to flee, only to be cut down by more 12 gauge flechettes delivered from Alfonso's shotgun.

Two men in the middle car managed to get out and lay huddled on the ground as .45 ACP rounds from Chikako's KRISS shattered the glass, blew through the thin Japanese doors and killed the two men on the driver's side.

Mark fired from a position behind an old stone well directly in front of the first car—ripping off rounds rapidly. The armor piercing ammo plowed through the windshield killing the driver and the man riding next to him immediately.

A man attempted to exit, but made it no further than placing a foot on the ground before hot lead ripped into his body.

A thug in the lead car staggered out—hit twice in the left shoulder—and crawled toward the ocean screaming, "I go! Don't kill me...I go!"

"Too late, motherfucker!" Mark shouted.

Moving from cover to a new position Mark changed magazines in his Colt Gold Cup—dropping a fifteen rounder and replaced it with another loaded with Hydra-Shok rounds.

Once behind a large coconut tree, he dispensed with the two

men laying beside the second car—tapping both in the head—sending a pink mist spraying into the night air. He then fired a round into the leg of the man crawling for the ocean.

As quickly as the firefight erupted, it ended.

"Mika?" Mark called out.

"I'm good."

"Alfonso?"

"Good."

"Hold your positions...cover me," Mark ordered as he dropped the second mag and loaded another.

Rather than march forward like so many movie heroes, he zig-zag sprinted to the bullet riddled suburban. He duck walked down the side and did a quick look inside. Everyone appeared to be dead. Adhering to a long time rule, he tapped each once to the head. Bone, blood and brain matter blew out the backside.

He repeated the action—rushing to the second car—to find no survivors. As he approached the dual cab truck. the drivers door opened and a man leapt out attempting to flee. Mark double tapped him—once between the shoulder blades, and then in the head.

"All clear...help me load the trash into the bed of the truck," Mark called out.

Both Chikako and Alfonso approached—weapons ready—as Mark walked to the man he had shot in the leg.

"*No mas...por forvor...no mas,*" the man kept repeating as he lay cowering on the ground—his empty hands held out toward Zorro.

Mark answered him, "You're right Poncho…no more. I told you not to come back…You should have paid attention."

The odor of fresh feces wafted up from the gangbanger on the ground as he groveled in fear.

"*Vios Con Dios,*" Mark said before shooting him between the eyes.

Mark retrieved the gang member's cell phone from his shirt pocket. "Get their phones…check 'em for any intel we can use."

"What about money?" Alfonso asked.

"Take it…we'll call it interest on whatever the resort owners lost before we got here and to replace our ammo."

Mark and his ICC tossed the last body onto those already piled in the bed of the pickup truck. A stack of weapons, cell phones and wallets lay on the ground behind them.

"Let's get these cars out of here. Alfonso drive up the road to that hill with the sharp turn. Run the truck off into the sea. Call Manny. Have him meet you and drive you back here."

"On it, boss."

After he had departed in the truck Mark and Chikako walked into the *champa* thatch-roofed cantina. He poured a shot of tequila for each of them. They clinked glasses before biting on a slice of lime and downing them in one swallow.

"That went well," she said with a smile.

"Better than I'd hoped." he answered as he scrolled through the saved numbers of one of the phones.

"Easy money."

Mark started laughing.

"What?"

"Easy money…I say that all the time."

"Great minds think alike. How long you planning on hanging around here now? Double or nothing…you know they will be back…and more of them."

"Still a few days before the client arrives. This is as good a place as any for us to lay back and relax," he said with a grin. "And…just look at that view." He nodded at the moonlit ocean breaking gently on the beach.

"Worthless for surfing, but romantic. Is your Colt modified for full auto? Sounded like full auto."

"Nope. Just years of practice and a happy finger. Start scanning the phones. Look for any numbers they have in common. Sure to have the boss on 'em somewhere."

PUNTA GORDA RIVER BASIN
Honduras Nueva Guinea

Nortino stood watching rebels joining his camp. They came in small groups of three, five and sometimes as many as twelve. Most had a weapon of some sort, a few had none.

Word had spread that the great Captain Nortino was going to crush a private army sent by foreign industrialists to rape their country for its gold. Rumor also had it that he would march on Tegucigalpa before he was finished.

Moving through the camp, Jorge and his men lead a pack of mules laden with the mortars and crates of ammunition from the army base they had overrun a few days after destroying the Oro del Christi mine. A smile came to the old warrior's face as he heard the sounds of men playing guitars, men and women laughing, calls of recognition between the new arrivals and those who had fought with him for years.

A cheer went up from the far end of the encampment then a chant. Collins...Collins...Collins...

Ah...the Americano has arrived.

***

CHAPTER EIGHT

RED PARROT
Teguciagola, Honduras

Taco Muerez waited at his usual table. A young working girl sat on his lap running her fingers through his hair when Bianca entered the bar. The ceiling fans rotated lazily—doing little more than stirring the heavy cloud of cigarette smoke·

In a corner near the front, the Colombian noticed two men—Maldinado and Hernadez—who seemed too interested in not noticing. *Every eye is on me except those two...and they're wearing new shoes.*

As she approached, Muerez sent the woman away from his table and pulled a chair over to the wall next to his. "I have the tools you requested."

"First a cold beer…and who are the guys in the corner?"

"Never saw 'em before. Both have pistols under their shirts." He held up his beer bottle and indicated to the bartender he wanted two more.

"Heard from Zorro?"

"No…One of 'em is making a call."

Kevin Maldinado—cell to his ear—glanced over. He diverted his eyes when he realized he was being watched.

Leo Hernandez faced their table wearing sun glasses—a dead giveaway in the darkened bar.

"How far?" Bianca asked as the waitress delivered the new drinks.

"The trunk of my car. In the alley."

"Back door?" Bianca drained half her beer in one swallow.

"Down the hallway to the rest rooms."

"You go first. Have the car running. You get a minute head start."

Bianca ran outside and jumped into Taco's badly rusted and battered blue '81 Chevrolet Impala sedan as he pulled in front of the door. They were turning out of the alley as Kevin and Leo rushed into the alley.

"Only here one day and already you have a fan club."

"Couple of Alan Matthew's gofers, I suspect. Maybe not…Lose 'em."

"*No problema*," Taco replied as he abruptly turned onto a narrow street, downshifted and floorboarded it. He quickly turned the wheel into the slide. As the vehicle straightened out he asked, "Why would he have a tail on you?"

"No idea other than a plan B."

They exchanged a look as he turned left onto a busy avenue and began rapidly weaving through the traffic. Bianca reached out the window and adjusted the passenger side mirror. She scanned the traffic behind them, looking for any pursuit.

Bianca closed and locked the door to her small third-floor apartment. "Put the bags on the bed."

He did as she requested, and then moved to a window overlooking the street. "We lost them. Even if they find the car it's two blocks from here."

"The sooner you get across town the better. If you hear from Zorro, tell him to call me...I don't want him walking into any surprises." She removed her blouse and draped it over the back of a wobbly wooden chair.

Taco could not take his eyes off her until she turned to face him. A lump came to his throat, but he managed to stutter, "Yes...yes, of course...I...I should be going."

"Do you have an associate who can be trusted?...Someone Matthews might not know?"

He stood at the door with his back to her and replied without turning, "There is Raul...I trust him. He's young, but very good in a tight spot..."

"Call him. Don't tell him what is going on other than I may need him to back my play."

EL CHICO DELFIN RESORT

The sun cleared the horizon and the soft morning light spread like golden honey across the water and beach. Mark lay sleeping while Chikako peered out the front window of the bungalow. Across her lap lay her carbine and her H&K .45 Tactical hung in a shoulder holster under her left arm. She reloaded the magazines quietly as possible while she kept her vigil.

The air conditioning unit that had seen better days kept the room reasonably cool. She looked over at him and felt a sense of belonging she had never known before. *Why this one? Why is he...so...* The sound of an approaching vehicle broke her train of thought.

Manny and Alfonso returned in the resort van. The ICC got out and headed for their casita. She quietly stepped outside with only a quick glance at the sleeping man. *If something seems too good to be true...Stop that! Live for now*

She closed the door behind her. "He's asleep. What is it?"

"I think I'd like to have my cousin join us...maybe another man as well."

"How soon?"

"Tonight, if I call them now."

He looked back at the road in front of the resort. Just across it a family group picnicked on the beach under a pair of brightly colored beach umbrellas. Further down a second group of Hondurans played in the surf—all unaware of the empending danger about to befall the resort.

"Call them. Another pair of guns is good."

"You were very effective last night. I get the feeling you have dealt with...these situations before. No?"

She ignored his question. "Anyone come around about the truck and cars you disposed of?"

"No...Are you former military?"

"Ha...Not hardly. It's been a long night. I'm going to get some rest."

"If anyone shows up...I will call you immediately."

Zorro opened the door wearing a pair of gray running shorts, a light blue tank top and joined them on the patio. He squinted in the glare of the sunlight and yawned. "Alfonso, who can you call?"

"We just discussed it. I am contacting two men to join us."

Mark looked to Chikako—a smile crossed his face. "Good enough. Don't tell 'em much...just arrive weaponed up."

"Of course. I'll be in the cantina. There is a good view of the approach."

Mark's cell phone rang and he nodded to Alfonso before going back inside. She followed him and closed the blinds before removing her outer garments. She stretched her back and legs for a moment before laying down on the bed.

"Zorro."

"It's Dog...You in country yet?"

"Yup. What's up?"

"The client will be arriving tomorrow and we just found out he's bringing his teenage son along."

"Oh, great' Call Hal."

"Did yesterday. He's majorly pissed."

"That's his normal state…Is he sending another agent?" Mark moved to a window and lifted one slat of the blinds and checked the view.

"Yeah, someone named Linebacker. Know 'im?"

"Uh huh, worked with him a couple of times' Good hand…Listen, I stumbled into a situation. Gonna be a day or two before I get there. Keep the clients and the kid in one cluster. Call Taco Muerez…I'll text you the number and get him to hook up with you and Blaster…Mantle with you?" Lowering the blind he turned and looked at the vision of loveliness laying near by. Her eyes were closed, but he knew she was listening. *I'm living in a dream. Even the scar on her thigh is hot.*

"Yep. We're with the Batt engineer, Malcolm Winslow. Mousy nervous kinda guy."

"What did you expect? He's an engineer…Call me when the clients arrive."

"Will do. If you don't mind me asking…What kind of situation you in?" Mike asked apprehensively as he recalled the hostage rescue in Bangkok and the terrorist incident in the Philippines the month before.

"MS-13." Mark sat down on the edge of the bed and placed his hand on her leg tracing the scar with one finger.

Chikako did not open her eyes, but moved slightly feeling his unexpected touch'

"Those guys are serious sons-a-bitches."

"Maybe so…They're down twelve so far, but I'm betting they'll be back…Brains are not a requirement for joining the club."

Mark heard a beep on his cell. "Gotta another call coming in, Dog. Reminds me...there will be a delivery any day. Sender is *Brilliant Technology*. Split the cameras between the house and the office...Heavy on the house. There's a debugger for each of you and a device for inspecting the vehicles."

He canceled the call with Sloan. Before answering the next one, he leaned down and kissed her stomach. She placed both her hands on the back of his head and held him close as she let out a soft moan.

A smile crossed his face as rolled over and she began to rub his forehead. he took the incoming call. "Hans...great to hear from you."

"The package should arrive tomorrow, maybe the next day considering taco time."

"You got my text about the WiFi camera system?"

"It is part of the items you are receiving. Total cost twenty-one thousand."

"And a bargain at that. I'll transfer the funds today. How hard would it be to link a laptop and a couple of satellite cells into your global system?"

"Not hard at all. What do you need?"

"I want to infiltrate the CIA."

"Uh huh? I see. We would want to create a roaming ping account. Never stay on any one site more than say...two minutes before bouncing to the next."

"But doable?" Mark said as he slowly caressed her—moving closer to her breasts with each kiss.

"Of course. How soon do you need it?"

"What time is it?"

Hans chuckled. "I have another contract...Should be completed by tomorrow late, sorry. Is day after tomorrow acceptable?"

"Sure...Run a test once you get it operational, then give me the link."

"I thought you were done with the CIA."

"I am...but according to Bianca, they ain't done with me. You remember her? Colombian?"

He felt her tense as he mentioned the other woman.

"The one woman I will never forget...besides my Francesca of course."

"Once you get in their system, see what you can find that pertains to me."

"Will do. Want me to lead them to Nigeria like the Triad?"

"No. They know I'm in Honduras...But get set up to bread-crumb me out of here should the need arise," Mark said as she began to pull his tank top over his shoulders. "Gotta go."

ORO del CHRISTI MINE

Crank, Rhino and Captain Mendez stood on the highest point inside the compound. The Nicaraguan soldiers were digging in and setting up mortars. The heat and humidity had everyone's clothing soaked in sweat.

Below, a sixteen foot Isuzu NPR van pulled in and parked near the military six ton cargo truck. The driver and man riding shotgun got out, moved to the back and lifted the roll-up door.

Five more men wearing jungle BDUs climbed out and began unloading their gear.

"They're early. I like that...Rhino hang here with Mendez. Get this target as hard as you can," Crank said as he started down the hill.

"Save a steak for me bro, a big one. Not like the last one the size of you pecker," the South Afrikaan replied.

"Bite me you brokworst rhinocerotidae!"

"Damn bro...you're using big words you are˙ Growing up to become a little Zorro?"

Crank turned halfway down the hill and with his patented smile, shot Rhino the bird while thrusting his arm upward and catching it on the bicep just above the elbow with his other hand.

"That's more like it...signalling your IQ for all to see," Rhino countered.

Crank approached the man giving the orders. "Stow your gear in that two-story building." He pointed to the burned-out employee's barracks. "There's chow. Get some, then see me."

"You Crank?"

"Last time I checked...and you?"

"Santiago. Zorro said you needed our services."

"Damn glad you're here. We're expecting a monster ball buster any time. We definitely need you."

"We brought five hundred rounds per man. Iron clad rule number two..."

Crank repeated along with Santiago, "Ain't no such thing as too much ammo."

They laughed.

"Get me a list of your calibers. I can arrange for resupply when needed."

"5.56...308 and 9 mil."

"Have your men set up along the edge of that rise. See me when you're dug in," Crank directed.

MURTALA MUHAMMED AIRPORT
Lagos, Nigeria

Fifi and his gang had flown to Nairobi to deliver funds for Madam X before continuing on to Capetown, South Africa, to catch a flight to Lagos.

They maintained a low profile in South Africa as the Big Circle Gang had no presence there and was, in fact, often in conflict with the three competing Triad groups.

Within an hour they had their luggage and were in cabs headed for the home of the only contact they had in Nigeria—the biggest narcotics dealer in the country. His little empire funneled large sums of capital back to his second cousin—Zing Phen Wu.

CIA HEADQUARTERS

Willoby and Walsh walked across the grounds of the facility. The afternoon sun blazed down on them and both men were sweating profusely in their suits. Walsh reached inside his dark blue jacket, pulled out a pack of Marlboros and offered one to his assistant.

"No thank you, sir. Trying to quit," Willoby said with a yearning look in his eyes.

"Good decision. I swear when I retire I'm going to give up these coffin nails." Walsh lit his smoke before going on. "Where are we on Zorro?"

"Nothing new to report. Still waiting on Matthews to make contact. Bianca is in country…no word from her either. We'll get him."

"Damn well better," Walsh replied as he exhaled slowly through his nose. "You haven't asked why yet?"

"I figured you would tell me if I needed to know."

"We have a line on El Cobra. He's in Bolivia."

"I see˙ I thought…"

"Just checking to see what you knew. I remember everything about the Cobra operation. I'm betting our old friend will want the contract."

"Contract? You're going outside the agency?"

"Distance ourselves from the deal. If it goes south' we claim we don't know anything. If it goes north? We win."

"Same old shuffle. Heads we win, tails you lose. What makes you think he'll take the contract?"

"He broke protocol to get the Lopez family out of the country. I'm betting he hooked up with the woman. Only reasonable explanation. Probably had a thing for her and when Captain Lopez bit the bullet...the door was open." Walsh lit another cigarette from the butt of his last one before tossing it to the ground and grinding it under his shoe.

"Whew...that's a bit of a stretch."

"Zorro got really close with the family. Hell, he went on vacations with them before the step-brother rolled to the other side. She's a twenty-six on a scale of ten. Connect the dots...That's why finding the family could be an asset."

"You think he'll take it to protect them? I got it but how would Cobra know where they are? I mean...if he did, he would have made a play already."

"That's the beauty of it Willoby. We find 'em and leak it if Zorro doesn't want to play. Then we tell him El Cobra is going after them. Either way' that son-of-a-bitch will take the deal." Walsh held his smoke between his lips and squinted his eyes to avoid the smoke drifting upward. He massaged his left hand—in particular the scar for his missing two fingers.

"Why do I get the feeling no one in the agency likes this guy? I mean...I worked with him. He was always a straight shooter no pun intended."

"That's exactly why. He has his own set of rules and won't get with the program when needed. There're two stars on the wall I'd bet were his doing."

"He killed two of our agents? I don't know, chief' That doesn't sound like the Zorro I knew..."

McCAMBELL'S OFFICE

Maggie was reading a Cosmopolitan magazine while eating chocolate covered cherries when the phone rang.

"McCambell Import/Export.

"It's Leo Hernandez. I need to talk to Hal."

"One moment please."

She placed the call on hold and used the intercom to speak to Hal. "Honey…Leo Hernandez is on the line."

"Well, hell. Wonder what the problem is now?"

"Now, calm down. He's probably just checking in. He's a nice young man…"

"If you knew half what all these nice young men do out there, you wouldn't be saying that all the time."

He took a moment before picking up. "What's wrong now?"

"The woman, Bianca…she made us."

"Well done, bonehead. Where is she now?"

"She gave us the slip. Met a local in the bar…"

"What did he look like?"

"Hispanic' five eight' fifties, pencil thin mustache…"

"Taco Muerez. He's an ICC down there. Worked with Zorro several times."

"What do you want us to do now?"

"Shit…not much you can do. What part of covert do you two not understand?"

"She picked up on us the minute she laid eyes on us, boss. Like she had our number before the game started."

"Imagine that." Hal sat stewing over the turn of events for a moment. "Here's what you do...I'm going to contact Zorro. Tell him you're down there to get with them on the contract. You two will just have to improvise how to keep the CIA getting their hands on him...You can improvise can't you?"

McCambell picked up a cigar and began chewing on it as he considered the options available. *Crapola! I'd trade every one of those damn boneheads for two Ingrams in a New York minute.*

He dialed Mike Sloan's number. As he waited, he swiveled his chair to view the world map. *Eighteen teams and they all act like Ned in the first reader. Jesus' no wonder I get heartburn.*

"Sloan here."

"I have another pair of guys that are going to join you."

"Yes, sir. Linebacker just called and Blaster has gone to the airport to pick him up."

"With the three new men and Zorro, there will be six of you...Don't fuck up' I'm already losing money on this contract...Am I clear?"

"Yes, sir. Why so many?"

"Just got the news the feds picked up Digna Valle Valle in Florida. With the leader gone, the drug gangs are going to be running wild down there."

"Who is he?"

"She...Digna is a she and the number one in the Valle crime group. They picked up her two brothers and her son last month.

So the playing field is wide open. That brings to question…did you do your background on Honduras before I sent you down?"

"Well…yes, sir' I mean not all of it. You sent us down early and…"

"Better step up your damn game, boy. You had two months to do the research. I suggest you stay out of the beer joints and tittie bars between jobs and get your young ass up to speed before getting on the plane."

"Yes, sir! I'll do that, sir!" Mike blurted out like the new guy he was. "What's the ETA for…" he looked at his cell phone realizing Hal had hung up on him. *Ah shit'''another strike.*

BATT ENERGY TECH OFFICE

Mike nodded to Winslow before stepping out into the hallway and calling Roger.

"Blaster."

"Hal is sending some help. Said there's about to be a turf war down here…"

"Call you back, Zorro's on the other line."

He ended the call. "I was about to give you a ring."

"Anything wrong?"

"No…nothing like that. I just got off the line with Hal' He's sending two more."

"Excellent idea. I just read that Dinga Valle Valle was arrested in Miami…Any idea who that would be?"

"She's the head of the Valle crime organization. Her brothers and a son were arrested last month," Mike replied as if he was up to speed on events.

"Well…well…I'm impressed. What about Linebacker? Is he on the ground?"

"Yeah, he is."

"I have an ICC coming in with me…"

"That reminds me…Hal told me to contact a Taco Muerez…Said you know him."

"I do indeed. We are about to become a small army it seems. Have the clients arrived?"

"Tonight at 20:00."

"Get with Taco as soon as we get off the phone. The most vulnerable time to kidnap a foreigner is upon arrival…Play it smart. Grab 'em up and roll to the residence. No stopping along the way."

"We don't have any hard vehicles."

"Taco will take care of that. Call him now."

Mike again realized he was holding his cell to his ear, but no one was on the other end. *This is getting crazy…first Hal, now Zorro acting like I know what I'm doing? Jesus H Christ!*

ZETA COMPOUND, HONDURAS

Oscar Puto stood on the balcony as Ting Long Ti's motorcade arrived. His men—armed with a variety of automatic weapons—were stationed at strategic points around the courtyard to provide security. Once the three vehicles were through the gates, a guard activated the electronic switch and they closed.

Ting was the last to exit the black Humvee and took his time straightening his Alfani Red custom-tailored suit, knowing full well the eyes of his new associate in crime were on him. He preferred his suits to be gray allowing him a wide selection of colors for his shirts—his dark purple silk pleased him.

A soldier, built like a tank, approached the Chinese contingency. He welcomed Ting Long, and then looked up at Oscar on the balcony. The ZETA leader nodded and walked back inside the mansion.

Ting and his men followed the soldier inside. As they walked down a long hall with marble floors it was impossible to miss the glass cases along each wall with numerous firearms on display. AK-47s of every model, pistols and revolvers of many brands, all intricately engraved or gold plated.

"There is a fortune in pretty guns here," the Ting's translator said.

"Only an enormous ego would need so many. Did you see the room on the left filled with stacks of money?" Ti replied.

"Yes, I did. Seems this Oscar Puto has no fear of his people stealing from him."

"You have missed the surveillance cameras." Ting looked up at one mounted on the ceiling.

Moments later, Ting, two of his men and the big soldier entered the game room. Four of Putos body guards stood quietly with their arms across their chests as the two respective leaders shook hands and sat down.

"It is good to finally meet you in person." Oscar offered a box of cigars.

The smallest Chinese man began to translate for Ting and continued to do so throughout the exchange as the two men spoke in their native languages.

Ting took a fine Nicaraguan Gran Habano cigar and replied to his translator, "And for me as well. Our first shipment of heroine will arrive tomorrow. I am instructed by the Dragon Master to meet with you at this time…it represents one hundred twenty million dollars."

After the translator relayed the words in Spanish, he waited for the reply.

"I see. Are there issues of trust?"

"Not at all. We trust you or you would not have been our choice for a middleman."

Puto lit his cigar and exhaled slowly. His body language said everything about his displeasure. "I will make arrangements for you to be present, but only my people will be allowed at our submarine base of operations."

The interpreter tensed as he spoke.

Ting relaxed and smiled—his facial features masked his dislike for the man with whom he was ordered to do business. "As you wish."

It was evident that Puto was annoyed with the bouncing back and forth of the conversation.

"No one can move the volume you want but me. I have a fleet of submarines and dozens of customs officers on my payroll." Oscar stood up and moved to the wet bar. "A drink?"

Ting waved his hand and shook his head before going on, "I look forward to a long and prosperous association. There is another matter. You received our communication concerning a man and woman we are seeking?"

Oscar moved to his ornate desk and opened a drawer. He removed the photos of Mark and Chikako and laid them on the desk. "What is your interest in them?"

"It is a business matter. If you happen to find them you will be richly rewarded."

"How richly?"

"One million dollars."

"You must want them very badly. The woman...she is one of yours?" Oscar held up the Yakuza's photo.

"No. She is Japanese."

"And the old man? Is he...what? Her father?"

"Looks often deceive. The silver hair belies his age, we suspect. If you find them I want to know immediately."

"What makes you think they are in Honduras?"

"That is the mystery. We do not know where they are so we look everywhere. The woman was last seen in Costa Rica...the man in the Philippines."

"Is the reward for both of them or either?"

The translator noticed the wry smile on his boss' face and turned his head slightly with a quizzical look.

"It can be divided if necessary. We are very patient. One will led us to the other."

***

CHAPTER NINE

SAN PEDRO SULA
Honduras

Carlos Pineda watched his three children playing soccer in the courtyard from his balcony. Two Pittbulls chased after the battered ball as well. The pair of muscular canines were attack trained, but gentle giants with the kids. A smile crossed the MS-13 leader's face when one of the dogs grabbed the ball and began to lead the others on a wild chase to catch him.

"Carlos...I have not heard from your brother today. It is not like Ramone to miss the daily conference," a frail Nicaraguan man said hesitantly from the doorway.

"Everyone else has checked in?"

"Yes, Don Carlos. Only your brother Ramone has not."

"I will call him," Carlos said dismissing his accountant. He called out to the children, "Get the ball! Attack!"

The three boys looked up, smiled and waved to their father before renewing their efforts to take the ball from the huge steel gray Staffordshire terrier.

Carlos picked up his phone and dialed. While he waited, he lifted a empty bottle of beer and held it for his mistress to see—indicating he wanted a replacement. She came out of the house and took the bottle and returned quickly to the interior.

EL CHICO DELFIN RESORT

Mark, Chikako and Alfonso relaxed in the champa cantina having a meal of fresh fish. A cell phone—one of the many taken from the dead gang members—on the table next to them began to ring. Mark held his first finger to his lips stepped over, picked the up the phone and activated the speaker.

"House of pain…what is your pleasure," he answered in Spanish with a distinctive gay lisp.

SAN PEDRO SULA

Carlos held the phone away from his ear and looked at it for a moment. *What the hell?*

"Ramone?"

"Ramone…Ramone? No…no one here by that name."

"Who the fuck is this? Where is Ramone?" Carlos asked hard edge in his voice.

"I am the emperor of pain. If Ramone is one of the lizard heads that showed up here looking for protection money…he's permanently unavailable."

Pineda sat stunned for a moment—his mind swirled around the unexpected news and the calmness of what sounded like a decidedly homosexual voice. As he stood up he yelled into the phone, "Now you listen to me you faggot fuck…I don't know who this is…"

"Pay attention, this is the emperor of pain…"

"Put Ramone on the phone…"

"He sleeps with the fishes."

The veins on Pineda's neck and bald head swelled. "Do not fuck with me punta! I will speak with Ramone…"

The voice lost the lisp and hardened. "The chances of that are about as good as you being any better looking than Ramone and his crew of tattooed freaks. Unless of course you can speak with the dead."

The gang leader sat down hard as the realization his brother might full well be dead settled in.

"There's a new sheriff in town. If any of your reptilian buddies show up here again…they won't be coming back either. You see I have an affinity for amateur tattoo…"

"Affinity?"

"Sorry…big word. I just love reaming tattooed chocolate highways to death. Something about the way their little mouths pucker…"

"I will find you and when I do…I will kill you myself…very slowly…"

The voice reverted to the gay lisp and Spanish. "I'll be waiting at the Chico Delfin resort. Gotta go now…time to feed the ducks. You know ducks…They hate to be kept waiting."

Carlos stood up and threw his cell phone so hard it cleared the wall of his courtyard and bounced down the street as it shattered into pieces.

EL CHICO DOLFIN RESORT

Mark laid Ramone's cell phone on the table. He looked to Chikako and Alfonso and smiled.

"Oh, you're just mean." Chikako laughed.

"Actually that was fun. I could nearly see the asshole's eyeballs bulging out of his inked head."

"One thing's for certain there will be more of them coming now." Alfonso turned up his bottle of beer.

"Right. But not before we make some arrangements for a proper greeting. I have a half dozen claymores in my golf bag. I don't expect them to rush in again, so let's set a surprise and make a big impression."

"The last time our suppressors insured no one would hear our activities. What you are suggesting now will certainly bring the local law," Alfonso said.

"Agreed. By the time they get here, we'll be gone. I took a little walk this morning…About two hundred yards behind the resort is a dirt road. We'll have Manny show you how to get there and drop your ride. We do the deed, hit the road...The client is coming in and we have a contract to fulfill."

"What about Manny and his family?"

"We'll drop a dime with the local law. If they don't take action, I'll figure something out. Well, boys and girls...let's get to work. Al, you place the claymores...interlocking fields and disguise 'em...I want the sacks of shit to walk through a wall of hot steel before we open up on them." Mark stood up and started for the casita.

"What about me?"

"Hey somebody's gotta stand guard, Darlin'."

SAN PEDRO SULA

Carlos yelled at his men in the courtyard below, "We go!"

The tattooed soldiers in the shaded courtyard entered the barracks and rousted their fellow gang members.

In less than five minutes four crew-cab pickups and Carlos' bulletproof car drove out the gates onto the street and headed north.

ORO del CHRISTI MINE

Malakhi was reassembling his TAR-21—a Israeli bullpup assault rifle—while listening to Jackal, Adom and Ido banter about who was going to win the World Cup.

"I think Nigeria will win this year," Adom said with pride.

"Yeah yeah…when hippos fly out your ass," Jackal responded. "Germany will clean the fields…"

"There is always an unknown team. You know the wild card. Like Cameroon a few years ago," Ido added.

"Wankers. I can see the Americans…"

Adom and Ido started laughing so hard that Jackal stopped.

Then in a goodhearted show of comradeship, he too began to laugh. "They be the real wankers…the Americans."

Malakhi smiled as he laid the bullpup down before pulling his Bowie knife from its sheath on his belt. The twelve inch blade reflected a band of light across Adom's face as he turned it in his hand.

The Nigerian lifted his right hand and shielded his eyes as he, Ido and Jackal looked to see what had caused the flash to occur. Malakhi proceeded to draw a nine inch long Wusthof diamond sharpener across the blade while he quietly repeated a Jewish prayer—unaware his companions were staring at him.

"Yehbow man…where did you get that giant pig sticker?" Ido asked.

"Zorro," the former Sayeret Matkal Major replied without looking up. A long battle scar on his right forearm—received during a covert insertion in Iran—bore testament to a man who had dealt with the enemies of Israel up close and personal. "He gave it to me after a contract in Kenya."

"Can I see it?" Adom asked.

"You blind?"

The men chuckled at his joke—each now transfixed on the heavy Damascus steel blade.

"Don't be such a Nigerian turkey lover." Adom reached out his right hand.

Malakhi looked over, smiled and answered in Yoruba, "Be careful not to lose a finger."

The black-as-coal Nigerian answered in the same native tongue, "You are such a swag puppy...Let me have it."

Malakhi flipped the knife—catching it by the blade—and held it out to his friend. "I am serious. It will cut through a man's forearm like warm butter."

"It is heavier than it looks."

"Hey...speak English. I don't understand that Nigerian jabber," Jackal said.

"You understood the Nigerian plunger dive well enough," Ido said in English as he laughed.

"Yeah, I did. Never had a whore give better head than that," Jackal replied.

"What is the story of the blade?" asked Adom.

"There was a famous knife fighter in the United States long ago. He designed that beast himself. His name was Jim Bowie. Hence the name...Bowie knife."

"I like it." Adom admired the weapon. "I will get me one."

"There's a company in Spain that still makes them."

Ido reached out to his friend—indicating he too wanted to see the blade. "You, Crank and Rhino speak of this Zorro as if he is some sort of god."

"In our line of work...he is."

"I would meet this man. He is a big man? Like Rhino and Crank?" asked Ido.

"No, he's different…cunning like a fox. Zorro is Spanish for fox."

Ibo handed the blade back to Malakhi. "How different?"

"Let me put it this way…when he learned Rhino was caught up in the coup to overthrow the President of Kenya, he called up some men and went in to extract him…"

"I remember hearing of that. There was a fierce battle at the president's summer estate. Right?" Adom questioned.

"The fiercest I've ever seen. We would have been lost if not for…"

"For extraterrestrial aliens," Rhino interrupted as he walked up. "And that's all we're going to say about that."

Malakhi and the big South African shared a look.

"We were discussing your brother, Zorro."

"That will take more time than we have right now. Hal has a load of new high-tech toys coming our way. Crank just got the manuals via text."

"Any pinup girls in the mix?" Jackal inquired.

"None. But you may be able to find some locals with the drone he's sending. Mud ducks are better than nothing," Rhino offered.

LAGOS, NIGERIA

Fifi and his men stood on the roof top of a local restaurant watching the crowded street below. The tattered orange awning over the sparse dining area did little to relieve the intense heat. His cell rang.

"Yes, Master Wu."

"What is your progress?"

"We search day and night. One would think in a country filled with black people, a white man and an Asian woman would be easy to find."

"They are there unless they crossed the border undetected by our people."

"Sing has been studying the images you sent...the airport in Brazil and here in Lagos. He thinks they may have been created and covertly inserted to deceive us."

"I will inform our technicians to reevaluate the footage...Until you hear from me, keep searching."

"Grand Master...there is a severe out break of Ebola in this area. The men..."

"It is not for them to consider. For you, there is but one goal...Find them."

"Yes, Master Wu."

Fifi placed the phone in his pocket and turned to his men.

"Fifi, there is a brothel that has western women..."

He shook his head. "For those who wish to risk catching Ebola or AIDS or what other disease lurks in this filthy country...meet me at the hotel no later than eight o'clock in the morning."

El CHICO DOLFIN RESORT

A heavy rain moved in just as the sun set and turned to a steady drizzle. The entire resort shimmered in the decorative lighting in hues of blue, red and green. A stray dog wandered across the front lawn searching for food. It stopped, staring at the road with its head cocked then turned and ran back into the scrubby foliage.

"Standby," Mark called over his radio. "Something wicked this way comes…"

"Did you see something?" one of Alfosno's men called back.

"No…the dog did."

"Shakespeare…Macbeth," Chikako interjected.

"What?" Alfonso's other man asked.

"I didn't know you were a fan of the Bard."

"A girl has to read something between jobs."

"What are you two talking about?" Alfonso asked.

"Literature. Time for business…Someone turn on the music in the cantina…Hold 'til I say fire."

They the sound of approaching vehicles. Each of the team rechecked their weapons.

"Mika. Any movement out back?"

"Nothing. Quiet as a graveyard," she answered softly.

Four crew-cab trucks and Cesar's armored Lincoln pulled to a stop on the road in front of the resort instead of driving into the turnaround like their predecessors. Heavily armed figures stepped out and took positions behind the vehicles.

"Everyone pick a truck…wait for my call," Mark instructed.

"What about the car?" Alfonso's other man asked.

"That'll be the boss. He ain't comin' in 'til his men have secured the area...Focus on the soldiers."

After a tense two minutes, the gang members moved from behind their cover and began to advance in a long uneven line toward the resort.

"I count...twenty," Alfonso called.

"Plus three behind the Lincoln. Easy...let's get 'em into the claymores. Now!"

Mark and Alfonso triggered one mine each, sending 14,000 steel balls flying into the men from either flank.

Those not killed immediately, fell to the ground seeking cover—they found none.

"Light 'em up!" Mark ordered. From his position on the left flank, he threw a phosphorus grenade into the middle of the attackers. A blinding white flash shattered the darkness and a deafening roar shook the thatch roofs on the resort casitas.

Several men scrambled to their feet and ran screaming toward the ocean—their flesh burning as it melted from the bone. They fell to the ground screaming and writhing in agony long before they reached the soothing waters of the Gulf of Mexico.

As the team opened fire, Carlos Pineda's car wheeled hard right and raced back down the roadway.

Shit! I was afraid big dog would run, Mark thought as he emptied a fifteen round magazine through his suppressed 1911. The shots had no effect, except to craze the rear glass.

Zorro could hear the sounds of Alfonso's two men firing their M-16s in short bursts. He had positioned his ICC on the right flank and assigned the two least experienced men to the middle. One was positioned on the tin roof of the office and the other behind the stone wall of the cantina. The suppressed shotgun was inaudible, but the effect on the gang members was devastating as steel flechettes shredded their bodies.

The last of the gang members tried to make a fight of it—in less than ninety seconds, it was over. The smell of gun powder, phosphorus, burning flesh and feces mingled with the cries of the wounded, gave witness to the slaughter that had occurred.

"Alfonso?" Mark called over his radio.

"I'm good."

He yelled to the two new men, "Anyone hit?"

"Good here," they replied in unison.

"Hold…let 'em bleed out. On my signal, move to the second position."

"What about the unused claymores?" Alfonso inquired.

"Not worth going after. There's always a chance one or more muthafucker out there is playing possum."

The four defenders waited. The dead lay silent—the grim reaper had come to visit and collect his due.

Five minutes passed before the distant sounds of a siren could be heard.

"Time to go boys. Mika, we're coming in."

Chikako replied over the radio, "Come to momma. The back door is open."

Silently, the four men retreated and faded into the darkness.

BATT ENERGY TECH OFFICE

Roger Mantle waited just inside the doorway when Kevin Maldinano and Leo Hernandez arrived in a cab. Sloan watched from the office window above.

"Hal sent us down to help out." Kevin shook Mantle's hand. "I'm Maldinano. This is Hernandez."

"Yeah, the chief called last night. Is that all you brought?"

The two men shrugged and nodded it was. Both had a small suitcase and a military duffle bag.

"The office is on the second floor. Mike is up there with Linebacker."

"Linebacker? Damn, this is shaping up to be a small army. Where's Zorro?"

"Delayed. Something to do with the MS-13."

"It's always something with him." Leo chuckled.

"Seems that way. You work with him before?"

"Couple of times…Never a dull moment," Kevin answered. "So…the five of us plus Zorro. Anyone else?"

"Taco Muerez."

"Taco? Outstanding. If anyone knows where the primo tail is it's Taco," Leo commented.

"Wouldn't know about that. First time to work with him. He showed up yesterday…Room 205. Up the stairs to the left."

TEGUCIGALPA, HONDURAS

Rain fell in sheets driven by a howling wind. Bianca Toro exited the run-down apartment building by the back stairs and entered the alley—greeted by the odor of rotting trash, canine and human urine. *Gotta find a way to stop running around in this shit.*

She wore a native dress—that concealed her voluptuous figure as well as her handgun and shortened shotgun. Her head was covered in a black cotton scarf and she wore a pair of cheap sunglasses. The only clue that she might not be local, was the rollaboard suitcase and her shoulder bag.

Three blocks down the alley, she waited until a bus pulled up and hustled across the street to board it. Sitting in the last seat, she scanned the street for a tail. Satisfied there was none, she removed the scarf and stuffed it in her shoulder bag, followed by her pistol.

The early morning streets were almost deserted. Only four other passengers and the driver occupied the bus. No one seemed to take any notice of her, but she profiled each out of habit. Sensing nothing amiss, she relaxed her hold on the shotgun's pistol grip and drew a gentle breath of relief.

Zorro said to meet on the south end of the Silver Bridge in Choluteca tonight. I cannot wait to see him again...

CHOLUTECA, HONDURAS

"Wake up." Alfonso nudged Zorro's leg behind his driver's seat.

Both Mark and Chikako awakened to see the fifth largest city in Honduras sprawled below them as they crested the hill on the Pan-American Highway.

"You made good time." Mark stretched and yawned.

"I'm starving. I could eat anything...except fried yucca," Chikako said.

"Yucca is the national food here. Fried, dried, boiled...pickled. It is very good mashed with pork," the driver commented as he slowed the SUV to the posted speed limit.

"Where'd you let the boys out?"

"Near their home. It was on the way. I told them you would send the money."

"You send it. Don't need any trail that leads to me...Once we get to the hide, I'll pay you. Keep your cell on...May need your help again."

"It will be a pleasure to assist you as always. I haven't had this much fun in years."

"Fun? Surfing is fun..."

"Mika, if that is your name...I used to work often with Zorro. But now, I am too long in the tooth for such things, it seems. An occasional adventure is more gratifying as one grows old."

"I'll keep that in mind. Never spent much time thinking about growing old...until lately." The Japanese woman looked at Mark.

The SUV pulled up to a small three story residence. Alfonso blinked the headlights, the electric gate opened, he drove in and parked under a metal awning on the east side of the house. The gate closed and the automatic lock secured it with a solid clank.

Mark and Chikako waited until the he had entered through the front door, moved to the side entrance and motioned to them. They only took a bag in each hand—leaving most of their possessions in the SUV—and slipped quickly inside.

Trombone, tasked with maintaining the safe house, met them in the kitchen and embraced Mark with a hearty slap on the back. "Long time, *mi amigo*. Long time. Who's the fox?"

"Too long. Meet my new shadow, Mika."

"Since when did you need a shadow?"

"Since I met her. She showed up like a lost puppy...I couldn't leave her behind."

"Hey! Who you calling a lost puppy?" Chikako popped him on the back of the head.

Trombone smiled. "She's a feisty one. You two can fill me in later."

"More like a pit bull. She laid lead on some MS-13 goons as well as any man I've met," Alfonso said.

"MS-13?" Trombone looked cautiously out the front window. "You followed?"

"No one left to follow us." Mark sat down on the worn couch and began to untie his boots.

"Can't be too careful these days. Those inked assholes are all over the place now. Just the other day they killed three police officers and hung them in the city square." Trombone pulled the drapes closed. He remained there peering out at the front gate and street.

The house was modestly furnished. The only item that reflected any recent expense, was the large flat screen sitting on a stand in the corner.

"You have cable?" Mark removed his second boot.

Trombone stepped away from the window, picked up a remote and tossed it to him. "You betcha! Cowboys and Redskins start in a few minutes…Channel 167."

"Help me get the bags and trunks in." Alfonso headed for the kitchen and the side door.

The two men made several trips hauling in the golf bags, foot lockers and duffles. They struggled up the narrow stairs and stored the equipment in a bedroom. Mark and Chikako's personal items were taken to the third floor—consisting only of one bedroom, a sitting area and bath.

By the time they had finished, Mark had the game on and was filling his shadow in on the nuances of American football.

"Number nine is the quarteback…Tony Romo. He's not as big as most of the quarterbacks in the league but he can scramble."

"What's a scramble?" she asked.

"Run around...on the loose to keep the play going. He's a great improviser."

"Sounds like some one else I know."

"We're going to make a run to the market. Any requests?" Trombone asked as he and Alfonso came down the stairs. "There's some Shiner Bock in the frig."

"Shiner? Damn you're good. Don't care what Hal said about you." Mark started to the kitchen.

"Seafood. Bring back fresh seafood and vegetables. No yucca. I'll stir fry dinner," Chikako replied. "And wine...I'm tequilaed out."

"Done and done," the retired operative said as he departed.

"Keep it local so as not to give any indication foreigners are buying...Pick up some yucca. Alfonso can take it with him when he leaves," Mark ordered.

"We'll be back soon." As Alfonso walked out the door, he commented over his shoulder, "I'll buy enough bottled water for a week."

Mark pulled his electronic detection device from his Camelbak hydration pack and began sweeping the residence for bugs. She followed him making visual checks through the windows at the surrounding homes and streets. Satisfied the place was clean, he stowed it and turned on the shower checking the water pressure.

Chikako wrapped her arms around his neck and melted against him. He held her close and gently caressed her back.

"How soon do you have to go?"

"New plan. I'm staying with you bijin..."

Chikako pulled away, with joy in her eyes. "Really? Bijin?…I'm a hot babe?"

"To the tenth degree."

She playfully slapped his shoulder before laying her head on his chest. "Seriously, how soon do you have to join your security team?"

"Last time I talked to one of them Hal was sending enough men to form an army. You and I are going to work out the mechanics of the Trailer position together."

She placed her hand on his check and smoothed a loose strand of silver hair back over his ear before kissing him. "If we have to work…this could be a great way to do it."

"We shall see, what we shall see…Let's get under the water. I could use a shower."

"Yeah, you could…I just didn't want to say anything."

***

CHAPTER TEN

LONE STAR SHOOTING SUPPLY
Gainesville, Texas

Buck 'Shoehorn' Stienke supervised the loading of crates into a cargo van when his cell rang.

"Shoehorn."

"Zorro...What's your ETA?"

"Loading the gear right now. I'll be wheels-up in an hour. Makin' a delivery to Crank before I get to you...Anything else you want?"

"Just what's on the list, but definitely a pair of those new M-16 pistol conversions with cans...couple of 300 Blackouts would be good."

"Done. You hooked up with Bianca yet?"

"Tonight…20:00. You sure you don't want me to tell her you're coming?"

The former USAF fighter pilot entered the cab and latched his seat belt. Though in his sixties, his 240 lbs of muscle clearly indicated why his call sign in the military had been Shoehorn. "Nah…want to surprise her. Hope she remembers me. It's been a while."

"Like she's going to forget the month in Belize…I'm betting an old dog like you always leaves 'em wanting more."

"Gotta get this gear in the sky. With all this shit, you and Crank could start a friggin' war down there."

"Or end one…See you tomorrow, old man."

"Who you callin' old man, kid? I can still whip your scrawny ass."

"I'm sure you can, Shoehorn, I'm sure you can. Oh…got someone new I want you to meet."

"Better be a woman. You go playin' for the other team and I'll call your dad."

"Ha, ha…You hear from him lately?"

"We can catch up when I get there. Look forward to seeing you again…and meetin' your new friend…Does she have any idea what you really do for a living?"

"Yeah, she does."

Buck hung up and turned the key in the ignition. One of his employees tapped on the window and held up a 8x10 envelope. *Oh, damn…Hal's documents.*

CHOLUTECA, HONDURAS
Mark's Safe House

The two men had returned with the groceries. They joked about the jobs completed as they stored the supplies.

"We need a fan. Maybe two or three." Chikako dried her hair with a thick white towel. "How long is this contract for again?"

"A year, but once the boys have it rolling smooth...We're out of here."

"Where to?"

"Back to hacienda. I didn't realize how much I missed that place 'til I got back...Besides, I want to get DeLeon's new house going in the right direction. After that?...Maybe you'd want to teach me how to sail."

"Does a panda shit in the bamboo? Hell yes I want to."

Mark's cell rang—he noted it was Bianca. "I need to take this...How would you feel about another roommate for a few days?"

"Depends...long as it's not Crank."

Mark nodded. "Bianca, are you in Choluteca yet?"

"Just arrived. I'll find someplace to hang out 'til we hook up at the bridge tonight."

"New plan. Jump a cab and get to the Juarez market. We'll met you there...Alfonso set us up with a hide."

"We?"

"Look for the old priest. My partner will be dressed as a nun. See you there in an hour."

Mark ended the call just as Chikako walked away and entered the bath room. He followed her in and placed his arms around her waist as she washed the coconut oil off her hands.

"I haven't said it yet, but you're the one…No one is going to come between you and me. Understand?"

She turned, put her hands on his shoulders and looked him in the eye. "I get it. We both have histories. Whatever she was to you in the past…Is your past. Don't forget I'm Buddist. True love is born from understanding."

"Ahh, so, grasshopper." He bowed slightly at the waist. "Do not dwell in the past, do not dream of the future, concentrate the mind on the present."

Chikako studied him with a sly smile. "You always surprise me. What other teachings of Buddha do you know?"

"A few but now it's time for us to become a priest and nun."

TEGUCIGALPA, HONDURAS
CIA Safe House

Matthews waited for Bianca to answer his call while Daniels shuffled papers at his desk.

"Shit…she's still not picking up," he said as he disconnected.

"Our search for Muerez hasn't been able to find him either. What the hell do you think they're up to?"

"Stay here and keep looking. I need to get back to Nicaragua. Call me as soon as you find 'em."

"Will do. What's the plan if we don't?"

"I'll pull in a favor from the Chief of the State Police. His uniforms will see them moving around even if they have left the city...Focus on the bitch. Put a double team on her once you have her."

Matthews walked out onto the roof and made a call. *I'm gonna nail his ass down for the chief and finally have a ticket out of this shit hole.*

"What do you want?"

"Your payment is late."

"I told you to find me a rich American. Until I get the Tarzanas out of the way there will not..."

"Bullshit! Our agreement is not based on any personal problems on your end."

"There has been another unforeseen complication. Half my men were murdered, including my brother. Someone ambushed them in Puerto Cabezas."

Matthews considered the new information as he lit a smoke. "And you have no idea who?"

"Some smart ass. First he sounded like a queer, then he didn't. All I know is he sounded American."

The CIA agent's eyes narrowed. "You're sure...an American?"

"Yes."

"Use whatever forces you have left. Find the American for me. He has long gray hair...about five eleven. You find him and this month's payment is forgiven."

"You think this man is the one?"

"How were your men killed?"

"Silenced weapons. Explosives. What is his name?"

"Sounds like him...He goes by many names. Find him for me and I'll forgive two month's payments."

"You must want this man very much."

"Alive, Carlos. I want him alive. And don't let the gray hair fool you. He's a stone cold killer. He may also be the one guarding the rich American...The one I am thinking of for your kidnapping plan."

"For twenty thousand I will deliver him to you alive. But after you are finished with him...He is mine. For the honor of my brother."

"No problem." Matthews hung up and lit another cigarette. *Right after Chief Walsh and General Sasacas...he's all yours Pineda. All yours...*

HAL McCAMBELL'S RANCH
North Texas

Hal just turned off the engine to his Ford Explorer when his cell vibrated. *Damn! A man can't get no peace any more.* Looking at the screen he saw it was Stienke.

"You in the air yet?"

"Wheels up. Transfer to the C-130 in Costa Rica then drop to Crank at the mine. See Zorro afterwards."

"Who did you get for your loadmaster?"

"Tarzan."

"Ah, jeez, Buck! You're bustin' my balls. That insane Jarhead?"

"Best there is. Even if you don't like him...I trust him."

"This contract is going to give me a heart attack before it's over. One more thing. Watch your ass in Honduras. I forgot to mention the Triad is looking for Plata."

"Oh, really...just plain forgot to mention it, did you? Why the hell are those slant eyes looking for him?"

"Long story. He can fill you in...When you finish this run, I have another..."

"Not with me you don't. I took this one to see Mark. I have no intentions of getting on your list of runs to Dante's Inferno."

"After all I've done for you?"

"Kiss my rosy, Hal. The only thing you ever did for me was...sell me half a ranch you wanted but were too damn stingy to pay for all of it."

"You're the most stubborn self-centered Kraut blooded Texan I've ever met...How about the time I set you up with that big sale to the Rhodesians?"

"Oh, yeah, the one where I had to fly out of Africa with fighter jets on my ass? That big sale?"

"Hey! How was I to know there would be a change in management in that shit hole before you landed?"

"Hal, swear to God, if I didn't know you were on the right side, I'd strafe your hacienda...after I warned Maggie to be gone."

"Well, aren't you a ray of sunshine? Why the hell are you calling me anyway?"

"Your check didn't clear the bank. If it hasn't by the time I'm ready to land in Nicaragua...I'll dump the load on the airstrip in Honduras."

"Buck, you know I'm good for it...Buck...Buck?" Hal looked down at his blank screen. *Damn! That sumbitch is as hard to get along with as...Jesse and Mark Ingram.* Hal started laughing. *Peas in a pod. If I had Buck, Tarzan, Jesse and Mark on one team, I could overthrow those socialist sons-a-bitches in Washington.*

PALAWAN ISLAND, PHILIPPINES

Jesse Ingram read the text: Call me you west Texas brush popper. I'm flying down to Honduras with Tarzan to deliver a load of tools to your spawn. If I don't hear from you, I'm headed to Palawan next. Time for you two to have a face to face before you're too damn senile to see him. LOL.

"Who that, Poppy?" The slender Filipina asked as she rolled over on the foam mattress and laid her arm over his chest.

"An old friend, Chique, baby...Wants to see me."

"He comes here? We have celebration?"

"I don't know. Maybe. Go back to sleep."

She got up and moved into the bathroom. Jesse could hear her flush the toilet as he walked out under the clear night sky. He sent a reply to his old friend: No money for phone calls. Don't bother coming. You won't find me. Give son my regards. If he doesn't slug you in the kisser, tell him Oroquieta village in

Zamboanga del Norte was some fun. I'm done with that life, buddy. Gonna live what's left in peace. Salamat.

He proofed the message before hitting the send key, smiled, and then sent a second message: If you want to do a final hoorah, consider meeting at Rocky's Rawhide in Bangkok. Just the old gang telling lies and draining his tequila vault.

AIR SPACE OVER THE GULF
McCambell Import/Export Jet

Buck felt his sat phone vibrate and pulled it from his shirt pocket. He could not help but smile as he read the message. He checked the autopilot before moving from the left seat. He gently shook his sleeping copilot.

"Wake up. Gotta take a piss."

"Yeah...okay," Jerry said sleepily. He looked down at the featureless expanse of the Gulf of Mexico and then at his moving map on his nav display. *Crap I must have dozed off for a hour or more.* The forty-five year old ex-Air Force pilot was feeling the aftermath of the late night rendezvous with a Dallas Cowboys cheerleader...*Hell, I can sleep when I'm dead.*

Once Buck was out of the cockpit, he replied to the text: Excellent idea. Rawhide Club for Christmas. I'll alert Rocky.

Ken 'Tarzan' Farmer—mid sixties, hard as nails inactive Marine lifted his cap as Buck walked by. "Whaat?"

"Gotta pee. Why? You want to hold it for me?"

"Let me find my tweezers."

"Not yours, Jarhead, mine. Did you pack our latest western novel for Zorro?"

"I packed the whole Nations series. That kid could use some educational reading materials."

"Had a text from Jesse," Shoehorn said from the head.

"How is the salty dog?"

"Elusive as ever. Invited him to join us for Christmas at Rocky's."

"You think the police are still looking for us there?" Ken said with a smile.

"If they are, they won't recognize us. It's been nearly thirty years, in case you haven't looked in the mirror lately..."

As Buck made his way back to the cockpit Tarzan replied, "Up yours! I keep it high and tight! Not like that hippie spawn of Jesse...If he wasn't so damn ugly, he'd look like a girl."

Buck paused at the door. "Reminds me...Zorro says he's got a new lady."

"About friggin' time. I was starting to worry 'bout his sorry ass. Thought he might be goin' sweet on us."

CHOLUTECA, HONDURAS
Mark's Safe House

Mark, Chikako and Bianca finished a breakfast of fried fish, eggs, tortillas, fresh squeezed orange juice and strong dark Costa Rican coffee.

"No surprise you still use the priest and nun disguise." Bianca smiled. "Remember when we waltzed out of Bogota?"

"Uh, huh…the federales just ran past us like we didn't exist." He took a sip of the coffee. "Any idea what Matthews is after?"

"You…No idea why, but he has a serious hard-on to lay his hands on you."

"And the list grows," Chikako said.

A long moment passed as the two women measured each other. Neither were inclined to blink.

"I want to find out what he is up to and why…then I'm going to finish it. He's long overdue on being put out of everyone's misery."

"How do you know him?" Chikako asked.

"He's CIA. We crossed paths a couple of times. Thinks his career took a wrong turn in Peru…and I caused it."

"Not to mention losing half his left hand," Bianca added.

"El Cobra did that…Not me." He stood up and set his cup on the counter.

"You trained the bastard," Bianca said.

"This just gets better by the minute," Chikako added.

"It was a contract. I trained him and ten other Colombian DEA agents to shoot long distance. He was the best of 'em."

"Matthews isn't the only one. El Cobra made it his trademark to shoot anyone he thought had betrayed him in the hand…He's twisted that way." Bianca glanced at Chikako.

Mark looked at the Colombian. "How do you contact Matthews…"

BATT ENERGY TECH OFFICE

Linebacker finished giving his orders to the team. "Everyone else stays with the clients. Sloan and I will be back as soon as we finish the meet with Zorro…Any questions?"

John Batt stood up. "I was informed by Mister McCambell that this Zorro was to be in charge…"

"He is in charge."

"When do I get to meet him?"

"When he's ready…We'll be back before your appointment with the Minister of Finance. Until then, everyone stays in the office. Clear?"

John's seventeen year old son, Thomas, stood by the window looking out at the city. "I didn't come down here to be cooped up in an office. When am I going to get to look around?"

"You'll get the nickel tour before you leave. Until Dog and I get back, stay here and keep away from the windows," Linebacker barked. "Hernandez take a walk around. The rest of you, lock this place down…Sloan, on me," the big man ordered as he walked out of the room.

On the street the two men hailed a cab. Sloan glanced up to see the kid shooting them the bird.

"The little turd is going to be trouble," Mike said.

"Yeah…stupid move bringing him down here. Daddy has no idea how quick wormy little shits like that can disappear."

"I'm looking forward to seeing McCallister again," Sloan said.

"Zorro's operating under the name of Steve Wilson on this gig…Remember that."

CHOLUTECA, HONDURAS
Central Downtown Park

Sloan and Linebacker stepped out of a cab on the south end of the park. They walked through the crowd casually—both men scanning for any danger—and for Mark.

As they neared the fountain, a ragged beggar approached. He was bent over with his face practically touching the top of his wooden cane—his torn and frayed palm-weave hat obscuring his face. On his back was a noticeable hump and he moved as if in constant discomfort.

"Spare change? A coin or two for an old man," the beggar asked in Spanish as he extended a battered metal cup with his left hand—covered by a dirty, worn and tattered cotton glove.

"I don't have any spare change old man. Move along," Linebacker answered in Spanish.

"Some small paper…"

"Move on, old man."

"That's a fine way to treat an old friend," Mark replied in English with a glance up to reveal his identity.

"Damn, Zorro. Didn't recognize you," Sloan said.

"Precisely the point. I'm going to get on a bus down at the corner. Follow me. I'll pick one that's nearly empty. Sit behind me. You don't know me…Got it?"

"Yeah...Damn good disguise old man. Damn good." Linebacker watched Mark hobble off.

Bianca and Chikako passed by just as Mark moved away. Both wore black habits complete with a white wimple and hood. They tossed a coin into his cup, each taking one of his arms and proceeded to assist him to the bus stop.

Bianca glanced over with a smile.

"Wow! Did you see the face on that nun? They didn't look like that when I was in Catholic school," Mike said.

"Leave it to Zorro to have women hanging on to him...Come on let's go."

On the bus, Mark picked a seat near the middle with an open bench behind him. The two nuns moved to the very back and the two men sat down as instructed.

Once the bus was in motion, Mark spoke quietly, "How's the client?"

"So good so far. The kid's a little prick, but his father is an ass...so go figure," Linebacker replied. "What's the deal on this set up?"

"I'm working on a new idea. You and the team just carry on like you would if I wasn't here. If you recognize me, don't let on you do. I'll be around...If shit hits the fan, we'll cover your six and provide a back door."

"Who's we?" asked Sloan.

"Our appearance will change...but for now, it's the two penguins in the back."

They glanced over their shoulders.

The nuns winked.

"Damn," commented Linebacker. "How will you know where we are or where we're going?"

"Sloan will text me every move you make…What's the itinerary today?"

"Batt has a meet with the Minister of Finance. The engineers are going over data in the office. Plan on keeping the kid with the engineers."

"All right, instead of three and a driver on the boss like we would normally do, just have two men with Taco driving. Keep the others at the office…I'll shadow ya'll."

The bus stopped. Mark got up and moved off, followed by his escorting nuns.

"Good thing he's on our side," Sloan remarked. "He's got that crippled old man shuffle down pat."

"Roger that. Let's get back to the office. I got a gut feeling the kid's planning something."

CHOLUTECA, HONDURAS
Building of Ministries

The colonial style building had been restored to its original state after hurricane Mitch in 1998 devastated the country—much of the country had not been lavished with such care after the six billion dollar storm. The white stone structure with red tile roof was surrounded by a wrought-iron fence and guarded by regular army soldiers—due primarily to the resurgence in activity the rebel forces.

Mark chose a spot under a large mahogany tree—out of the blistering glare of the sun—and sat on a stone bench. He held his head up enough to see, but not enough to be recognized—his tin cup outstretched for any passerby to drop in a coin or two. The old faded serape provided perfect cover for his pistols in their shoulder holsters as well as the short barreled over and under shotgun strapped to his right thigh.

Chikako and Bianca strolled casually up and down the street—stopping frequently at one shop or another to avoid notice by the military personnel across the street.

"I had forgotten how damn hot this disguise was," Bianca said as she wiped her forehead with a small white handkerchief. "I'm doing the skimpy dressed hooker next time."

"Imagine adding body armor," Chikako added.

"You have body armor?"

"Zorro rule number six."

The two passed behind the old beggar and paused.

"How much longer?" the Colombian asked.

"Any minute now. How you two girls gettin' along?"

"Fine now that we established Amazon woman will hunt me down if I hurt you and I will slice her up like sushi if she makes a move on you," Chikako replied in Japanese.

Mark chuckled and answered her in Japanese, "Thats good...Play nice, children. Just one big happy family..."

"No fair. I don't understand Asian." Bianca laughed.

"I was saying you two need to harness the estrogen flashes and hold 'em for the bad guys."

"Really?" Bianca shot back.

"Funs over. The boys are pulling around the corner. Cross the street. Separate…Get close to the entrance…and be ready. Comm check." Mark activated his mic.

"Loud and clear," Chikako answered.

"Ten by ten," Bianca added as the two started across the street. "Oh, and when do I get body armor?"

"Stienke special delivery service."

"Stienke? Buck Stienke? You wouldn't joke me would you?" Bianca replied with a tone of excitement in her voice.

"The big Shoehorn himself."

"Who's Buck Stienke?" Chikako asked.

"Later. Focus on the team."

Taco stopped the hardened limo at the front gates. Sloan and Linebacker stepped, out followed by John Batt, carrying a small Halliburton aluminum case in one hand. The two nuns were positioned twenty yards to either side of the limo.

As the men and Batt exited the vehicle several attackers rushed to cross the street with weapons firing. Their rounds bounced off the bulletproof car. Sloan and Linebacker shoved Batt back inside the limo.

"Give 'em hell ladies." Mark fired at two men on his right. Both fell onto the cobblestone road and tumbled to a halt. No one heard a sound from his suppressed Gold Cup.

Chikako slipped her pistol out of the loose sleeve of her nun's habit. In quick succession, she dispatched three men in front of her with two rounds each, center mass. Without pause, she returned the weapon into the sleeve and walked away.

Bianca fired and dispatched a man on her right with a pair of Glaser rounds to the chest. Seeing a dark green sedan speeding toward the scene with a man leaning out the passenger window, firing at the client, she emptied her weapon. The shooter slumped over—his pistol bouncing down the road.

Mark stuck the barrel of his S&W from under his serape and emptied it into the vehicle as it roared past. The driver's head exploded, jerking violently to the side—his body fell behind the steering wheel. The car swerved hard to the left, across lanes of traffic and crashed into the fence in front of the Ministries building.

It was over before any of the military guards realized what was going on. The duty officer ran around screaming orders to his men who gave a great impression reminiscent of the Keystone Cops as they rushed to secure the area.

When the chaos settled, Linebacker and Sloan got out of the limo and scanned the area before hustling Batt through the gates and into the building.

"Outstanding ladies. Hustle back over here and get inside the ice cream shop. Cool off 'til the package is ready to depart."

"Okay boss," Bianca replied.

"Thank you, Buddha. I'm going to lose ten pounds wearing this outfit and the armor plate is rubbing my breasts raw," Chikako commented.

"After you cool off, there's a little bodega on the corner. Pick up a pair of gel shoe inserts."

"How the hell are shoe inserts going to do anything for my breasts?"

"Trust me…It's a little-known trick for protecting boobs."

One hour later, Batt, Sloan and Linebacker walked out of the building. They paused on the front steps until Taco pulled to a stop on the street. Once the limo was at the gate they descended the thirty stone steps and entered the vehicle.

Chikako and Bianca—again positioned on either side of the gate—waited until the car departed, and then walked across the street and met Mark at the bus stop.

"Smooth as ice."

"I'm cooking in this robe. A bucket of ice sounds great," Bianca mentioned.

"I'll get Trombone to pickup some before we get to the hide. Fill the tub on the second floor and slide in," Mark said. "How 'bout you, Chikako?"

"Cold shower and a massage for me."

As the three entered the bus, a man who had been taking photos of the team and Batt climbed in after them. The bus moved off with a cloud of blue smoke before everyone was seated. Mark stumbled into the photographer causing him to fall on the floor between the worn bench seats.

"*Lo sinento mucho.*"

"You should be you filthy beggar," the man answered. As he started to pull himself up his camera hung on the seat. "Damn."

"Let me help you," Mark said as he karate chopped the man's neck.

It took only a second to disable the photographer and relieve him of his camera. No one on the bus paid the incident much mind—except the two nuns.

Mark nodded to his accomplices, moved to the front of the bus and stepped out at the next stop. The ladies followed.

On the street Bianca hailed a cab. All three got in and were gone before the bus had turned the corner.

"Nice camera," Chikako said in Japanese—knowing there was little chance the cab driver would understand her.

MARK'S SAFE HOUSE

The three had the taxi drop them two blocks from the house and walked casually down the street. As they approached the gate, Trombone opened it from inside. They entered the small driveway.

Inside everyone stripped off most of their disguise and sat down in the living room. The keeper of the safe house served a round of ice water and set a pitcher on the table before moving to the window to watch the street.

"Let's see what's on the camera," Mark said after draining his initial glass of water.

Chikako removed her armor before hitting the playback feature and scrolled through the photographs.

All were images of the Batt Energy office and the coming and going of the clients and the team. The last dozen were of the incident at the building.

"Interesting. How did you know?"

"Noticed him before the team arrived. He was too busy being disinterested. Then boom…picture time."

"We should have questioned him."

"Waste of time. There are over fifty known gangs operating in Honduras. We can't go after all of 'em. Have to play defense with a twist ladies."

"A twist?" Bianca asked.

"Yeah. Instead of just trying to hold the line…the three of us are gonna to blitz the bad guys. Sack 'em up and throw 'em for a loss."

"I like it," the former DEA operative said.

"Very nice. I've been on the hitting team before. Sliced the security team up and snatched the client without any difficulty. But this? Wicked," Chikako added.

***

CHAPTER ELEVEN

CIA SAFE HOUSE

Matthews stormed into the main office like an angry bear in a china shop. "Zorro's here. The son-of-a-bitch surfaced!"

Daniels and two other agents looked up at the agitated leader with surprise.

"You sure?"

"Sanchez just called. Said an old beggar jumped him on a bus." Matthews banged around the room. "Has Bianca checked in?"

"Not yet. What makes you think…"

"Sanchez was documenting the movements of an American businessman in Choluteca. He told us there was an attempt to kidnap him and they were shot to hell by a pair of nuns and a beggar...Get packed. We're going there now."

"You're the boss, but getting mugged by a beggar is an everyday event in Central America...Kind of a stretch linking the two," Daniels said as he began to pack a bag with extra ammunition and surveillance gear.

"Call it a gut feeling. The rest of you stay here. Finish those reports for Washington. Step up the pressure on our contacts to find Bianca!" The angry head of operations turned and headed out the door.

"I get the feeling this one is personal," one of the agents mumbled as he went back to preparing his report.

ORO del CHRISTI MINE

It was after midnight when Chuck Watts landed his Kazan transport chopper. Before the blades stopped rotating, men rushed forward and began downloading the new equipment and supplies from McCambell.

"Care to stay over? The cook makes some mean breakfast burritos," Crank asked as he opened his door.

"There's a pair of babes waiting for me. Got three days off and I'm going to wear 'em out," Sundance replied.

"Thanks for the haul. When we get this rodeo rolling right I'll be looking to you for introductions to some of Honduras' finest."

"Done deal."

Crank ran bent over to avoid any contact with the slowing blades. Rhino was waiting for him with a cup of coffee and an update on activities while he was gone.

"Watch out, it's hot. Nothing much happened since you left. Kept Jackal and another man out on the river. No sign of the rebels yet."

"That's some good news. Once we get the drone up we won't need anyone forward."

"Who's that?" Rhino nodded at a passenger disembarking the chopper.

Crank looked back and smiled. "Ahhh…Grasshopper. Hal sent him down here to get the high tech whiz bang operational and give us some training."

"Skinny little runt. Can he shoot?"

"Not likely. Hal has an army of geeks that rarely leave the US. Keeps all of them safe in some underground bunker near Dallas. This is the first stamp on his passport."

"Oh shit! The way things are going we won't have a job soon. Some flip-flop wearing sissy will be doing it from a computer halfway 'round the world."

Tom 'Grasshopper' Conroe walked up carrying his shoulder bag and a laptop case. He claimed to be five nine, but was little more than five seven and weighed a whopping 140 lbs soaking wet. His red hair and freckles made him look younger than his twenty-five years. "Where's the restroom?"

"You're standing on it." Rhino laughed.

Conroe looked around confused for a moment then laughed as well. "No, seriously, I need to take a dump."

"Ah…that would be the tin shed over there. Take a flashlight and watch out for spiders, snakes and scorpions. They seem to be more active after dark," Crank said.

"Oh…I ah…I'm afraid I didn't bring one. Hal said I'd only be here for forty-eight hours."

"Did he tell you it would be a piece of cake?" Crank asked with a smile.

"Yes he did."

Rhino and Crank looked at each other, broke out in a hard laugh and started walking away.

"What? What's so funny?"

Rhino turned back and tossed a flashlight. "This is my first official operation for Hal McCambell, but his long time ops will tell you…if he says it's gonna be a piece of cake…hunker down and pray…Cause it ain't."

Grasshopper fumbled to catch the flashlight, dropping his shoulder bag on the ground and struggling to hang on to his computer. By the time he reovered, Crank and Rhino were gone. "Hey, where do I sleep?"

Out of the dark he heard, "Anywhere you like."

When the sun came up, Crank found the computer geek sleeping on top of a crate delivered the night before.

"Up and at 'em, sunshine. Long day ahead of us. Chow in five."

"Oh…my back."

"I'll have the men assembled at 07:00 for your geek class. Find Malakhi and let him know what you need."

"Okay." *What the hell have I gotten into? I have to call Hal.
This just won't do. Won't do at all.*

NUEVA CHOLUTECA AIRPORT
McCambell C-130

The newest airport in Choluteca was in poor condition
compared to most in the US, but was considered excellent in
Honduras. The 4,100 foot gravel strip boasted no navigational
aids, tower or hangars. It sat on a flat patch of coastal plains
thirty kilometers from the Nicaraguan border.

Buck lined up on the strip and prepared to land. "Toncontín
ATIS says the altimeter's 29.95 and winds are from the north at
six. Give me flaps fifteen and gear down."

"Roger that." Jerry rotated the landing gear lever to the
DOWN position and followed shortly thereafter with the flaps.

Buck continued the descent to 1,600 feet, about what the
intercept altitude was for an ILS glide slope. Without any
airfield navigation facilities or VASI, he used the GPS to set up
the three degree glide slope to the lat/long for the rudimentary
airfield. At five miles out, he spun the airspeed marker bug
down to approach speed and made the call, "Full flaps, before
landing check." He eased the four throttles back slightly and
simultaneously lowered the nose a tad as the aged workhorse
responded to the massive flaps extending out of the back of the
wing. He thumbed the elevator trim forward to counteract the
bird's natural tendency to climb.

"Gear, down, three green, Flaps full, props full increase. I reckon we're cleared to land...ain't nobody fired a missile at us." Jerry chuckled.

"Not yet, but the day ain't over," Buck said without a hint of a smile.

Coming in low across some semi-swampy looking land, he put the main gear down firmly only 250 feet from the approach end and quickly followed up by shoving the yoke forward and putting the nose wheel on the center of the ninety-eight foot wide strip. He slammed the four throttles back to idle range as he applied the brakes and then almost instantly brought the props into reverse. For a couple of seconds, the runway in front of him disappeared in a cloud of red dust.

"Ninety, sixty, forty, twenty..." Jerry called out using the GPS ground speed readout.

Buck brought the props out of reverse. In short order, the dust dissipated and he taxied to the right edge of the runway. Using the nosewheel steering, he made a quick 180 degree turn near the departure end of the strip.

As the cargo plane rolled to a stop, Stienke could see a dark green GMC SUV pulling out a side street near some houses and moving his way.

"Stay sharp and keep the engines running. If this turns into a goat fuck, I want us to be back in the air before we end up guests of the state."

"Ten four that, El Capitan."

When the SUV rolled to a halt, Mark stepped out and gave the hook 'em horns sign with his left hand. Shoehorn couldn't help smiling at his younger friend's signal. He was more excited to see Bianca follow him onto the gravel parking area. *Damn! She got finer with age, she did.*

Chikako stepped out last, wearing a long rain coat and moved to a position to offer cover. Alfonso opened the back doors to the vehicle and stood ready to transfer the cargo from the aircraft to the SUV.

Buck brought the Hercules to a stop on the unpaved parking area and quickly shutdown the turboprops. In less than a minute, the crew entrance door opened as the rear cargo ramp lowered to the ground.

Stienke was the first one off the plane, wearing his usual attire, a pair of starched Wrangler jeans and a custom tailored short-sleeved chambray shirt. He had even donned his signature Stetson once he shed the pilot's headset and boom mic.

"Shoehorn! You're a sight for sore eyes my friend," Mark said as he extended his hand.

Buck ignored the offer and wrapped his arms around Zorro's upper body and picked him up in a bear hug. "The hell you say...I'm glad to see you're still kicking, kid."

"Uggg...easy old man. You're gonna crush me. What the hell kinda workout are you doing these days?"

Buck set Mark down. "P90X. You should try it, you skinny ass runt. Might do you some good. Now...ya'll get busy offloading. I need to say hello to the jewel of Colombia."

Bianca moved up and was standing to the side of the two men. Her aviator-style glasses hid the look of joy and lust in her eyes. "Long time no see, Buck," she said with her lyrical Latina accent.

"Well, by God, I'm here now and we're going to catch up, sweet thing." He didn't hide his exuberance in seeing the beautiful woman—picked her up and held her close.

Bianca wrapped her arms around the big pilot's neck and returned his affection with a kiss that lingered. Her legs wrapped around his thighs as the pair seemed to melt into each other. "Is that a promise?"

"Have plane will travel. Wherever you want to go, darlin'."

"Texas?"

"Easy as pie. If you don't have a clean passport...I know a guy who can get you one."

"Okay you two, quit suckin' face, let's get this gear loaded and get out of here before someone arrests you for lewd behavior." Mark laughed as he slapped Buck on the shoulder and headed for the plane.

"Oh, I don't do any heavy lifting, *mi amigo*. I just fly."

"Alfonso...chop chop! It's just you, me and your cousin," Mark called out in Spanish. Then in Japanese, "Chikako, eyes wide open. Sound off if we have any company."

"Okay, boss," she responded in kind.

As Mark neared the rear of the plane he heard a familiar voice calling him.

"Well, Hollywood, took you long enough."

"Tarzan?"

"In the flesh. Let's get this load of toys off the plane and get the hell out of here. Feel like a turkey the day before Thanksgiving sitting out here in the open."

"Tarzan, you son-of-a..."

"Don't you go talking ugly about my mother. I'll have to whip you like a redheaded step child," Farmer said as he stepped into view.

The two men embraced heartily for several moments. Ken pulled back first and eyed him. "Plata you still look like a girl with that pony tail. Does your daddy know you're playing for the other team?" Tarzan reached around and lifted his hair up.

"What are you doin'?

"Always wanted to know what was under a horses' tail."

"Bite me." Mark grinned. "Damn good to see you again. Let's get this done and boogie to the hide...Got a bottle of tequila with your name on it...When we're done, Rolando and your copilot will baby-sit the aircraft for us."

"Sounds like a plan," Farmer agreed. "We'll lock this baby up tighter than a drum. Don't want anybody messin' with our ride."

ORO del CHRISTI MINE

Rhino, Cheyenne and Malakhi drove up to Crank as he listened to Grasshopper's dissertation concerning the new drone. He turned as they pulled to a stop.

"Sure you're okay with us going off base?" Rhino asked.

"You guys earned a little R&R...Don't make me come bail your happy ass out of some beaner lock up."

"We'll be good as choir boys," Cheyenne replied.

"See your rusty's in three days," Rhino said as he put the vehicle in gear.

"Malakhi, I'm depending on you to keep these two slackers out of trouble."

"Oh, man! How the hell am I suppose to do that?"

"Improvise, adapt...overcome." Crank laughed before turning back to the drone tutorial.

Rhino stepped hard on the gas pedal and drove off, throwing a cloud of dirt and pebbles in his wake.

Crank turned and shot his buddy the bird to the sound of the SUV horn indicating Rhino saw his salute.

The sun was low in the western sky when Grasshopper lifted the Devil Dog drone vertically off the ground and headed it forward. The fact that the new high-tech item was at the mine gave evidence to Hal's deep pockets. The five million dollar craft was a new level of expense for McCambell and a statement in how he intended to expand his security empire.

The two hundred and seventy-five pound aircraft accelerated to seventy knots in only fifty feet and climbed rapidly. The modified Israeli Plug-In Optical payload began sending back data in a matter of moments.

The computer guru had designed a perfect surveillance craft and this was its first field application. Unknown to Grasshopper, Hans was linked in and online as soon as the craft was airborne.

"How long will that bird be able to patrol?" Crank asked.

"Nine hours at best," Tom answered as he monitored the screens in front of him.

"How long to relaunch?"

"Depends on how fast your men can refuel."

"Get Badger and Katana up to speed on operating the toy. Sooner they know how, the sooner you go home."

"I was told forty-eight hours…"

"Hey…'Til these two can fly her, you're not going anywhere." Crank moved off to the mortar crew.

PUNTA GORDA RIVER BASIN

Captain Nortina and Collins—former Green Beret now rebel advisor—studied a map illuminated by a kerosene lantern. The sandy-haired American towered above most of the Nicaraguans at six feet.

"If we hit them from the north and east at the same time we could overrun their positions…"

"You're nuts, Nortino. From what your men told me the guys defending this mine ain't amateurs. Probably former military turned mercs…Any frontal assaults will end up like your last goat rope," he said with an eastern Oklahoma drawl.

Nortina thinly disguised his anger. He never cared for the American and was jealous of his popularity with the rebel forces. "What do you purpose?"

"The mining corporation has workers there now rebuilding the damage you inflicted. We infiltrate. With some of our men on the inside we do a Trojan Horse."

"Trojan Horse?"

Collins smiled considering his associates lack of military history. Realizing the instability of their new alliance, he refrained from causing any discomfort for the aging Nicaraguan.

"It's an assault from the inside to open the gates for our attack from without. You said the military has a mortar team. If the tubes were disabled, they would be useless. From your passdown about the last attempt to overrun the mine they have heavy machine guns. Right?"

"Yes. Fifty caliber and some M-60s as well."

"What if they could be put out of commission? The defenders would be reduced to small arms."

"They had claymores."

"With the right combination of stealth and intel, they could be disabled as well." Collins lit a small black cigar. He allowed the smoke to drift before continuing, "No mortars, no machine guns, no claymores...Then we have them."

"What if the military sends attack helicopters to support the mortar team?"

"I brought Stinger missiles. One goes down, the other bastards will scatter like chickens. Pick ten of your most trusted men. Have them gain access as laborers."

"I will do this, but...I must be the supreme commander of this operation. It will be my last campaign."

Collins smiled and walked away. "Of course.

MARK'S SAFE HOUSE

Mark and Chikako sat on the forth floor rooftop patio, the sounds of the city slowly fading as the clock ticked off the 02:00 hour.

"Your friends made little haste in going to the bed," Chikako said with a hint of humor. "Ken is odd man out it seems tonight."

"Huh, don't worry about him. He's probably making notes for his next award-winning novel, but don't worry...he'll change our names to protect the guilty...maybe."

"How do you know them?"

"Friends of my dad."

They sat silently for a few moments. Chikako poured another glass of Concho del Toro red wine for each of them.

"You never talk about your father." She sensed a slight stiffening. "Is he still alive?"

"Must be. Half dozen people have brought him up lately." Mark stood and stretched before turning and completing a three hundred sixty degree scan of the city skyline. "You saw the photo back at the hideout? The one over the fireplace?"

"Hard to miss it. I recognized you. Who were the others?"

"My grandfather, my dad and brother. We were on a ranch in west Texas."

"Is you grandfather alive?"

"No."

"What about your brother?"

"No."

She studied his face carefully. "Just you and your father. What about your mother?"

Mark took a deep breath and sat down. "She died giving birth to me."

"Oh...I'm sorry."

"Dad never seemed to get over it. Ended up leaving David and me with our grandparents and just...wandered off."

The night chill began to settle on the city. A light breeze picked up and ruffled the trees below.

Chikako realized she had broached a deep subject. A smile crossed her face knowing how much Mark was opening up to her. "Do you think you father blamed you?"

Plata just looked at her.

Mark woke to the sound of an incoming text. He rolled over, picked up his cell and read a message from Sloan: Client is nervous. Wants to meet. What are your instructions?

He lay back on the pillow and considered the options. *Not going to the office or the house. Blow our cover all to hell...Museum...That's the ticket.*

As he sent a reply, Chikako threw her arm over his chest. She snuggled close and whispered, "We go?"

"Just you and me. No reason to disturb the love birds."

"I doubt you could wake them. They were at it all night."

"Wear your short wig and the business suit...and put the pad Buck brought under your trauma plate. Don't want to rub those tattas raw."

She sat up and punched him in the shoulder. "They're already raw. You need to talk to your body armor friends and suggest some modifications for women."

"Excellent idea. Maybe I could get some sort of royalty. Make 'em like Madonna's, only bullet proof."

McCAMBELL'S OFFICE

Hal drank his third cup of coffee while reading a message from Crank: Mine secure. Drone operational. Grasshopper out of here as soon as team functional on Devil Dog. Rhino and two men first to take three day leave. Send more chow and ammo.

A smile crossed the old Scotsman's face. *Damn! The hippie kid is growing up. Might make a hand after all.*

He called his wife on the intercom. "Maggie, get on goggle or whatever and find me the best big wave surfboard you can."

"Oh, Hal, it's Google and you're too old to be surfing. Lord have mercy…what are you thinking about?"

"Not for me…for Crank. He deserves a bonus. Hell…ain't no way I'm going trolling for great whites."

"That's good, honey. You need to take care of yourself."

Hal hung up and chuckled. *Trolling for great whites. I gotta remember that one.*

CIA HEADQUARTERS

Director Walsh dismissed two subordinates when Willoby stopped in the doorway and knocked. After the men departed, he placed a folder on the desk.

"New intel on El Cobra. He's worked his way up and is now suspected of having direct contact with Senator Rojas in Colombia."

"How firm is this intel?"

"Level Three…There are a half a dozen photos in the folder. Seems our boy is working Bolivia and Colombia now."

Walsh looked at the photographs, and then closed the folder. "What's the latest on the Alpha team we sent?"

"No contact in three days."

"Have the Delta team suit up. Put them in play immediately."

"Yes, sir. ROE?"

"Find Cobra and kill the bastard!"

"Yes, sir. What about the Alpha team?"

"If you don't hear from them in twenty-four hours, consider them expended. Hold off on any official statement as such, but…gone four days? They are dead or worse."

"Yes, sir. I'll get right on it, sir."

As Willoby passed out the door Walsh called him back. "What's the latest on Zorro or Bianca?"

"Not a word from her and the ghost is still…a ghost."

"Damn! All right then, contact Matthews and light a fire under his ass. I want something and I want it yesterday!"

THE CASA de la CULTURA MUSEUM

Mark and Chikako wandered through the museum located in the former colonial house of Jose Cecilio del Valle. He wore his Sonny Bono disguise—black wig, fake mustache and an off-white suit complete with a stiff new white Panama hat. She wore the same disguise she had when she entered the country—a wig with short bangs and blue pinstripe business suit.

The museum was empty except for the staff when they entered. Zorro slipped the front door attendant a few bills and told her to direct the team and client upstairs when they arrived. From the balcony, the entrance was visible.

As soon as Linebacker, Sloan and John Batt entered, the attendant approached them. They looked up and saw Mark nod.

Chikako remained on the balcony. The others gathered in what had been a small sitting room converted to a library. Mark introduced himself.

"Steve Wilson. I understand you wanted to meet."

"Is this a joke? You look like a pimp," Batt blurted out.

"Keep your voice down. What do you want?"

"Who is she?" asked Batt.

"Need to know. Get to the point."

The wealthy American stood measuring the man in front of him. Though several inches shorter and fifty pounds lighter, the figure in front of him was intimidating. Batt was used to being in charge and Mark's attitude had him off balance. "I was nearly killed yesterday…"

217

"I was there. You were never in any danger."

"You were there? I never saw you…"

"Who do you think took out the gang bangers? Rocky and Bullwinkle?"

Linebacker snickered at the exchange. John turned and glared. Sloan walked out to join Chikako to avoid being caught laughing.

"How's it going in there?" she asked as he approached.

"Batt's getting his first lesson in Zorroism."

Chikako looked back, but could not hear what was being said. "Zorroism?"

"That's what Rhino called it in Bangkok. I'm Sloan," he said as he extended his hand.

"Mark told me. You did a good job yesterday."

Batt's face flushed and his voice raised a full octave. "I was told you would be in charge of security while I was here…"

"I am in charge. Yesterday should have covered that question for you."

"I expect employees to…"

"Easy now…you're about to step in some deep shit."

"What? You insolent bastard…I'll have you fired!"

Mark took one step forward and hissed. "Lower your voice."

John took two steps back and looked to Linebacker. He smiled and turned away moving to join Sloan.

"I…I…"

"Not going to tell you again. If you want to opt out of the contract that's fine. Just pack your staff, your kid and your happy ass up. We'll see you to the airport."

Batt stood staring. He was angered to the point that he began trembling. "I'm calling Hal McCambell. He'll have another team down here in…"

"No, he won't. After I call Hal and explain the situation that there are fifteen to twenty gangs looking to kidnap your ass…Hal will cancel this op. He's never lost a client and that's a record he's really proud of."

The two stood eyes locked on one another for a long moment. Batt was the first to blink.

Still hissing, "Now…sir…you get back to your business. I'll take care of mine. First order is…the kid goes home today. This is no place for testosterone charged little boys…Am I clear?"

"I don't like you, Mister Wilson. Don't like you at all."

"I don't care…I agreed to keep you safe and that's what I'm going to do…My way."

As Batt and the team left the building, Plata joined Chikako at the balcony railing.

"So how did the Zorroism go?"

"What?"

"Sloan said you were giving the client something called Zorroism."

Mark laughed. "I'll have to remember that one for my memoirs."

"Looked a little heated from here."

"Some clients need a bit of schooling. Have to keep in mind they're all alphas. Wouldn't have the money to hire us if they weren't."

"I see. Zorroism is…rich alpha meets bad ass alpha?"

Mark laughed again. "Have to remember that one too. Let's get back to the house and out of these outfits. Buck and Bianca should be up by now and Ken's probably ready to roll on back to Texas."

MARK'S SAFE HOUSE

Buck, Ken and Bianca were just finishing brunch when Mark and Chikako returned.

"I see you're keeping banker hours down here," Mark jested. "How'd the bed hold up?"

"I thought the floor was going to cave a couple of times," Ken cracked.

"It's too damn short I can tell you that. Where have ya'll been?" Shoehorn took a bite of *huevos rancheros*.

"Working. Some of us have jobs."

"Why did you not wake me?" Bianca looked to Chikako.

"Best we could tell, you two were doing the horizontal mambo 'til an hour before we left. Doubt you would have been much help." Mark grinned.

"Don't mind him. He's just jealous," Chikako said.

"Want me to cook you up some lunch? I was looking at the grub and I could make some more mean *huevos rancheros*.

Throw in some fried *papas* and bacon." Buck started to clear the table.

"I could go for some of your cooking...Did I tell you he's one of those gor-met cooks, Chikako?"

"Gourmet...numb nuts." Buck threw a biscuit at him.

"No. No, you didn't. Seems you have skills, big guy." She pulled off her wig.

"What's up with the valley pimp outfit?" Ken poked.

"Had to meet the client. Didn't want to blow our cover."

"Cover? You call Sonny Bono a cover?" The retired Marine laughed. "Damn son! Your dad's really gonna be disappointed in you."

Mark and Chikako shared a look. She started up the stairs undressing as she went. Bianca got up and followed her.

After the two women were out of hearing distance, Buck brought a cup of coffee to the table. "Damn that woman is fine. Too fine for you."

"Ya think? Don't tell her or I'll tell Bianca your secret."

"What secret?"

"Hell, I don't know yet, but I'll make something up."

The three men shared a laugh.

"If I had a woman like that, I'd be thinking about retiring," Ken said with a twinkle in his eyes.

"Strange you should mention that."

"Smartest thing you ever did if you do, kid. It's time you moved on. It's been what...ten, twelve years now?" Buck commented

"Twenty-one. Next month it will be twenty-one."

"It's clear she's into you. God only knows why…You're just a skinny-assed Jarhead with no future…But she definitely is…so run with it," Ken added.

They sat quietly for several moments and could hear the two women talking upstairs, but were unable to make out the words.

Plata looked at Shoehorn. "You mentioned Jesse. Do you know where he is?…I'm thinking I should reach out."

"Not exactly. Somewhere in the Philippines. Reminds me…he said to tell you that was a hell of a rodeo in Oroquieta. Whatever that means."

Mark spit his coffee out and set the cup down. "What about Oroquieta?"

"Hell, I don't know. He said you'd know."

Two days passed without incident. There were no other attempts to kidnap Batt or his engineers and the son had been sent home, simplifying the team's life.

Bianca spent most of her time with Buck, like lovers on holiday. Ken spent his time pounding away on his laptop—frequently pausing to say some bit of dialogue out loud. When he didn't like it, he revised and repeated, 'til he did.

Mark and Chikako continued to work on polishing the role of the Trailer. The contract was settling into a good rhythm.

ORO del CHRISTI MINE

Grasshopper found Crank talking with Striker and Pablo. He was anxious to be out of Nicaragua and intended to make it happen soon.

"Striker, I lasered that hilltop there to the south. Nine hundred meters. Take Pablo and the two Nigerians up there and scout it. Set up a fallback."

The sniper looked to the hill then back to Crank. "Good choice. On it."

"Provisions for a couple of days. I'll have someone resupply you."

"Crank, I think your men are ready now. When can I get out of here?" asked the young technogeek.

Crank turned to the frail man and smiled. "How about as soon as Rhino and the boys get back?"

"I'm packed. When are they due?"

"Tonight or tomorrow. I'm disappointed you are in such a hurry to desert us here at the resort. Think of the stories you will be able to tell your nerd buddies."

"Funny. Very funny. Like I said…I'm packed."

Striker and his team reached the top of the hill just past 10:00 hours. The men dropped their packs and sat down in the shade gasping from the climb in the heat with a hundred pounds of gear each.

"Take ten, then we dig in," Striker said as he scoped the mine below.

223

"How come Crank sent us up here?" Adom took a long swig of tepid water from his hydration bag.

"He's a Zorro protégé. Just doing what he's been taught."

"I very much want to meet this man, Zorro," Ido said.

"I think we need mules to carry our shit," Pablo said as he massaged his knees.

They shared a good-natured laugh at the Nicaraguan's comment.

"I too wish to meet him," Adom added.

"I remember thinking the same thing. Everyone talking about him. Zorro did this and Zorro did that. One word of advice when you meet him...Don't ask too many questions. He'll tell you what he wants you to know when he wants you to know." Striker laid his scope down.

"We will do that." Adom looked to his friend Ido. He shrugged his shoulders and smiled. His white teeth looked like pearls against his black skin.

Ido smiled back and tossed a small pebble Adom. They started exchanging rocks and soon escalated to golf ball sized ones.

"Knock off the grab ass...Pablo find some brush and cut us some cover. You two get set up behind those boulders above us. Ido...Once you're done, scout a back trail off this hill. If we have to boogie out of here, I don't want to be running blind."

***

CHAPTER TWELVE

MUNICIPAL JAIL
Managua, Honduras

Rhino stood at the bars—shaking them in his massive hands—while Cheyenne and Malakhi lay on steel beds bolted to the floor.

"Hey! When do we get out of the shit hole?" the big South African kept repeating.

"Give it a rest. You been at it for two hours now," Cheyenne grumbled.

"Yeah, you're giving my headache a headache," Malakhi chimed in.

A skinny policeman in a baggy uniform walked into the cell block and eyed the three men with a wry smile. "You gringos want to go home now?"

"No...we love the decor and outstanding room service," Rhino spat back. "When do we post bail or pay a fine or whatever the crap you people do here?"

"You go before the magistrate tomorrow. But...if you have some moneys? Maybe...I could assist you."

"Now we're getting somewhere. How much to check out of this Nicaraguan hotel California?"

"So you have some moneys?"

"Damn straight. Bring me my wallet." Rhino's veins on his neck began to bulge.

"What wallet, gringo? I don't see no stinking wallet."

"I had ten thousand Cordobas when you arrested me."

"Five thousand for me," Cheyenne said.

"I must have had at least five or six," Makakhi added.

"No...No wallets. You had no wallets when we arrest you."

"Bull fucking shit...I want to see the Capitan!" Rhino roared.

"El Capitan no here today. He here tomorrow when we take you to see the magistrate. But...you no have moneys the magistrate will give you maybe one month for the damages you do in the bar and another month for resisting arrest."

"I want to make a phone call!" said Rhino.

"This is Nicaragua, my friend. There is no phone call for prisoners. I see you again tomorrow...maybe." The jailer laughed, turned and walked out.

Rhino shook the bars again with all his strength. Dust fell from the ceiling as the steel rattled.

"Hey…get over here you two. Give me a hand. We can pull this rotting shit down."

"Then what? Fight our way out with our bare hands?"

"Whatever it takes, Malakhi."

They looked at one another for a moment, and then got up and joined him. The three pushed and shoved, loosening the bars with each action.

"Lay your backs into it, damn it!" Rhino growled.

"What if the guard comes back?"

"Fuck 'im. I'll beat his greasy ass to death with these bars." Rhino smiled wickedly.

ORO del CHRISTI MINE

Crank squatted under a gravity-fed stream of luke-warm water in a improvised field shower. His wristwatch vibrated. He stood up straight and eyed the time. 1800. *Finish this shit, shower, shave and have a few beers with a nice thick steak…*

"Crank! The drone has movement headed this way!" Badger ran up.

He stepped out of the four foot-by-four foot tin roof structure without turning off the water. He jammed his feet into his boots, grabbed his clothes in one hand, rifle and Molle vest in the other and started to the drone command center at a dead run.

The construction workers could not help but pause from their labors, seeing the nude blonde giant race across the compound.

"What you got?"

"Looks like a half dozen boats coming down the river. Hard to say for certain...maybe twenty men in each." Grasshopper didn't look up from the monitor.

"Badger ring the bell. Get every swingin' dick to their duty station."

"Yes, sir," he said as he ran for the bell hanging on a pole nearby.

"That's not all, look here." The geek turned the drone to the east. "Didn't see this until I spotted the boats."

Crank could clearly see armed men crossing a small stream headed toward the mine. "Shit!"

"Ah...do you know you're buck naked?" Grasshopper snickered nervously.

"Fuck you...Get on the horn. Call Rhino and tell him to get back here ASAP!" Crank sat down on an ammo can, yanked off his boots and put on his utility pants. He hopped around on one bare foot, and then the other as he pulled them up. Sitting down again, he pulled a pair of socks on his damp feet, followed by his boots again and zipped them tight.

"There's a world of hurt headed our way, kid. You know how to use an M4?"

Grasshopper looked up with a mixture of shock and fear in his eyes. "I...I uhhh took the mandatory McCambell firearm's course."

"Well that's just spiffy...Did you pass?"

"I scored a 160 with a M16."

"Jesus…160? Out of 300? Wow! You better pray they don't break the wire." He walked away. "Santiago, let's go! Captain Medina, we have contact headed our way."

The security force rushed to man their positions. The construction laborers ran to their vehicles and began to drive off, en mass to the sound of the alarm bell. The infiltrators broke away, slipped into the hides they had selected and waited for their rebel brothers.

"What's up ol buddy?" Striker called on the radio. "Looks like a bee hive down there."

"Incoming. Down the river and another force moving in from the east."

"Roger that. How many?"

"A shit load…two, three hundred maybe."

"Get out. Get out now. We'll cover you."

HANS SCHOEPKE'S RANCH

The computer guru rushed into his operations room as soon as he heard the buzzer ringing—only one reason it would. His Devil Drone invention was picking up signals that meant danger for the McCambell men.

He sat down in his chair and brought up the same feed Grasshopper was viewing thousands of miles away.

"Not good. Not good at all."

He picked up his secure phone and called Hal. As he waited, he began a computer run to estimate the forces advancing on the mine.

"Now before you start in on the bank transfer…"

He interrupted Hal, "There's a large force headed toward your team at the mine. Computer count is two hundred fifty…three hundred twenty-five and counting."

"Christ! Have you called Crank?"

"I'm seeing the same images he is."

"Damn! Gotta go, Hans."

The screen continued to show red images coming out of the jungle and crossing the stream as the ground force advanced.

"God be with you boys. God be with you…"

MARKS SAFE HOUSE

The ring tone told Mark the Scotsman was calling.

"Bag pipes?" Chikako asked.

"Hal. Probably wants to chew my ass out for the meeting with Batt. I better take it."

Zorro stepped out the back door as he answered. "*Hola, mi amigo.*"

"Crank's getting ready for an Alamo."

"What?"

"There's an big ass army, maybe five hundred headed his way right now. Hans just called…"

"Whoa…slow down. What's Hans doing in Nicaragua?"

"He's not, I bought a drone he designed. Crank has it and Hans is monitoring it from his ranch in Chili."

"Are you authorize me to pull out of the Batt contract?"

"No dipwad! I'm calling to ask you to the Marine Corps ball. Jesus! How long 'til you can get there?"

Mark stood in the midmorning sun, calculating the situation. "Buck is still here. You say it's a go for him to fly…"

"Done. Have him call me if he has any problems with it. Just get there. Who can you take with you? Any of the boys there capable?"

"Yeah…but that would put Batt in harm's way."

"Damn it to hell!"

Zorro could almost see Hal's face turning red. "I'll call you when we're wheels up."

Mark walked back into the dining area, everyone could immediately tell there was something wrong.

"What's up ol buddy?" Buck asked.

"Crank's about to be hit with a shit storm…I gotta go. Shoehorn, Hal said he'd pay you to fly me down there. How long 'til we're in the air?"

"Soon as we get to the airport. The plane is fueled."

"I'll get my gear." Chikako started for the stairs.

"You're not going. You and Bianca are staying here and keep the trailer going…"

"You can shove it right there, mister! You may big dog to everyone else and boss them around…but you don't tell me."

Chikako stood staring with fire in her eyes.

"No place for you…"

"You will have to beat me down to stop me. And even if you do, you'll be in no shape to help Crank. I'll be ready in ten."

She didn't wait for a response, but started up the stairs.

"I think you've been put on notice, big dog. I'll get my bag and wait for you in the car," Ken said with a hearty laugh as he slapped Zorro on the shoulder and started for the stairs.

"No way I'm going to miss out on this one," Bianca added.

"Ken! How many parachutes do you have on the plane?" Plata asked.

"Five. One for me, Buck and the copilot. Two extras," he replied as he kept moving up the steps.

Buck looked down at Bianca. "Well there you go, Darlin'. Only two chutes." He stopped at the top of the stairs. "You're serious. You're really gonna to jump in?"

Mark shot him a look. "No time for passport checks and highway miles."

"Well, I sure as hell am not staying here…I'm in for the ride. Buck, wait for me," Bianca called out as she took the stairs rapidly.

Mark shook his head and mumbled, "It's wonderful to be in charge."

ORO del CHRISTI MINE

The team had secured their positions and waited for the assault they knew was coming. Pantera, Jackal and Katana made last minute checks on their Browning machine guns. Their gunners mates ran back and forth from the munitions bunker—a shipping crate covered with a triple layer of sand bags—with additional cans of belted ammo.

Crank made the rounds of each position, encouraging the men. *What would Zorro do? What am I missing? Christ, I wish he was here.*

He paused half way up the incline to Captain Medina's mortar team and pulled his sat phone from the holder on his vest and dialed.

"Zorro. What's your status? You as hard as you can get?"

"Ain't good. Beau coup bad guys moving on us."

"Hang in there. You stay cool. Keep your head on a swivel. I'm about to take off…"

"Take off?"

"For your position. Text me the coordinates. Shoehorn flew some equipment in for us after the drop to you. He's giving us a lift."

"Wait a minute. How do you know…"

"Hans called Hal. Hall called me. Said you're about to see the elephant. So we're headed your way."

"Who's we?"

"Chikako and I."

The sound of her name flashed through his memory like a flash of hot white light. *Chikako? What's she doing with…*

"Oh man…you hooked up with her didn't you?"

"Hey…be like old times. Except it'll be beaners instead of China men."

"You bastard. Hell, should have known."

"I'll fill you in when we join the party."

"Better make it fast. According to the drone geek we'll be up to our ass in yucca heads by dark."

"No you won't. They'll wait 'til sometime after midnight. Let you sit and stew. Play with your nerves. Probably do a couple of probes to test your firepower."

"Yeah…yeah, you're right…What else am I missing?"

"You got this Crank. You're the best. Do you have any barrels of fuel? Or propane tanks?"

"Maybe twenty fifty-five gallon drums of diesel. There's a half dozen twenty-five pound propane tanks in the mess hall."

"Move the diesel out near the perimeters. Rig a grenade with a trip wire to everyone of 'em. Same with the propane. Spread 'em to the most likely points of assault."

"Should've thought of that…On it."

"You would have."

MARK'S SUV

Mark disconnected and turned to Buck who was speeding through the traffic with the flashers on and laying hard on the horn. "When's the last time you've been to Brazil?"

"I don't know. Four…five years why?"

"Bianca, you still want a vacation?"

"I do but…"

"You three need to go on down to outlaw's hideout. Kick back. Ken, you can tune up my horses. Lakota Moon acted a little squirrely the last visit…gettin' cranky 'cause nobody's ridin' him…When's the last time you went skinny dipping in a stone tank, Buck?"

"Jeez, not since high school."

"Then it's settled. The three of you fly down to my hacienda and we'll catch up when this is over. I'll call DeLeon and tell him you're coming."

"How you figure on jumping in on Crank's position with all the gear we loaded?" Ken asked.

"That's the beauty of you going ahead. Chikako and I take only what we can carry. You haul the rest back home. Win...win."

AIRSPACE OVER HONDURAS

Mark and Chikako worked preparing their gear for a drop. Bianca and Ken assisted. Tarzan checked the spare chutes. Not satisfied with the date on the packing tag, he repacked both. They were shouting to be heard over the roar of the engines.

"I'm going to check with Shoehorn on our ETA. See if he can come back here and check us out on the Dolos Quick Detach barrel system."

"Do we have to jump with the Armor500?" Chikako asked as she stuffed her jump bag.

"Damn straight, sunshine. Stuff it in your gear bag. We'll put it on once we're on the deck."

Mark entered the cockpit to hear Buck talking to Hal. "I'll leave the C-130 in San Jose. Pick up the Gulfsteam. You can hire a pilot in Brazil to fly your jet back to Dallas." He looked up at Zorro with a big smile. "You hired me to do Nicaragua and Honduras. I did. Now it's back to Nicaragua. So this is a new contract."

Mark looked out the plane at the weather front moving in from the west. *Great...now we have to race the storm.*

Buck put his cell to his chest. "Hal's trying to do the ol' pop-goes-the-spinning-weasel trick. Give me a minute."

Mark nodded and turned back to the cargo hold. He smiled seeing the two women working together.

"I'm hungry," Chikako said as he returned.

"There's some MREs in the gray foot locker. Have to eat 'em cold," Ken answered.

Bianca looked up. "That sucks."

"Where we're going, it will taste better than lizards," Zorro added.

Buck entered with a big smile. "Took some square dancing but finally calf roped the deal. We leave the jet in Rio. Can your man pick us up?"

"Reminds me, I need to call DeLeon. How 'bout giving us the Buckster short-short on that Dolos first?"

"More than happy to. The Dolos system consists of this threaded adapter that attaches directly to the upper receiver on any standard AR or M-16 upper, and these proprietary free-float fore ends. They use any regular AR barrel that you want, but I put these 10 ½ inch ones on for compact concealment. Each backpack has two barrels, as you might have noticed. The one with the flash hider is in 5.56 while the one with the muzzle break is in 300 Blackout."

"You're thinking subsonic...for wet work, I assume. That looks like a Yankee Hill quick-attach break."

Buck grinned. "Uh huh. Anyway, line up the gas tube on the barrel with the hole in the upper. Slide it in and twist the forend until the three cam slots in the barrel assembly mate with their counterpart cams on the adapter. Turn it clockwise until you hear the ratchet engage, locking the whole shebang together, like this."

Buck demonstrated the assembly, then he reached into the backpack and pulled out a suppressor. He slipped it on the muzzle break and twisted it until it locked. It made a sound like the Dolos forend engaging. He let the bolt assemble fly forward and then held up the entire weapon for the group to admire. "Only thirty six inches long when fully assembled and it fits in this backpack or a standard briefcase when pulled down."

"Nice," Bianca said.

"Thought you'd like it." He winked at her. He handed the parts to Plata.

"Got it. What a sweet inovation." Mark said at the end of Buck's tutorial. "Man I could have used one of these babies a dozen times…got any Blackout ammo loaded?"

"Three twenty rounders in the backpack. The 5.56 is Hornady V-Max forty grain. Got some Surefire sixty round mags in there…already loaded and ready to rock and roll."

"Damn, Buck you are one crafty bastard…for an old fart."

"Yeah, but I wish I'd been born rich instead of so sexy and good lookin'."

"And modest…" Bianca added with a wink.

Buck smiled. "You know, humility is not one of my many virtues."

Ken chuckled. "Hell, it'll be perfect for your jump. Hit the ground and slam it together lickity split. How much ammo you going to haul?"

"All the drop bag can carry. You know the rule?"

Buck and Ken laughed and repeated. "Ain't no such thing as too much ammo."

Ken turned to Chikako and asked, "Kinda a weird time to be asking, I know, but…you ever jump before?"

"We jumped together in Hong Kong. She's good to go."

"Hong Kong? Why the hell were you parachuting into Hong Kong."

Mark and Chikako shared a look and a smile.

"Long story." Chikako didn't look up.

"Wait a minute…Hong Kong? Has this got anything to do with the Triad?" Buck asked.

Again, the two shared a look before Mark answered. "How do you know about the Triad?"

"Hal mentioned it to me on my way down here. You know those guys are bad to the bone?"

"We keep hearing that…How you coming on the chow?…If there's a ham and eggs, I'll have one."

ORO del CHRISTI

"The fuel drums are set. Where do you want the propane?" an ICC asked.

"Fill the gaps. Set 'em far enough back to avoid any cook off from the diesel when it goes."

"Crank, the boats have landed," Grasshopper radioed.

"Heads up guys...won't be long now," Crank called to the men on the radio. "Expect perimeter probes."

"You're starting to sound like Zorro," Pantera called back.

"Striker...movement?" Crank asked.

"Too much jungle."

"Watch your three and six," the team leader replied.

"Roger that."

MUNICIPAL JAIL

The steel bars came loose at the ceiling and the three men pushed with all their strength. The steel cage began to bend. Five minutes later there was a space big enough for the two smaller men to slip out.

"Man I never thought we could do it." Malakhi placed his hands on his knees and tried to catch his breath. "How we going to get your lard ass out?"

"Up yours, kosher breath. Make some noise. When Pancho comes in to find out what's going on, relieve him of the keys."

They positioned themselves on either side of the door and began yelling.

When the guard came in, Malakhi put him in a headlock and choked him down.

"Keys. Let's get this show on the road. Crank's going to ream us good."

"Probably have you filling sandbags after I tell him why we ended up in the brig," Cheyenne replied.

"Never figured you for a snitch," Rhino answered.

"You two can discuss who's on first…once we're on the highway. Let's get the hell outta here," Cheyenne said.

ZETA COMPOUND

Oscar Puto rode his favorite stallion in a manicured arena, under floodlights, when his trusted intelligence gatherer arrived. The MIT graduate stood at the fence admiring the horse and rider as the ZETA leader put the pure breed Iberian stud through his paces.

Passing by, Oscar nodded but continued the ride. Always seeking to show his skills off to an audience, dropped the reins on the horse's neck and extended his arms out to the side, shoulder high. With a unnoticeable cue with his legs the horse accelerated from a lope to a canter.

He called the horse to a halt.

"Magnificent, isn't he?"

"Yes…yes he is."

"If I were to give you a photo of someone, how long would it take for you to identify them?"

"Depends on how much information is on the net. Someone who is, shall I say…normal everyday…"

"I would like to find two people actually. And they are not normal everyday."

"Why are you looking for them if I may ask?"

"Our new allies, the Triad, desire to find them. I would like to know why…A pawn in the game if you understand me."

The well-dressed man paused before answering, "Give me the photos. I will see what I can do."

"Excellent. Stay for lunch. I have three new girls from the Netherlands that just arrived."

"How could I refuse such a generous offer?"

"You can't." Puto laughed before riding off.

AIR SPACE OVER HONDURAS
McCambell's C-130

Mark did a palm smash to his forehead.

"What?" Chikako asked.

"The team. I must be getting Alzheimer's. Forgot to let them know we're gone."

He grabbed his satellite phone and sent a text: Big trouble Nicaragua. Call Hal for details. Trailer team en route. On your own. Maximize use of the WiFi cameras. If it gets too deep, get out.

"Linebacker can handle it," Bianca said.

Over the intercom Buck alerted the passengers.

"Crossing the border. ETA one hour. Anybody call for lawyers, guns and money?"

Mark chuckled at the reference to the Warren Zevon song. "Doubt lawyers will do us any good where we're going."

Chikako opened a suitcase and began rummaging through her clothing. She held up a pair of tan utility pants and gray shirt. "This?"

Mark looked over. "Nope." He flipped open a foot locker and removed a set of jungle tiger stripes and laid them on a bag before pulling out a second set. "Try these on."

"I'm going up front while you two get your fashion show worked out." Bianca moved forward to the cockpit.

Ken smiled then turned his back.

Zorro stripped off his clothing and put the distinctive Vietnam black and green utilities on. He removed his preferred bush boots—knee-high brown leather packer outfitters—from a footlocker, pulled them on, tucked pant legs in and began to lace them up.

Chikako had her utilities on and turned to Mark. "Kinda baggy. Don't suppose one of you have any skills tailoring?"

He could not help but laugh seeing the pants legs and shirt sleeves draping off her smaller frame. "Actually, we both do. Now where's that sewing kit?"

Thirty minutes later he and Ken had altered the uniform and stepped back to admire their work.

"There ya go, Darlin'. All ready for the dance," Tarzan said.

"Thanks. What else do you want in my drop bag?"

Mark opened a crate, removed two frag grenades and quickly tossed them to her. She caught them easily and laid them beside her bag and turned just in time to catch the first of several phosphorous grenades.

"Hey! Slow down."

"Load 'em up in these shoulder bags." Mark tossed empty claymore bags. "How many rounds of .45 do you have?"

"Six mags."

"Good to go. Load ten more mags for the M-16. Shove them in this bag."

Ken moved to help. "Put two tracers in first. Shit's in the fan, it lets you know the mag is done."

"I want you to carry the over and under. I'll put the ammo together. A dozen rounds will about do it." Mark pulled the snake blaster and holster out of a case.

Buck and Bianca came back from the cockpit.

"Reminds me of the time I hauled your dad to Bolivia. Only he had a team of knuckle-draggers. You?…You have a heavenly ninja."

"Yakuza, Buck. I eat ninjas for breakfast."

"Ouch. My bad."

"Take your wakizashi." Mark pulled his from a suitcase.

"May I?" Shoehorn asked as he reached for the blade.

"Don't cut your dick off."

"You shouldn't ought to talk to your elders that way," Buck said as he caught the three-century-old short sword. Removing the sheath, he balanced it in his massive hands for a moment, then did a series of moves—each perfectly performed.

"Nice," Chikako said with admiration.

"I was stationed in Japan a couple of tours. While my pilot brothers were raiding the hostess bars in Kabukicho I used my off time to learn some more, uh…practical skills," he answered in Japanese.

Chikako replied in same, "I bow to your wisdom, oh, wise one,"

"And I bow to you capturing the heart of my young friend."

243

"Hey, English or Spanish," Bianca chastised.

"I'm packed," Mark said as he zipped up his drop bag and attached a line. "I'll take the wakizashi. Chikako, strap yours to your thigh. If we need to shed the chutes quickly...cut the rigging."

ORO del CHRISTI MINE

A flare shot skyward north of the mine alerting the defenders the enemy had arrived. Almost immediately, one arced high in the night sky on the eastside.

"Captain Medina, stand by," Crank called over his radio.

The munitions bunker exploded. A rebel—one of the infiltrators—had thrown a grenade inside and ran toward the communications shack intending to disable it.

Crank pulled his revolver and shot the man center mass. The Glaser Safety Slug penetrated and exploded—shredding the man's internal organs. He bounced once like a rag doll before the grenade he carried exploded.

"Ahh...shit, shit, shit!" Grasshopper screamed.

"Get on the horn. Find out ETA on the choppers General Sacasa promised." Crank calmly took aim on a second rebel running towards them.

"I...I can't do this..."

Crank fired, sending the second attacker to the ground, turned and pointed the .44 magnum hand-cannon at the geek. "Cowboy the fuck up! Make the call or I'll shoot you myself."

The other infiltraters made their moves—each attacked the heavy machine guns. Before the defenders realized the threat, two of the three weapons were blown to pieces and the crews killed.

"Fuck!" Crank yelled.

A rebel fired an RPG from the tree line at the mortar team's ammo. The resulting series of explosions tore the hilltop apart killing most of the Nicaraguan soldiers in one fell swoop.

Crank stood momentarily stunned by the chaos swirling around him.

Grasshopper grabbed his arm. "No answer. No one is on the radio!"

"What? Forget it kid. Grab your rifle. Follow me," he yelled over the explosions. "Striker! We're coming out."

As Crank and Grasshopper ran for the south perimeter the remaining machine gun team joined them.

"This is one giant cluster fuck," Pantera yelled as he ran with his gunner's mate…

***

CHAPTER THIRTEEN

HANS SCHOEPKE'S RANCH

The computer genius stared at the monitor. Realizing no one at the mine was operating the drone, he logged in and began controlling it himself. His eyes grew misty as he watched the destruction unfold. His hands shook as he moved the joy stick and picked up his phone and voice dialed.

"Zorro. What you got, Hans?"

"It's over."

"What do you mean over?"

"The whole place went up in flames. Explosions…so many explosions."

There was a long moment of silence on the other end.

"Wait…wait a minute. I see images moving to the south,"

Hans said as he picked up the signatures of Crank and the survivors headed for Striker's position.

"Can you identify who it is?"

"No. At night it's infrared. Just make out images."

"Damn," Mark replied. "Okay Hans. How long can you monitor the situation?"

Hans checked the drone data before answering, "Only another couple of hours fuel. Then I'll have to terminate it to keep it out of the wrong hands."

"Call me every fifteen minutes with an update."

"Yes, yes, of course. Zorro...I'm sorry."

AIRSPACE NICARAGUA
McCambell's C-130

Everyone sat or stood waiting for Zorro to brief them on what Hans had relayed. They knew by his body language the news was not good.

"We're too late."

A silence hung like a heavy cloud on the group.

"Survivors?" Ken asked.

"Hans said there's a few running south."

"Then we can still help." Chikako placed her hand on Mark's shoulder.

"Maybe. How much longer to the drop?"

Buck checked his GPS Nav display. "Thirty minutes best case scenario."

"My brothers are down there. If anyone is still alive I owe it to them to jump."

"Semper Fi!" Ken said as he continued to load magazines.

HAL McCAMBELL'S RANCH

The Scotsman woke to the ringing of his cell phone. He rolled over and checked the screen while rubbing his eyes to clear the blurred vision.

"Honey, what is it? Who would be calling at this hour?" Maggie asked.

"Hans. Gotta take it." Hal sat up. "What do you have?"

"The mine has been overrun. I see a few survivors moving to the south. Maybe three hundred images descending from the north and east."

The old man's shoulders slumped and he rested his head on his left hand. "Jesus."

"I called Zorro…he's still going in."

"What is it?" Maggie asked with concern.

"The mine is…is gone. The men are gone."

"Oh, dear Lord."

AIRSPACE OVER NICARAGUA
McCambell's C-130

The mood was somber as Mark and Chikako made the final check on their gear.

Zorro moved to the back of the plane and made a call. *Come on Surfer. Pick up.*

Crank answered in a whisper. "Battery's about to go. We've been overrun. Bad guys on our tail. Headed southeast into the Cerro..." The line went dead, leaving only static.

"Damn!"

The two women responded to his outburst with concern, neither wanting to ask, but both wanting to know what had upset him.

Mark speed dialed another number.

"Bro! How goes it?" asked Rhino.

"Where are you? Where's Crank?"

"He's at the mine. I'm headed back from a three-day furlough. Why?"

"It's been wiped out. Where are you?"

"What? No friggin' way! Wait a minute...how do you know?...Come on, man, you're jerking me off."

"I don't have time to jerk you off. What weapons do you have and what's your ETA to the mine?"

"Not a damn thing. We got in a bit of trouble and the fuckin' cops took our tools. We checked ourselves out, but couldn't break into the gun locker."

"Jesus! How FUBAR up can things get?" Mark considered the situation. "Where can you get your hands on some weapons?"

"All our gear is at the mine, mate."

Mark paced back and forth as he yelled into the phone. The drone of the turboprops made it almost impossible to hear.

He leaned against the bulkhead, drew in a breath and exhaled slowly.

"Call Hal. Tell him you're alive. Call me back." Mark hung up, leaned over and rubbed his temples slowly in small circles.

He flinched when he felt Chikako's hands on his shoulders and looked up to see her smiling down at him.

"We can do this. I know we can."

Mark relaxed as she massaged the tension away. "Crank's alive."

"Of course he is. You think a few hundred rebels can kill the mad surfer?"

Mark could not help but grin, and then he laughed. "Yeah, you're right. But…the jungle he's headed into sure can. Some of the darkest shit on earth."

"Well…figure it out. How do we save him?"

NICARAGUAN JUNGLE
Four Clicks East of Oro del Christi

Crank shoved the sat phone back into its holster and looked over at the men with him. The battered team was in a defensive circle.

Captain Medina and his mortar crew had gone in one huge explosion. The other Nicaraguan soldiers and four ICCs died moving to or during the brief skirmish at the fallback position before the survivors were pushed into the jungle.

"Ido," Crank called softly.

The Nigerian crawled over—a compress bandage on his left shoulder. "Yebo, boss."

"How far did you scout a back door?"

"Another three clicks. The jungle closed in. Could see a ridge line that might take us four or five more clicks."

"Take the lead. Adom's on you. Pass the word. We move in five."

Ido slinked off silently. He tapped his buddy on the shoulder and they started into the jungle on a game trail that continued to wind down into a narrow canyon.

"Five meter spacing. Don't fire unless fired upon," Crank called out only loud enough for the team to hear as he circled his left hand above his head, and then pointed in the direction the Nigerians had taken.

The survivors fell in quietly. Crank took one last look behind him, tightened the blood-soaked bandage on his right calf and followed...

AIRSPACE OVER NICARAGUA
McCambell's C-130

Ken sat quietly preparing an improvised Griswald bag for a M-16 Dolos near the cargo door. Bianca had moved to the cockpit leaving Mark and Chikako alone. She was still rubbing his neck when his cell rang.

"Zorro."

"I just got off the phone with Rhino...I can get them weaponed up in Managua..."

"When?"

"Said they could be there in four hours…"

"Shit!"

"Hold your horses, cowboy, I have a chopper pilot in Managua. Goes by the call sign Sundance. I can have him fly the boys to you. He'll call you for the coordinates."

"I talked to Crank. Where he's going there won't be any place for a chopper to set down."

"Get your head in the game. Two words…fast rope."

"You ever been to the Cerro Wawashan? Cause that's where Crank is headed."

"No."

"Triple canopy…some of it over swamp."

"Best we can do…I have a call coming in from Hans."

Chikako sat down and shook her hands—throwing off the bad energy from Mark's body. "What now?"

"Hal's sending in the cavalry. Looks like you won't need to jump after all."

"We had this conversation already. You jump? I jump."

Mark sat staring at her with a mix of concern and admiration. "Yeah…How's your knee?"

"Good to go."

"Take the fall on your right foot as much as you can. Once we hit the ground, we're on our own. Don't want to have to carry you…"

"I walked out of Costa Rica." She moved to the parachutes and began to put one on. "I wonder what Stranger's doing?"

Mark couldn't help but marvel at her give-a-damn attitude concerning the world of hurt they were about to enter. "She's sleeping. Probably on our bed."

She turned and smiled. "I like the sound of that. Our bed...Better chute up."

Ken joined them and adjusted their rigging. "Did I ever tell you about the time Jesse and I jumped into Laos?"

"No...no you didn't. How'd it turn out?"

"Command decided it was too hot for extract when the time came. We had to walk out."

"That sucked."

"Not as much as it did for the major that made the call to leave us. Your daddy marched right into the officer's club and beat him so bad before the MPs could subdue him the prick was sent stateside for recovery."

Bianca knelt between the pilot and copilot seats watching the approaching storm. "Can we make it before that hits?"

"Have to. Mark'll jump even if we don't. He's as hard-headed as his old man."

"I want your chute."

Buck turned to her. He took a long look at her beautiful face while she was focused on the storm. "What about Brazil?"

"You're rich. You can fly down when this is over. I'll meet you there."

Stienke didn't like what he was hearing. "What will you do for tools?"

"Did you see all the toys Zorro has in those cases and foot lockers?"

She entered the cargo compartment carrying her chute. "I'm coming...Don't give me any of your mucho macho bullshit, the discussion is over...Open the toy chests and weapon me up."

Chikako gave Bianca a high five. "Three's a good number. Isn't that what you said in Hong Kong?"

Mark moved to a case and pulled his Remington 870 out. He opened a foot locker and began to extract ammunition, a suppressor and web gear for the shotgun.

"I have to be out of my mind. Jumping into hell with two women."

"Shove it, blue eyes. I was raised in the jungle, I could teach Sheena a few tricks," Bianca said with a smile. "You'll need my skill sets down there."

"There's gonna be a book deal and a movie," Ken said as he snugged Zorro's rigging. Once satisfied with the adjustments he removed a length of eighty pound test line from his pants pocket and tied the improvised Griswald bag to the harness. "This should get you operational once you hit the ground."

"Check me." Bianca walked to Ken.

"Have to carry the scatter gun on your side. Too damn long to strap across your chest. Besides those huge melons would be bruised on impact." Ken grinned as he worked his jumpmaster skills.

ORO del CRISTI MINE

Nortino and Collins stood where the mortar teams had been, watching their men ransack the dead for anything that could be hauled off.

"That was easier than I expected," Nortino said.

"We should get the hell out of here. Come daylight there will be Nicaraguan soldiers all over this place," Collins replied.

"Yes, of course. What we cannot carry…we'll destroy."

Collins looked at the rebel leader with disdain. *Fucking idiot. No wonder they lost the war.* "I'm taking my men north. If you move swiftly, you can be upriver before dawn."

"I am going after the men who fled to the east. I want to crush them…"

"They've been crushed. Why put your men in danger following a few survivors into the jungle?"

"You Americans never understood my people. It is a point of pride to eliminate every one of them…Even if a few must die doing it."

"Suit yourself," he said as he slung his Thompson over his shoulder and started down the hill. He paused and looked back at Captain Nortino standing alone. *If I his followers wouldn't shoot me I'd kill that pompous ass right now.*

"Collins. It was a good plan. I salute you on it. Why not join our forces and march on Managua?"

Lunatic. A raving lunatic. "Next time. For now…it's time to run and hide."

The Nicaraguan never answered, nor did he look at him as he walked down the hill, calling his men to move out.

A pair of rebels ran up to Nortino.

"There are only a few of them. They are headed east into Cerro Wawashan," one man said between breaths.

"Excellent. We shall either find and kill them or see the jungle has killed them for us. I want thirty men to take the spoils of our crushing victory back to our camp. Have the others join me on that hill."

They looked to each other. One said, "The Wawashan is not called the jungle of lost souls for nothing."

CIA SAFE HOUSE
Managua, Nicaragua

Matthews lay on his bed smoking a cigarette. The ashtray was overflowing with butts.

A subordinate knocked on the door.

"What?"

"Sir, there's a lot of chatter on the military channels. Seems the Oro del Christi mine has been attacked again."

Matthews sat up and downed a half-filled glass of rum, then lit a new smoke from the butt of the nearly finished one. "I'm coming."

MISTRESS MENDOZA'S RESIDENCE
11 Marsellas Circle.

General Sacasa slept in Lucia's arms when his cell rang. The old man rolled over and checked the screen to see who would be disturbing him at such an hour. Lucia moaned and moved closer, pressing her breasts against his bare back.

He sat up and rubbed the sleep from his eyes. "Yes."

"My general. We had a call from Captain Medina."

"Go on."

"That is it sir. I could hear the sounds of gunfire, then the line went dead."

"How long ago was this?" The general stood up and moved to the balcony.

"Half an hour…"

"Why the hell did you not call me sooner?"

"Sir, you ordered us not to interrupt you when you are with Lucia."

"Get the attack squadron ready. I will be there in twenty minutes."

When he entered the bedroom again, his mistress was sitting up on the bed holding a sheet over her body. "What is it, my love?"

"I am surrounded by incompetence. I must go."

"But you promised to take me to…"

"Another time." He hopped back onto the balcony as he was pulling on his pants and yelled down to the soldiers, "Get the car started! We must get to the air base immediately."

AIR SPACE OVER NICARAGUA
McCambells C-130

Buck entered the cargo area to find his three passengers sitting quietly and prepared for the jump. Mark and Chikako were both meditating. Bianca walked over to Shoehorn.

"They're doing some Asian mind drill. Haven't said a word in ten minutes."

"We'll be over the mine in five. Better wake 'em up. Are you positive about…"

"We'll meet again, big boy." She placed a hand on his cheek.

He grabbed her around her waist and pulled her close. "I'm going to hold you to that, Baby Cakes. You get in and get out, hear? I have plans…"

"What sort of plans?" She smiled and looked into his eyes.

"Big ones."

"Yeah. You fly boys always think your plans are big."

"I'm serious…You and me, girl. No more bullshit adventures. I have enough dough for the both of us."

"What if I told you I don't want to live in the United States? What then?"

"Fine by me…The way the president and his socialist cabal are destroying the goddamn country, I got no problem leaving."

"What's the ETA on the DZ?" Ken asked.

Buck and Bianca continued to hold their gaze before he answered. "Five minutes. Hey, Zorro, you bring this Colombian wildcat back or I'll hunt you down, boy."

"There's a long line ahead of you." Chikako stood up.

"Seems to get longer every friggin' day…Don't worry ol buddy. We'll make it out. Have a big old reunion at outlaw's hideout. Hell, may just let you guys build a couple of shacks there…Be good to have a pilot and another jarhead living close by."

Stienke released his hold on Bianca and started back to the cockpit. "Knowing your dad, I have to ask…what's it going to cost me?"

"We'll start with your left nut…"

"Buck's going to need both nuts." Ken laughed. "At his age he'll definitely need 'em both."

"A man just can't get no respect around here," he said with his best Rodney Dangerfield impression as he straightened his imaginary tie. "I'll have you know I have more juice in one nut than any man half my age."

"Yeah, yeah," Mark replied as he shifted his harness and attached the line to his drop bag "Let's get ready girls before Buck starts rutting season."

Shoehorn paused at the cockpit door and looked back. "You're a chip off the old block. Just as loony as your old man…and then some."

"I want to met him," Chikako said with a sly grin.

"Christmas. Gonna be a celebration to remember. I wouldn't be surprised if Jesse showed up and kicked Zorro's ass all over Rocky's Rawhide bar. When this is over, I'm flying us all to Bangkok."

Mark's sat phone rang. It was Hans. "What've you got?"

"The assaulting force left the mine. Half headed north. The other half is on the trail of the survivors."

"What sort of lead do they have on us?"

"Last images showed three miles. The drone is down…ran out of fuel."

"Whose satellite feed could you hack into?"

"Anybody and everybody's. I'll get on it."

"Hans, I'm turning off my sat. I'll turn it back on every hour to see if you have an update."

"God go with you, Mark."

CRANK'S TEAM
Cerra Wasawshan

The men paused at a slow moving stream. Those who had hydration packs filled them from the muddy flow and added purification tablets. They were tired but alert.

"There are caiman." Ido pointed at the far bank.

"You know more about 'em than anyone. How do we get across?" Crank asked.

"Toss a grenade in and haul ass."

"Assuming it's not too deep. How about a grenade and two men cross?…Pull a length of the rappelling rope Striker has and tie it off in a tree. We tie off here and use a carabiner to cross above the stream."

"Great idea. Ain't interested in getting in the water. Gives me the willies just thinking about it," said Grasshopper.

"Maybe you could rig some sort of high tech gizmo and we all fly across. You know, a McGiver thingamajig," Crank joked. "Need two volunteers."

"Ido and I will go," Adom said as he peeled off his pack and tossed it to Santiago.

Pantera arrived as the men prepared to cross the brackish water. "They're coming. No idea how many, but from the noise they're making, it's a goddamn lot of 'em."

Crank tossed a frag and the two Nigerians moved into the brown water almost immediately. He then fired at the reptiles on the bank and was joined by the rest of the team. The water was filled quickly with thrashing crocs. Some injured, others not, all intent on having a meal.

Once the two men were across, Ido climbed a tree and tied of his end of the rappelling rope. Santiago and Pantera pulled it tight and secured the other end.

One by one, they made the perilous trip suspended above the stream—hand over hand, pulling themselves across.

On the far bank, the team gathered at the top of the embankment while Striker cut the rope—allowing it to fall and deny the pursuing force the opportunity to use it.

"This is as good a place as any to set a claymore. Top of this bank. Hit them as they climb up from the stream."

"On it."

"Ido, keep heading east." Crank swatted a mosquito on his neck. "Damn. Big ass suckers."

"They get bigger the deeper we go," Santiago said as he passed. "And they are always hungry."

NICARAGUAN ARMY AIR BASE

General Sacasa arrived to find his Hind 24, four Hind 17 helicopters—motors running, blades turning—and fifty well-armed men waiting. He exited the vehicle and walked to his chopper without speaking. The others boarded their choppers and the squadron lifted off into the early dawn light.

The formation climbed quickly and raced to the Oro del Christi mine.

CIA SAFE HOUSE
Managua, Nicaragua

Alan Matthews listened to the scanner tracking military movement. The chatter between the chopper pilots and the air base indicated a force was definitely on the move.

The subordinate rushed into the room. "Sir, a contact left a message. I just discovered it. Someone matching the description of Zorro was seen at the airport in Choluteca boarding a McCambell Import/Export cargo aircraft."

"Where's he headed?"

"Filed a flight plan for San Jose, Costa Rica."

"Get me a flight immediately. Send a message to Emerson Walsh advising him."

"Yes, sir. Anything else?"

"Contact our man in San Juan. Have him standby at Juan Santamaria airport. Follow Zorro, but do not approach."

"Yes, sir."

Matthews ran up the stairs to his room and began to throw clothing into a travel bag. Grabbing the bag he opened a small safe and removed his passport, a backup pistol, three boxes of 9mm ammo, a Mac 11, several magazines and supressor. He dumped them all into a large canvas shoulder bag and took the stairs two at a time to the main floor.

"Did you want to fly business or economy?" The subordinate asked as Alan passed on the way to the door.

"A private plane you fool. How the hell am I going to get on a commercial flight with hardware?"

"Oh…yeah right. Sorry, sir."

"Call me with the details as soon as you have them. I'm gone." Matthews charged out the door.

AIR SPACE NICARAGUA
McCambells C-130

Tarzan stood with his hand on the cargo door control button. "These chutes are the new and improved 101st Airborne T11. The square design will allow you to guide your descent more effectively with your risers. Also, they'll give you a slower descent speed. Don't forget to use one of the Capewells quick release devices as soon as you hit the deck. It'll collapse the chute. Don't want your ass dragged around like a rag doll. Use the quick release in the center of your chest. Rotate it, punch and press." He demonstrated. "The leg and shoulder straps will release simultaneously…"

"We know all this," Mark said.

"Shut your pie hole, Marine. Until you step off this plane I'm the boss. Lastly, disconnect the waist web belt."

"Anything else?" Bianca asked.

"Yeah…when you kick your drop bag off the ramp there's no turning back. Oh…if your chute don't open?…Kiss your ass goodbye and take back to the factory."

Buck came over the PA system in his best airline pilot voice, "Thanks for flying McCambell's piece of crap airlines. As you exit the plane note the storm rolling in from the west. Suggest you open low. Wind gusts could take you over the Gulf of Mexico if you don't…Two minutes to target."

Ken hit the green button on the controls and the ramp began to open. The noise factor increased tenfold.

"You hear the one about Chesty and Superman?" Ken yelled.

"No," Mark replied.

"They once fought each other on a bet."

"And?"

"The loser had to start wearing his underwear on the outside of his pants." Ken smiled.

"Who's Chesty?" Chikako asked as the two men laughed.

"It's a Marine thing. Just think God…Happy hunting, jarhead," Ken said.

"Go. Go. Go," Buck called.

Mark kicked his bag off the ramp and followed it into the dawn light. Chikako looked to Ken and did a fist bump before following Zorro. Bianca jumped last.

"Definitely a book and movie deal in this," Ken said before calling to Buck on the interphone. "Packages away. I repeat…packages away."

***

CHAPTER FOURTEEN

HANS SCHOEPKE'S RANCH

Hans worked feverously at his keyboard. After several attempts, he hacked into a Russian satellite feed of Nicaragua. He zoomed in on the Oro del Christi mine. Seeing something as he did, he clicked back slowly until he could make out what caught his attention—four helicopters flying toward the mine.

"Oh, shit."

HAL McCAMBELL'S RANCH

"You remember the play in Angola?" Hal asked.

"What about it?" Buck answered.

"I have a contact in DC, our Senator Coleman. I think I could get permission for you to land at the US field in Honduras and load up some ordnance."

"I know where you're going with this. I'm willing and pretty sure Tarzan would be too."

"It could be the wild card that gives Zorro a chance."

The line was quiet for several moments.

"You still there?" Hal asked.

"Yeah. Just running it by Ken. How exactly do we keep the Nicaraguan Air Force on a leash? And what's the financial reward to the guys crazy enough to try this?"

"A hundred thousand each. If Coleman approves this, he'll keep the Nics out of it."

Another long pause ensued before Buck answered, "Two-fifty apiece and you draw up the standard million dollar insurance policy for all of us."

"Done. I'll have to forge your signatures on the policy…"

"I'm turning this bucket of bolts around. Call you back with details after the ape man and I have a chance to work 'em out. You make damn certain the fighter pilots down here don't lock in on our ass."

NICARAGUAN AIRSPACE
Free Fall

Mark had positioned himself well ahead of his companions by keeping his arms in close to his body as soon as he stabilized the exit from the C-130. He looked back quickly and saw the two women behind him several hundred feet.

He checked his altitude on his watch. At one thousand feet, he deployed his chute. The canopy opened and jerked him hard into a vertical position. *Sixty seconds.*

Tugging on his the risers, he directed his descent toward the center of the demolished mine complex. He glanced and could see both the chutes above him were deployed. *So good so far.*

The last thirty seconds seemed like an hour as he dropped the final five hundred feet to the ground. Zorro could see there wasn't anything moving below, but imagined there could be a number of rebels hiding in the wreckage of the overrun mine.

He hit the ground standing up a few seconds after his drop bag and quickly collapsed his chute. As he disengaged, he instinctively pulled his Gold cup from its drop leg holster.

He completed the removal of the chute just as Chikako and Bianca landed nearby. The Colombian landed at a run and tripped. Her chute began to drag her and her drop bag across the ravaged ground. Without hesitation, Mark pulled his K-Bar from its sheath and sliced the cords.

"Thanks."

"No problem. Weapon up."

Chikako landed on her feet, but on top of her drop bag. The distraction caused her to fall hard on her left knee. She stood up and tested the knee gingerly before extricating herself from the harness. She opened her Griswald bag, removed the M-16 and assembled it all the while scanning the area. "This place looks like Dante's inferno," she said viewing the fires from the fuel drums.

"Yeah, it does. Move to the two story building." Mark grabbed his bag and hustled to cover.

Once inside, they started collecting their gear from the bags.

"Hans said the survivors headed south. That hill over there looks like where I'd have set a fall back position."

"What's the plan?" Bianca asked.

"We cut their trail and follow. Move fast. Move silent. Chikako, you cover nine to eleven o'clock if we run into any bad guys. Bianca, you take one to three. I'll cover the center."

The two women nodded affirmative as he took off at a trot.

CRANK'S TEAM
Cerra Wasawshan

The men paused and moved to the side of the animal path at the sound of the claymore explosion and screams of the dying or injured rebels behind them.

"Sucks to be them," Crank laughed.

"That'll slow them down," Santiago said.

"Maybe. Take five. Ido, find us a route to the ridge line," Crank said pointing to the his right. "Time to get out of this canyon."

NORTINO'S REBELS
Cerra Wasawshan

The men lay in the jungle expecting incoming after the explosion. Several minutes passed. The wounded called out for help, but no one moved to assist them until it was evident there was no further danger.

The men in the water fired at the circling reptiles in self defense. One man felt the viselike grip on his thigh and screamed as he was jerked below the surface. The others frantically pushed on to the far bank.

"See to the wounded," Nortino ordered as he pulled out a map.

"We have no doctor," one rebel replied. "What of the men too badly hurt to move?"

"Leave them. Make them as comfortable as you can."

"But…if we leave them they will…"

"We leave them," the Captain said with a cold hard voice. "Three men will stay with the wounded. When we finish killing all the enemy, we will return for them"

"Yes, my Capitan."

MARK'S TEAM
Cerra Wasawshan

The three fell to the side of the trail at the sound of the explosion and waited quietly.

"Crank's slowing 'em down," Mark said softly.

270

"How many do you think are following him?" Chikako asked.

"No idea. Reminds me. I need to check in with Hans. Move up the hill." He indicated the direction with a hand signal. "Set a defensive. We'll take five."

They crawled through the dense foliage twenty yards and settled into a cluster of boulders.

AYSEN REGION, CHILE
Hans Schoepke's Ranch

Hans answered his phone on the second ring. "You want the good news or the bad news?"

"There's good news?"

"Hal called. He has your friends headed to Soto Cano air base in Honduras to pick up some ordnance. Could be back to assist you in twelve to fifteen hours."

"The Angola plan. That's some good news...Bad news?"

"There are helicopters landing at the mine as we speak. Looks like fifty to sixty men securing the area."

"Uh huh, figures. Cranks team. Can you get a fix on them?"

"I hacked a Russian satellite. I have the survivors about five clicks ahead of you, due east."

"We just heard an explosion in that direction."

"The rebels are two clicks ahead of you," said Hans.

"How many?"

"Maybe a hundred...More bad news."

"How's that?"

"The men from the helicopters are coming up behind you. The choppers lifted off and are headed your way as well."

"This cluster just keeps getting better by the minute."

The connection ended. Hans sat staring at the computer.

"Hans, what is wrong?" Francesca asked.

He turned to see his wife standing in the doorway. "Mark and his friends are caught in a squeeze play. Please make a pot of coffee."

"Of course, darling. What else can I do to help?"

"Pray. They are headed into Nicaraguan hell."

Francesca moved to her husband, wrapped her arms around his neck and placed her check against his. "You should rest. You've been up all night, my love."

"I can not. I must be here to assist however I can. The coffee please, dear."

She kissed him on the check and walked out of the room.

Hans sat staring blurry-eyed at the screen. *Dear Lord in heaven. Watch over and keep them safe.*

CRANK'S TEAM

At the highest point on a ridge the team halted and set a defensive position. Crank used his compass to set a course. Looking in the direction ahead of him, all he could see was the top of the dense green jungle. *That's some nasty shit up ahead. Really nasty.*

Santiago joined the him and sat down. "You know what they say about that jungle?" He jerked his head in the direction Crank was looking.

"Enlighten me."

"They call it the *Jungle of Lost Souls*."

Crank raised his eyebrows slightly. "Suggestions?"

"With the enemy behind us? We have no choice but to enter. A day's travel from here, there is a swamp. We should be able to lose them there."

"Great. How do we cross?"

"There are a few native villages. Maybe we could enlist the use of their canoes…If they don't kill and eat us."

"You're a real bundle of joy."

"A storm is about to hit."

"Crapolla. We got maybe a hundred rounds per man. Swamp, cannibals and a storm. Out-fucking-standing." Crank swatted at the mosquitos.

"And mosquitos are always hungry," Santiago said.

The two men shared a look then began laughing. A clap of lightning flashed and thunder rolled across the sky.

MARK'S TEAM

They paused and pulled ponchos from their packs as the first splattering of rain began to fall.

"Gonna get messy now," Mark said.

"And slippery," Bianca added.

Chikako laughed. "It'll be like a spa day without the fun."

273

Mark and Bianca glanced her way, and then burst into laughter.

"Keep your weapons covered as best as you can. Watch your step. Last thing any of us need now is to twist an ankle or knee."

"Remember the rain in Serrania de Chiribiquete?" Bianca asked.

"Yeah. Five days and nights. Worst storm I ever saw. Even the damn frogs were climbing trees."

"Where is Serrania de...what ever?" asked Chikako.

"Colombia. Zorro and I were chasing El Cobra."

"Did you find him?"

"No. Lost him and the FARC fuckers he was with," Mark answered in a growl.

"FARC?"

"Fuerzas Armadas Revoucionaries de Colombia. Communist rebels," Bianca offered.

"What was El Cobra doing with them?"

Bianca and Mark shared a look. "He rolled to the dark side. Was a member of the Colombian DEA, but had a better offer."

"Is he still alive?"

"No idea where he is...or if he's still kicking. I ever find out...I'll hunt the bastard down and finish him. He led us into a trap and killed Marta's husband to cover his betrayal...Would have killed me, but I made a forty foot leap into a river and was carried downstream."

"Is there anywhere you don't have enemies?" Chikako asked softly.

"Yeah, right here. With you two."

The sky opened and a torrential downpour began.

"There's an overhang...there," Mark said pointing up the side of the hill. "Let's go."

NORTINO'S REBELS

The Captain stood under an improvised shelter—devised from a pair of surplus US military ponchos—fuming at the delay caused by the heavy rain.

His men and women took shelter wherever they could—some under ponchos, others under rock overhangs. The storm caused a drop in temperature—all were shivering and miserable.

"Capitan, the men are wondering if it would not be wise to turn back. This jungle will surely..."

"We will press on. We must catch them before they reach the swamp...With it in front of them and us behind...we will annihilate them." He closed his hand into a fist. "Tell the men we wait." He turned his gaze on one of his subordinates. "Shoot anyone who attempts to desert."

"I will tell them," the man replied before moving from under the shelter. He ran toward the nearest group of his compadres and slipped on the sloppy ground—falling on his right side in a puddle of muddy water.

"The army is sure to have arrived at the mine. What if they follow us?" Nortino's second in command asked.

"They would not risk soiling their pretty uniforms. I suspect they are already back at their base. Besides, if they did follow us…they are unable to move any more than we are."

"But…"

"Do not question my orders! What better ending to our success at the mine than to lure the Nicaraguan army into the jungle and slaughter them? Imagine the new followers who will rally to our cause…"

McCAMBELL'S OFFICE

"How long ago did you lose eyes on?" Hal asked.

"The drone went down four hours ago…"

"Damn! Four hours?"

"Let me finish. I managed to link into a Russian satellite feed about an hour later. Then the storm moved in off the Pacific and I have not had a visual since," Hans said.

"Have you had any contact by sat phone?"

"Not since the storm hit. I can assure you of one thing…No one is moving on the ground. Your C-130 barely made it to Soto Cano before it was socked in. What's the status there? I will advise Zorro when he checks in."

"Still waiting on Senator Coleman to get the clearances arraigned. Coleman's a former Marine and understands the need for immediate action."

"I'll call you when I have anything from here. Try to relax. If anybody can do this, Zorro can."

After hanging up, the old Scotsman began pacing around his office. He lit a cigar—something out of the ordinary as he normally just chewed them in his office. He paused at a black and white photo. Jesse, Buck, Ken and other hard men standing beside a C-130 on a dirt airstrip in South America.

The fucking road goes on forever. Only the players change. The original Zorro, Buck and Ken in 1984. Now the new Zorro, Buck and Ken. I gotta get out of this business. Too damn old.

Maggie's voice came over the intercom. "Senator Coleman on line three."

Hal charged to his desk and lifted the hand set. "Tell me you have the clearance…"

CRANK'S TEAM

The four men sent to set the fall back position had taken their packs with them. Those who evaded the rebels in the heat of battle had only their weapons and ammo. A pair of shelters constructed from four ponchos was better than no shelter at all, but only marginally for the nine men.

"Enrique will likely not make it much longer. His wound is through and through, but it hit his intestines," Santiago said while blowing into his hands to warm them. "Two…three hours."

Crank reached into one of the pouches on his vest and pulled out a morphine lollipop. "Have him suck on this. It will ease his pain."

"A lollipop?"

"Laced with morphine. Latest greatest pain killer being issued to Navy Corpsmen."

After Santiago moved to the other shelter Crank passed the word to send him any sat phones the team members had. Only three arrived, but all still had battery power. *Finally some good news. Let this storm pass and give Hal and Zorro a call.*

"I did the inventory you wanted," Pantera said. He held a flashlight with a red lens in one hand and a piece of paper in the other. "Seventy-three rounds of 556 per man. Striker has thirty-one rounds of .338. Adom and Ido have three 40 mm grenades each for their M203s. One man has twenty-six rounds for his shotgun. We have forty-three rounds of 9mm per man."

"Grenades? Claymores?" Crank asked.

"Only four claymores. Used most of them on the perimeter back at the mine. Six frags, three phosphorous, two smoke and a pair of flares."

"Santiago said one of his men is going down soon. Distribute his ammo as needed."

"You have any idea what's up ahead?" Pantera asked.

"According to Santiago, some bad shit."

"You want me to look at that?" He pointed at the wound in Crank's calf.

"Nah. Checked it as soon as we covered up here. Ain't as bad as it looks."

Pantera reached in one of his cargo pockets and produced a lightweight thermal bag—preferably to be used inside a sleeping bag. He opened the zip lock pouch and began to unfold it. "You need to get inside this. Wind and waterproof half-millimeter polyester film. Last thing we need is for you to go down."

Crank looked at the bag then the wounded man. "I'm good. Get Santiago's man in it."

"He's dying. You're the boss. Don't make me call some of the guys over and stuff you in here."

They shared a long look.

"Okay. Set a watch. I'm going to catch a couple of hours shuteye." He slipped into the bag.

SOTO CANO AIR BASE
Honduras

Only six hundred US troops were stationed at Palmeroia Air Base—the commonly used name for Soto Cano. The force was a mixed Air Force, Army and Marine detachment known as Joint Task Force Bravo. It is the best twenty-four hour airfield in central America.

Due to the intense tropical storm, it was impossible to take off, no matter what the JTF-B command claimed.

Buck and Ken waited inside a second story briefing room in hanger B. They could occasionally see their C-130 when a flash of lightening lit the sky.

"Any word from Hal?" Ken asked as he woke from a short power nap.

"Nada. Wouldn't matter if we did. Ain't no way to fly in this soup."

Ken rolled over and sat up on the temporary cot. "You would think if we can put a man on the moon, someone could invent a damn cot that didn't break your back."

"If we get clearance to raid the munitions bunker, how many men do you think you'd need to handle the payload?" Buck asked as he poured another cup of liquid mud that passed for coffee on the base.

"At least one. Two would be better…Make it three and we're in the money."

"Last thing Hal told me was he intended to pull the security team Zorro was running. They have to still be here. When McCambell calls I'll request he loan us some of them."

"Ask for men with former military experience. Some of them are FBI suits. Useless as tits on a boar hog in a pinch."

"I'm going to see if there's a shower in this hanger. We could both use a triple S."

"Shit, shower and a shave? Why not? A change of socks would be nice too."

An Air Force major entered the room. "Don't know who you guys are, but someone loves you. Just received a message from command that you are to have carte blanch. Get me a list of what you want. Soon as the weather breaks, I'm to see you get it."

"Looks like Colonel 'Raving Mad' Coleman has some pull after all," Ken said with glee.

"We'll have a wish list in a half hour…Where can we get cleaned up?" Buck asked.

"Right this way, gentlemen."

CIA HEADQUARTERS

Director Walsh was listening to the play-by-play of a Washington Redskins game on his radio when his secretary called on the intercom.

"Alan Matthews, line four, sir."

Finally. Better be some good news. He turned off the game and lifted the handset. "What have you got?"

"We had some intel that Zorro had been spotted boarding a McCambell Import/Export cargo plane in Honduras. Logged a flight plan to Juan Santamaria International."

"Tell me you alerted our man in Costa Rica."

"Yes, sir, and I jumped a private down here as well. Problem is…I arrived, but the McCambell plane never did."

"So you still have no idea where he is."

"No, sir. There's been a terrible storm in off the Pacific. If the C-130 hit the shit I did, it could have gone down."

"Could have? Maybe? Possibly? I'm sick of this crap, Matthews. Find this guy or your next posting will be…Borneo or whatever shit hole I can throw you into." Walsh slammed the handset down.

McCAMBELL'S OFFICE

Hal looked like he had been ridden hard and put away wet. His hair was ruffled, he had a three day beard and his eyes looked like they were going to bleed.

Maggie entered the room with a fresh cup of steaming coffee. "Emerson Walsh is on line two. I told him you were busy, but he insists on talking to you."

Hal looked at the phone and saw the light blinking. "Nothing from Stienke?"

"Not yet," she said as she closed the door behind her.

He took a sip of the coffee. It was so hot he burned his lower lip and tongue causing him to spill a generous portion of the liquid on his lap. "Damn! Damn it to hell!"

Without pausing to collect himself he picked up the phone. "What the hell do you want now, Walsh?"

"I have reliable intel indicating Zorro boarded one of your cargo planes in Honduras…"

"Never heard of her."

"Funny, Hal, very funny. The plane was suppose to fly to San Jose, Costa Rica, but never arrived."

Hal sat silently waiting for the CIA Director's next move.

"You still there?"

"No, I'm in Siberia. Tell you what you son-of-a-bitch. Tell me why you want to see someone I don't know and I'll consider finding him for you."

"You're stubborn if nothing else. Is this a secure line?"

"It is on my end, but my tech gizmo tells me your end is recording."

There was a significant pause while Walsh digested the realization Hal had the ability to recognize his best equipment was not transparent.

"I am led to believe to indicate a man known as El Cobra is operating again. I think your man might be interested."

Hal swiveled his chair one hundred eighty degrees and picked up a photo of himself, Mark and Ken Farmer on a shooting range in Colombia. Standing behind them were ten DEA agents wearing shooting jackets with long range rifles. Visible between Mark and Ken was the face of El Cobra.

"So fucking what?"

"We think he may be looking to finish his vendetta on his family. Thought out of professional courtesy, I should let your man know."

"You wouldn't know professional or courtesy if they bit you in the ass."

"Okay. No skin off my balls. But…if the family ends up dead, don't blame me."

"If you are so damn certain Cobra is alive why haven't you taken him out? Oh, wait a minute…back in the Medina to Mena cocaine runs, he use to be your boy," Hal said with sarcasm so thick it would take a chainsaw to cut it.

"Different time, different war. I have to go. You know where to reach me if you change your mind."

The line went dead leaving Hal with yet another problem to ponder. *If the shit gets any deeper I'm going to need my hip waders.*

***

CHAPTER FIFTEEN

HANS SCHOEPKE'S RANCH

Hans sat exhausted in front of his array of flat screens with arms crossed. Having set the alarm clock to wake him every hour, he tried to rest. He reached over and picked up his secure phone on the third ring.

"Hans."

"Any contact with the boys?"

He looked up and checked the progress of the storm before answering. "None, Hal. Looks like another three to four hours before the weather breaks."

"I need you to gather some information for me. This is strictly between us...don't say anything to anyone...Especially Zorro."

"What is it you need?"

"There was a drug enforcer in Colombia. Ran by the name of El Cobra..."

"I remember. As vile a human being as I have ever heard of...What interest is he to you?" Hans rubbed his itchy, burning eyes.

"There's a rumor he has surfaced again. I want to know where he is...What he is up to...Everything else you can find."

"How did you hear this?"

"The Company."

"Ah...Interesting. Zorro asked me to hack into their database before he flew off to Nicaragua. I'll see what I can find on their servers."

"Mark has enough on his mind right now. Report to me directly. When the friggin' rodeo is over, I'll fill him in."

"Understood."

MARK'S TEAM

The two women lay near the back of the out crop overhang, sleeping fitfully under their ponchos. Mark sat cross-legged, feeding small pieces of semidry wood into his BioLite. His satellite phone was plugged into the charging unit on the side of the small stove.

He had rigged a wind break at the entrance—using a length of paracord tied to brush—and secured the bottom with a few rocks. The howling wind outside shook the poncho and managed to send a significant spray of moisture around the edges.

Sailing around the world is sounding better every minute. He had the shorty M-16 field stripped with the components lying on his pack. He methodically dried each piece then wiped them down with a light coat of gun oil. He ran a wet patch through the barrel and chamber.

He worked methodically under the red light of his head lamp. Satisfied, he began to reassemble the weapon.

The rain had slowed to a steady downfall—lightening and thunder had subsided substantially. Chikako moaned, causing him to turn around. The illumination from the stove was marginal, but his lamp allowed Mark to make out that she was still asleep.

He moved to her and gently touched her shoulder. In a move so fast he was unable to avoid it, she wrapped her arm over his, rolled him over her hip and placed her Samurai short sword at his throat.

"Whoa. Nice and easy, now," he whispered.

"Uhh…I thought…"

"You were having a nightmare."

"Ha…and now I wake up in one."

"What? What is it?" Bianca sat up—her pistol in hand.

"You can release me now," Mark said. He rubbed his shoulder to ease the discomfort created by the takedown. "Anyone want coffee?"

"Yeah, me," Bianca answered.

"Never acquired the taste for it, but count me in. At least it's hot," Chikako added.

"Have to be black," Mark commented as he rummaged through his pack. "I have some raw sugar, but we may need it if anyone gets nicked."

CRANK'S TEAM

The rain ended and the cloud cover had begun to break up just as the sun went down. Rays of light set the sky on fire with brilliant hues of red, yellow and orange. Sounds of the jungle begin to return—signalling the natural inhabitants were moving and hungry.

Santiago had been checking the back trail and whistled to let the team know he was coming in. Hearing one of his ICCs, answer, he moved forward and stopped at Crank's shelter.

"Any sign?"

"Nothing. The moon will be up soon. This tree canopy will be light enough for us to move."

Crank eased out of the thermal bag with a groan. "All right. Alert the team. Move in ten."

Pantera sat up. "Not 'til I check that leg."

Crank began to remove the bandage. "Send a man down the trail fifty meters. If he sees anyone, have him beat it back here on the double."

"You got it," Santiago replied.

Pantera lifted the bloody Telfa pad and set it aside. He used a clean wad of cotton torn from a T-shirt and dousing it in hydrogen peroxide, carefully cleaned the area. "This is looking…not so good, Crank."

"Clean it. Pack the wound with sugar. There's a small bottle in this pouch." He pulled the container out and handed it to Pantera.

"Another forty-eight hours…you're going to need more than sugar."

"Just do it. Wrap it tight. Keep quiet about this." He turned on one of the sat phones he had collected from the team and dialed. He flinched hard when the bandage was replaced. "Ahh. Jesus!"

"Who is this?"

"Hal, it's Crank. My battery is dead. Using one of the other guy's phones."

"Details."

"We had to evacuate the mine. Some of the construction crew were infiltrates. Took out our…"

"I got all that from Hans. Where are you? How many men? Where the hell are you going?"

"There's nine of us. One man's dying from wounds. There's a superior force on our ass. We're headed into the Cerro reserve."

"All right, listen up. Zorro and a couple of friends jumped into the mine compound early this morning. No idea how far behind you."

"He's headed right into the rebel force. You have to warn him."

"It gets worse. Last satellite images Hans picked up shows an army unit behind Zorro."

"Oh, boy," Crank said dejectedly.

"There is some good news. The men that delivered your last shipment of munitions and supplies are in Honduras loading the 130 with ordnance. Too late for them to be any support today, but they will be able to be overhead by dawn. Do you have any flares or smoke?"

"Two smoke...two flares."

"Find some high ground. Hunker down..."

"We're headed into a swamp, Hal. If we dig in on any high ground between here and there, we'll be overrun before your fly boys get here."

"Okay, text your coordinates, then turn off your phone. Check for my messages every half hour."

"I have two other phones. I'll text you the phone numbers for all three. I'll use this one 'til the battery dies."

"You're learning, kid."

"Hal, I'm sorry for the mess..."

"Stow that shit. You're doing fine. Now buckle the fuck up. It's going to be a bumpy ride, but we're coming for you."

Crank felt a lump rising in his throat. "Really screwed this operation up big time..."

"I said stow it! I'll get you out of there or my name isn't Hal McCambell. When you check for messages from me, send your

289

new coordinates. You're a Goddamn Navy SEAL, Crank…Act like it."

The line went dead. He checked the screen and realized the battery had died.

"Good news?" asked Pantera.

"Zorro's behind us. Hal is sending in some air cavalry to support us," he replied, and then addressed the team. "Alright you guys, we move. Ido, Adom…point. Keep us headed east. Break this position down. We're moving."

"What about our dead man?" asked Santiago.

"Sucks, but we gotta leave him. Rig the body with a grenade." Crank stood up and tested his leg.

AUGUSTO CESAR SANDINO AIRPORT

Chuck 'Sundance' Watts waited beside his helicopter with Hal on his ear-mounted cellular. "Yeah, I got the tools. Your boys haven't arrived…check that. I think this is them," he said as a cab pulled up and three men got out.

"You Sundance?" asked Rhino.

"The one and only. Ya'll get on board. I don't want to have anyone check our manifest."

"About damn time," Hal grumbled. "You have everything?"

"Got it all. Already rigged the chopper to deploy a rope."

"Get those men to Zorro in time…there's a bonus waiting for you."

"Bonus is good. Why not deliver them to Crank?"

"He has a team. Battered, but still in the fight. Zorro only has two operatives…and he's caught in a squeeze play."

"How's that?" Sundance climbed into the cockpit, strapped in and started the engine.

"Nicaraguan regular army behind him and a rebel force in front. Crazy son-of-a-bitch parachuted in with two women."

"I like this guy already. Alright then…we're outta here." The blades began to rotate. "I have Crank's phone number…"

"His battery went dead. Soon as I get one, I'll call you back. I'm sending you Zorro's last known by text."

Sundance felt a tap on his shoulder as Hal hung up and looked back to see Rhino pointing at a airport security vehicle headed their way.

"Got company."

"Buckle up." Without waiting, he powered up and lifted off the ground.

NORTINO'S REBELS

The men hunkered around a half dozen small fires cooking rice and warming salted pork. The wet wood created a heavy dense cloud of smoke.

"Get the men ready to move," Nortino ordered.

"The rice is not yet cooked," Jorge replied. "It would be wise to allow them to eat."

Nortino studied his men. It was evident morale was low. "Fine, let them eat. When the moon is up, we go."

MAYANGNA VILLAGE

A pair of hunters trotted into the village and moved directly to a hut in the center. A three-quarter moon and a few torches lit the village. The chief came out to greet them as they excitedly informed him of the danger headed their way.

The villagers gathered slowly to hear what had created the disruption to the normally calm cluster of wood and thatch homes built on stilts. Women picked up their small children and held them close. The older men whispered among themselves.

"Strangers are coming. Small numbers. Mostly foreigners," the older said.

"Another group...Nortino rebels follow them," the younger hunter added.

A gasp went up from the crowd. This particular splinter group of the Mayangna tribe had fled their ancestral homelands to the north to evade the incursion by rebels and the army that hunted them.

"Gather the women, elders and children. Use the canoes to move into the swamp. When they are safe on Diablo Island, come back for the men," the chief ordered the teenagers. "All others, gather your weapons. We go delay the invaders," the chief ordered.

Without a question the women and older girls ran to their huts and gathered all that they could carry. The boys prepared the canoes and filled containers with fresh water. The entire process was over in less than thirty minutes.

While the exodus took place, the men and older boys gathered their bows and arrows as well as the half dozen rifles taken from fallen enemies. Once armed, they melted into the jungle headed for the oncoming threat.

MARK'S TEAM

The three finished with a meal of cold MREs and hot coffee—nothing more than placing a small amount of freeze-dried powder in their mouth followed by warm water and sloshed around 'til the two mixed—the three collected their gear and checked weapons one last time. Mark turned on his phone and dialed.

"Hans, what have you got for me?"

"I have the coordinates for Crank and his men."

"Text me. Anything else?"

"The Nicaraguan army is still following you. They started moving again fifteen minutes ago."

"Stienke and Farmer?"

"They are still in Soto Cano."

"Good to know. How about Rhino and his pals?"

"What are your coordinates?" asked Hans. After receiving the data, he calculated the distance and ETA for the chopper's arrival. "They will reach you…in one hour if not intercepted by the Army Hinds."

Hearing movement on the trail below, Mark whispered, "Gotta go."

He motioned the women to be silent and pointed out positions for them to take. Both moved and lay down near the entrance to the overhang.

A moment later, three rebel deserters that been detailed to stay with the wounded passed below them. It was evident they were in a hurry and showed little inclination to move quietly.

"Who were they?" Chikako whispered.

"We should have eliminated them," Bianca added.

"No. Just learned there's a Nic army unit coming our way. When those three meet them...we'll have an alarm. Let's rock and roll."

With packs reloaded, they moved to the east end of the overhang. They insured no other travelers were on the trail below them.

Mark hand signaled that they would move along the ridge line rather than the trail below. *If these guys were a point unit I don't want to be on that trail.*

It was slow going through the brush and the incline was slick from the torrential rain. They still wore their ponchos to avoid being drenched by the moisture-laden foliage. The floppy covering protected them to a degree from the mosquitos. They managed only a half click in an hour before Mark signaled a halt.

"Take five, then move down. If anyone was coming behind those guys, we would have seen them by now."

"What's the latest?" Bianca asked as she sat on a small bolder and leaned back against a larger one.

"Got Crank's location from Hans…At least where he was at the time. Rhino and a couple of others will join the rodeo soon." He checked his watch. "The Buck and Ken show will be overhead with whatever the hell those two have concocted."

"The rebels?" Chikako asked.

"Ahead of us. No idea how far. The Nic army is…"

The sound of automatic fire floated through the jungle from behind them. The firefight was brief.

"The Nics are that far behind us. Bianca, take a claymore." Mark pulled a pair from his pack. "Set it up on the hill above the trail. We can gauge the speed of their movement by how long it takes them to get from the gun fight to here."

"On it." She moved toward the trail.

Mark noticed Chikako massaging her left knee. "How you holding up?"

"I'm good. The knee's a little tender…but I'm good to go."

"Pull your pants leg up," Mark ordered as he dropped his pack and began to look in a pouch.

"No, I'm good."

"Bullshit. You go one-legged on us we're screwed. I have a big roll of Vetrap in here," he answered as he sorted through his medical gear. "I'm going to wrap the knee. Give you some support."

She untied the draw strings to the pants leg and pulled it up mid thigh. Both she and Mark immediately saw the knee was slightly swollen.

"You said you were good?" He gently touched her knee.

"Oww."

"Liar."

He rummaged through his first-aid bag and removed a small bottle, and then the green bandage. "I'm going to rub it down with some Polar Bear…"

"You have Polar Bear oil?"

"Long time, friend…Strip your pack. Keep the magazines, your poncho and your MREs. Give me the grenades and anything else you have hiding in there that's heavy."

He gently applied the liniment to the knee. "When did this start swelling?"

"Landed on my drop bag, lost my balance and twisted it…a little. It was tender, but did not start swelling until we laid up during the storm."

"Hold on while I get this started."

Bianca joined them as he began the final wrap. Seeing what Mark was doing, she immediately said, "I'll take some of her weight."

"We'll split it."

"Yeah, I got it. If I could dump the armor…"

"No. There's going to be lead flying before this is over…The armor stays."

CRANK'S TEAM

They had been on the move for three hours. Ido and Adom were the first to contact the men of the Mayangna village. One minute they thought they were alone—the next they were surrounded.

The natives rose up like wraiths, with bows drawn, rifles aimed. The chief—one of the few who spoke Spanish—ordered the two Nigerians to lay down their weapons.

Adom answered, "No comprende Espanola."

For a moment time stood still. Without a word the Mayangnas backed into the jungle and disappeared just as the rest of the team arrived.

"What is it? Why've you stopped," Crank asked.

"Did you see them?" Ido answered.

"See who?"

"I don't know who. Wild looking men. Bows, arrows...wild looking," Adom replied.

Santiago moved up from the rear. "The natives I told you about. How many?"

"No idea. I didn't think to count."

"Which way did they go?" Crank asked.

"They just melted into the jungle like smoke."

The team assumed a defensive position. The moon slipped behind a cloud and total darkness descended on them. When the lunar orb slipped free, the Mayangna had reappeared.

"Shit. Hold your fire. You speak their language?" Crank asked Santiago. "Tell me you speak..."

The chief again ordered the men to lay down their weapons. "*Establcer sus armas.*"

Santiago replied, "We mean you no harm. We are being pursued by Nortinos. We need your help."

The tribal leader relayed what was said to his men. No one spoke. Not one man took his aim off the team.

"Why do they pursue you?" he asked.

"They are our enemy."

Again the chief informed his men what had been said. He lifted his hand then slowly lowered it palm down. The tribesmen lowered their weapons.

"Tell him if he helps us, we will help him," Crank said.

Santiago relayed the message. Several moments passed as the Mayangna tribesmen discussed the offer.

"Come," the chief said, and then turned and started back toward his village. His men once again disappeared silently into the jungle.

Crank motioned the team forward. "This is some spooky shit right here. Pantera, rig a trip wire and a grenade."

MARK'S TEAM

Two hours after placing the claymore on the trail, it detonated. The distance to the explosion obscured the screams.

"We've got a couple of hours lead on 'em."

"How long 'til daylight?" Bianca asked.

"Soon. I'm going to rig another trap," he answered as he dropped his pack. "If the army boys still follow the training manual, a willie pete will do some damage."

After hanging the phosphorous grenade in a tree, he strung a length of paracord thirty meters before stretching it across the trail. Carefully laying bits of foliage to conceal it, he armed the surprise.

When he returned, Chikako and Bianca had moved another twenty meters up the trail and were holding his pack for him.

"That's going to hurt," Chikako said with a wicked smile.

"And it burns, burns, burns…the ring of fire…the ring of fire," Zorro sang as he adjusted the pack straps and took his rifle from Bianca.

"I didn't know you liked country western music."

"Prefer jazz, but couldn't think of any song that applied."

"Jazz? How about *Smooth Operator?*" Chikako offered.

CAPTAIN ROJOS SPECIAL FORCES

The claymore shredded the three men on point and dropped another two following them. Placed above and directed down at a forty degree angle, it destroyed the trail below. They were completely exposed to the thousands of deadly steel projectiles.

Captain Rojos signaled his force to take cover. As the injured men called for help, their brothers in arms waited for the ambush that never came.

"Sergent Guzman. Take two men…scout ahead."

The men moved forward cautiously. By the time they reached their fallen comrades, they were dead.

Waiting for his scouts to return, he radioed his commander. "General Sacasa, we are pursuing the enemy. Our progress is slowed by booby traps…"

"You must complete the mission, Captain. I am about to be airborne again. Send your coordinates every half hour."

"We engaged three of the rebels earlier. They died before I could interrogate them. Do you have any new intel on the enemy's strength?"

"Not at this time. I impress on you once more. The complete elimination of the rebel force is imperative. Do this and I will see that you are fast-tracked to my personal staff."

"Yes, my general. Thank you, sir."

"Once I am promoted to commanding general all of our futures will be very bright. Finish all before you."

***

CHAPTER SIXTEEN

McCAMBELL'S C-130

Ken, Sloan and Mantle worked all night modifying the aircraft for their new mission. They had cut a small opening on each side of the fuselage and mounted a pair of M-240 machine guns on makeshift pintel stands at each—creating a deadly duo of belt-fed .30 caliber weapons per. A pallet of green ammo cans filled with belted 7.62 rounds, loaded with one tracer per every four steel-core FMJ was strapped to the floor of the cargo bay.

On the tarmac, just outside the ramp, specialized trailers with 250 pound bombs waited to be loaded. Beside them were cases of arming fuses and wire.

"How long 'til we're wheels up?" asked Buck.

"We're done with the torch and welder. Only have to hump the bombs on board. Go a lot faster if you were to help," Ken replied.

Buck smiled, raised one eyebrow and held up his left hand with first finger extended. He pulled his cell and dialed. "Major, we're ready to load the bombs." He paused for a moment. "Thanks. The boys in uniform will be here in a moment. I suggest we have another cold beer while we wait." Buck moved to an ice chest and tossed each man a bottle of ice cold Coors.

Ken popped the cap and took a long draw. "Ya think a hardworking man could at least get a Shiner Bock. I keep hearing about all this exercising you're doing, but haven't seen you lift shit."

"That's because I don't lift shit, ol buddy...Ain't in my job description. I'm going to do the preflight inspection while you direct the troops."

The major arrived with ten men. "Sloan, Mantle...keep an eye on Tarzan. Don't let him do any heavy lifting...You know, his age."

"Up yours, melon head." Ken turned to the new arrivals. "Let's go girls. We ain't operating on civilian time here."

Mike and Roger stepped back and watched the bombs being loaded.

"I gotta give it to that old man. He southern engineered this plane pretty damn fast," Sloan said.

"He did, he did. Those two make me feel like we're in some sort of grumpy old men time warp."

Sloan laughed and blew beer our his nose. "Let's hope Buck flies as good as Ken southern engineers."

"You boys wanna get aboard or keep playing with your peckers?" Ken asked as the last bombs rolled up the ramp. "The Nicaraguan express is leavin' the station."

MAYANGNA VILLAGE

Crank's team and the villagers entered the cluster of stilt homes. A half dozen dogs greeted them aggressively before realizing their masters had returned.

"You...go there." The chief pointed at the largest structure.

"Crank, think we've entered the twilight zone," Grasshopper whispered.

"Maybe so. Santiago...tell the chief we want to send a couple of men back down the trail to act as sentries."

Santiago spoke to the village leader, and then followed the team into the building. "He says he left three men behind to be the alarm...Also, said he will have some food for us soon."

"I could eat," Ido said.

"We all could," Crank remarked. "All right then. Cover three sixty and get some rest."

An hour after the men had eaten a meager meal of watery stew—consitsing of rice, yucca, beans and fish—the young boys returned with the canoes.

Pantera gently shook Crank. "The chief wants a pow-wow."

He sat up slowly. His face was pale and showing signs of distress from his wound. "Okay. Let's do it."

With Pantera's help, Crank limped out onto the porch. Behind him, the men exchanged looks of concern.

"The chief says the villagers are going deeper into the swamp. There is room in the canoes for us." Santiago nodded at the dugouts.

"Then we go. Have to let Hal and Zorro know. How long do we have?"

"They're ready now."

"Alert the men." Crank pulled a phone from his pocket. He sat down on a log bench. After listening to Zorro's message, he left his coordinates and a brief pass-down.

Grasshopper came out and sat next to Crank. "We should change your bandage."

"Yeah. Get my gear." He called Hal.

"About damn time. What's your position?"

"I'll text the coordinates…Met some natives. They're taking us by boat further into the swamp…Don't think the rebels will be able to follow."

"The 130 will be in the air soon. They rigged some sort of ordnance load. All they need is the drop location."

"Zorro's behind us, Hal. Can't go dropping bombs on him. Jesus!"

"Jesus ain't got nothing to do with what's going to happen. You keep me informed where you are. I'll work with Zorro on the drop."

Crank started coughing.

"You don't sound so good. You all right?"

"I'm okay. Gotta go."

Grasshopper and Pantera helped Crank to his feet and assisted him off the porch to the canoes after cleaning and rebandaging his wound.

"Set a grenade trap where the trail enters the village. Make that three. Space 'em out," Crank said to no one in particular.

"I'll take care of it, boss." Ido motioned to Ado to join him.

The chief approached Santiago with a rolled-up leaf. He opened it and exposed the carcass of a small rat covered in maggots. He nodded to Crank, and then rolled the foliage back up before handing it to him. "Your man will die if he goes into swamp."

"He'll die if he stays here."

"Ain't nobody dyin'," Crank said in Spanish. "Let's get this show on the river."

McCAMBELL'S C-130

Ken and the two men had the cases of arming devices open when Buck entered the cargo bay.

"These babies need to go off on impact so we're setting the fuses to arm in five seconds."

"Will we be out of range by then?" asked Sloan.

"Armed in five seconds. They won't detonate 'til they hit somethin'."

"How do we activate the fuse?" Mantle inquired.

"With these." Tarzan opened a tube of arming wire. "We insert the wire before we roll the bombs off. When they reach the end of the wire...I'll be holding the other end. Once it's removed, the fall will activate the propellers and viola...armed and dangerous."

"Just got off the horn with Hal. I have the last known position of Crank and his team," Buck said.

"What about Zorro?" Mike rotated the blades on a fuse, setting it for five seconds.

"No idea. Last known location was over an hour ago."

"We'll have these bad boys ready in twenty. Don't guess you could have some hot flight attendant brew us some Joe?" asked Ken.

"I had the good major make us a couple of thermoses of coffee. Stored them in the forward bins. As for hot flight attendants?...Zorro took 'em."

"Is one Asian?" Mike stood up and screwed a five foot pipe extension into one of the 250 pounders, followed by a fuse.

"Yeah. And a equally hot Colombian number."

"Damn, you know how to hurt a guy." Roger screwed a fuse into another pipe extension.

"Put the safety clip in unless you want to blow us all to hell," Ken snapped, seeing Roger failed to do so. "Forget hot women 'til this is over. Fuck up one of these bombs...You won't have a dick to piddle with."

A moment passed, then everyone laughed. Buck turned back to the cockpit and left the men to finish with their preparations.

"How did you guys meet?" Sloan asked.

"Buck was a fighter pilot back when you two weren't even a wad in your daddy's balls. Got shot down over Nam. Zorro's dad and I were on the DPR that went in to extract him."

"DPR?" Roger asked.

"Down Pilot Retrieval...Flew in hot. So hot the choppers left us on the ground. When we found Bucko, he had a broken femur...That was a long night. Gooks all over the place, lookin' for us."

"You know Zorro's father?"

"I do...The original Zorro. You think Mark's a hard ass? You ain't seen hard 'til you met Jesse Ingram...He invented it."

"You made it out though. Right?" Mantle asked.

"Nope. We all got killed and ate by tigers...dumbass."

Mike and Roger exchanged a look.

McCAMBELL'S OFFICE

Maggie entered with a fresh cup of coffee to find Hal with his feet on the desk, leaning back on his leather chair asleep. She carefully set the mug down and moved toward the door. With one look back, she smiled and eased it closed behind her.

She sat down at her desk and made a call. "Jack, please get Hal's Lear ready to go."

"Yes, ma'am. How soon does he want to take off?"

"I don't know just yet...Just be ready."

AIRSPACE OVER NICARAGUA

Cheyenne, Malakhi and Rhino sorted through the bags selecting the weapons, gear and attire provided by Hal.

"How did he get all this crap collected on short notice?" Malakhi pulled on a pair of camouflage cargo pants.

"Zorro told me the old man has a bunker full of shit located just about everywhere his teams work. Sort of a safe house for mercs." Rhino inspected a Springfield SPG M1A Scout rifle.

"There was a couple of hours study when we were first hired that covered the bunkers. Never seen one, but the slides and video of a couple of them gave me a hard on." Cheyenne collected magazines for the M4 he had selected.

"Oh, yeah." Malakhi lifted a Saiga full-auto 12 gauge out of a weapons bag. "Gonna have me some fun."

"Hal has a way with acquiring, he does." Cheyenne looked with envy at the black AK variant.

Digging into the weapons bag, Malakhi pulled out several eight and ten round mags followed by a twenty round drum. "Hope he sent an assortment of ammo. Definitely want some flechettes." He began to dig out boxes of shotgun rounds. "Well looky here...must have intended this for Zorro. There's some of everything...*Macho Gachos*, Terminators...even a half dozen flash bangs. Who knew?"

"What...no double-ought buck?" asked Rhino.

"Not a one, but there's plenty of triple."

"We go light. Nothing more than a three-day pack. Heavy on the grenades and claymores." Rhino opened a crate and started filling a shoulder bag with various explosives.

The three men looked forward when they heard a whistle. "Twenty minutes. We have a squadron of Hinds coming up our ass...Be ready," Chuck yelled as he pushed the high-powered turbo-shaft engine up a notch. The whirlybird responded flawlessly and accelerated with a surge.

"Ten-four," Rhino replied. "Show time, children. Anyone see any fokin' gloves? Bare-handed fast rope is a no-go."

HIND SQUADRON

General Sacasa tapped his riding crop on his left thigh. He looked out the chopper to his left, and then right to insure the Hind-17s were flanking him as ordered.

"How much longer?" the commander asked.

"One hour, sir."

Loaded in the attack craft, another fifty members of the Nicaraguan Special Forces accompanied him as the squadron rushed to battle.

Sacasa smiled as he calculated the outcome. *I will crush Nortino like a cockroach. Then hunt down Collins and his forces. No one will defy me as Supreme Commander then.*

McCAMBELL'S OFFICE

Hal was awakened by his secure line ringing. He rubbed his face with both hands, and then slapped himself briskly to clear his brain fog.

"What is it?"

"The helicopter you contracted is minutes away from delivering the men," Hans answered.

"About damn time. What about Crank?"

"No idea. The jungle coverage is too dense to pick up any recognizable infrared images…There is another problem."

"Give it to me."

"I have visual on the military helicopters closing in on yours. They are maybe thirty minutes out."

"Dammit to hell…What about the 130?"

"I have them visually. For now they are in no danger from the military squadron."

"Have you alerted Crank or Zorro?"

"I sent text to both…No response as yet."

"Call me on my secure sat from now on. I'm leaving the office," Hal said before hanging up. "Maggie…get my jet ready to go."

Maggie came to the door. "I had Jack get it ready a couple of hours ago."

"Don't know what I'd do without you, honey."

"I've got a travel bag packed for you, already in the car. You be careful. I'm too old now to find another good man. Don't do anything crazy…"

"Who me?…I'll be back. Just want to be there when our boys come out. Some of them may need to visit our friends in Costa Rica."

"I'll let Doctor Riggioni know. I'll pull the employee records and make sure they have the blood types and previous medical history for everyone."

"If this gets as ugly as I think it will, you should alert that bone surgeon...Arellano. Hell, call Salazar as well."

ZORRO'S TEAM

Sitting in the undergrowth to the right of the trail, Mark studied the stream carefully. The two bodies laying on the incline across the way, were a cause to halt and insure there weren't any living rebels left.

Chikako moved up beside him and knelt slowly—favoring her tender knee. She slapped a mosquito on her right check then another on her left hand.

"Hungry suckers."

"Yeah, they are. Look in the middle pouch on my pack. There's a small bottle of citronella and coconut oil." Mark turned slightly to allow her access.

Bianca arrived as Chikako finished spreading the oil on her hands and face. She applied some, as well, before handing the bottle to Mark.

"Whew...anyone within fifty meters is going to smell us coming," the Colombian said.

"At least we'll die smellin' good," Mark replied.

A castellana—venomous relative of the copperhead snake—slithered up the bank and moved directly for the three as they lathered the oil on. Chikako was the first to see it and swiftly pulled her wakizashi from it's sheath. In a blur, the blade struck the snake just behind the head—severing it from the body.

Mark had been focused on the far bank and did not see the approaching danger until it was decapitated. "Nice move."

"How deep do you think it is?" Bianca studied the creek.

"No idea, but where there's one snake…there's more."

What appeared to be a floating log lunged out of the stream and clamped its jaws on the leg of a dead rebel. The seven foot caiman pulled the corpse into the water with ease and began its death roll.

"Shit," Chikako said. "What next?"

"We have to cross or the Nics will be up our ass. I see a downed tree to our right. Let's see if it'll support us," Mark replied.

They moved off silently. Arriving at the dead tree Mark tested the two foot diameter trunk first. As soon as he started to cross several caimans slid off the far bank and slowly moved his way. Their reptilian eyes and snouts were barely visible as they swam closer—anticipating an easy meal.

Chikako fired a .300 Blackout round into the head of the closest and it began to thrash wildly—creating a diversion that attracted the others.

Mark sprinted the last few feet and leapt to the muddy ground. He quickly knelt and fired four quick shots into as many of the reptiles. The wounded predators turned on each other in a viscous feeding frenzy.

"Any time, girls."

Chikako had made nearly three fourths of the distance when a large piece of rotted bark broke free. She fell hard on the downed tree, but managed to stay centered and gripped it with both hands—but her right leg hung in the water. Her rifle hung to one side on its two point sling, dangling in the muddy flow.

Bianca fired into the turbulent mass of crocs with her suppressed 870. Mark unclipped his rifle and dropped it before running to Chikako. He grabbed the pack and jerked her to her feet. The act of lifting her had both of them doing a balancing act—that would have been funny, except for the consequences if they fell in.

Once collected, they moved to the bank. Mark motioned for Bianca to join them as he retrieved his M-16.

She crossed without incident and leaned against a tree.

"Well, that was interesting," Chikako said.

"Not that much," Mark replied. "How's the knee?"

"It's good. Thanks."

"You two looked like amateur wire-walkers."

"Let's just hope we don't have to come back this way," Mark said.

The near-death experience by prehistoric reptile brought each to a new realization. The jungle of lost souls was testing them...

RHINO'S TEAM

Chuck called Rhino to the cockpit. Once he was seated, the chopper banked to the left.

313

"We're about two minutes out from your buddy's last location. Call…get his present lat long." Sundance scanned the sky to his left.

Rhino dialed and searched the sky as well, hoping the oncoming Hinds were not in sight.

"Zorro."

"What's your twenty bro? We're getting close."

Mark gave the coordinates of the trail at the stream crossing. "Be advised the creek is full up on crocs."

Rhino studied a map before indicating to Chuck where they would rope in. "This looks like the best we're going to get."

"Ten-four. I don't see the Hinds yet, but we need to get you offloaded soon. I got nothing to defend with."

"Zorro, there looks to be a clearing…half a click ahead of you and a quarter click south. We are going to fast rope in a small clearing there."

"I don't hear your blades yet. We're moving now."

Rhino looked back to Cheyenne and Malakhi. "Down in ten, guys. Be ready to drop the line on my command."

The Kazan chopper hovered at thirty feet when the rope dropped. Rhino went first, followed by Malakhi. Cheyenne provided cover as they made the descent. Once they were clear, he followed. He turned to Sundance and gave a thumbs-up before disappearing from his view.

You guys are some crazy mother fuckers, Sundance mused as he pulled up, trailing the rope. *Gonna look pretty suspicious landing with a thirty foot rope dangling off my ass.*

JUNGLE HILLTOP

The clearing was only 30 yards in diameter, but afforded a opening in the triple canopy. Zorro greeted the arrivals with a feeling of newfound energy. The addition of three more warriors was cause for a brief celebration.

He stepped out of the jungle and motioned the men to join him—they spread out and moved quickly. Mark brought them up to speed on the situation.

"So, we have rebels in front and the Nicaraguan army behind." Rhino adjusted the sling on his rifle.

"That 'bout sums it up," Mark replied.

Cheyenne and Malakhi could not help but size up Chikako and Bianca.

"I see you're recruiting women now," Malakhi said.

"Don't let their looks fool you. When the nut-cuttin' starts, you'll be glad they're on our side."

"You must be the Yakuza Crank's been talking about," Rhino said as he extended his hand. "Fabian Rheinhart."

"Don't believe everything he said."

"Bianca Toro. Your legend proceeds you, Rhino."

"I have a legend? Ha! Whatever Plata told you is a figment of his overactive imagination."

"Cheyenne, Malakhi good to see you again." Mark extended his hand.

"We have to stop meeting this way. When do we hookup on a deserted island with palm trees and dancing girls?" Malakhi joked.

"Long time, Zorro. Which way? I'll take point," Cheyenne offered.

With the Native American in the lead and Malakhi on tail, the group headed back to the brush. The jungle was denser, more entangled and darker than the terrain surrounding the mine. Cheyenne hacked a path with his WWII Marine bolo machete when necessary—the going was slow.

Everyone looked back but were unable see the white ball of fire produced by the phosphorus grenade Mark had set as a trap. They knelt—facing different directions—until he motioned them forward.

"That slowed them up," Rhino softly said to Chikako in front of him.

"Coming up next for them…the crocodile crossing. Death stalks all who enter here."

CAPTAIN ROJAS SPECIAL FORCES

The first five men in the formation had passed the grenade before the point man tripped the paracord trigger. One man behind Captain Rojas took a chunk of white hot phosporus to the back of his head and another between the shoulder blades. He was the lucky one. The other four fell writhing in agony as the phosphorus burned through their flesh.

"Down! Everybody down!" the officer yelled as he dove into the tangled foliage.

Further back in the column, a man screamed—not from a grenade wound but the bite of an ultra-deadly fer-de-lance snake. Unable to control his fear, he ran down the trail yelling at the top of his lungs. He did not run far.

The Nicaraguan Special Forces unit began to feel the jungle closing in on them.

"Collect their weapons...ammuntition and provisions. We push on," Rosa called out as he stepped back on the trail.

ZETA COMPOUND

Oscar Puto, Ting Long Ti and the interpreter sat on a balcony overlooking purebred horses in different pastures. A pair of large ceiling fans stirred the humid air and several citronella candles burned to repel the ever-present mosquitos. Standing just out of hearing distance, two of Ti's men and four of Puto's watched.

"Your first delivery was a great success. We are prepared to increase the volume," Ti said.

"Excellent. How much would you like to have shipped?"

"What is the capacity of your submarines?"

"Ten tons."

Ting and his man exchanged a look.

"I will have ten tons here in one week."

"*Magnifico*. I am pleased with our new partnership." Puto poured another shot of tequila into his crystal glass.

"As are we."

"I have something else you are interested in. The old man and the woman." Oscar paused and lit a cigar. He exhaled slowly, drawing out the moment. "One of my men works maintenance at the new airport. He tells me the two you seek were seen boarding a cargo plane."

"How long ago? Where was it going?" Ti asked showing the most emotion he had expressed in their conversations.

"Not long. It was flying to Costa Rica."

Ti nodded to the interpreter who stepped to the balcony railing and made a call. He spoke in Chinese, but Puto was certain the conversation was one of excitement.

"I have someone looking for them now. I suspect you can acquire the money we discussed in a timely fashion."

Ti returned to his collected demeanor. "Of course. It will not be a problem."

***

CHAPTER SEVENTEEN

SHENYANG, CHINA

Zing Peng Wu paced his office with renewed energy. The recent sighting of Chikako and Mark was exhilarating after months of discouragement.

He sat down and used the intercom. "Pon, come in here immediately."

Zing barely lifted his aged finger from the button when his assistant entered and bowed.

"Yes, master."

"Call Fifi. Inform him the Yakuza woman and the American are in Costa Rica again. Arrange for their flights."

"Yes, master." Pon backed out of the room and closed the door. He leaned against the wall and released a huge sigh. His hand shook as he dialed, then waited for Fifi to answer with nervous excitement.

"Yes."

"Grand Master Wu has ordered me to arrange for your transportation to Costa Rica. The woman and man you are seeking have been seen. Your contact will be Wong Chi. I will text you his number."

"Excellent. We are ready to leave as soon as the tickets are available.

CRANK'S TEAM

The natives pushed the canoes slowly through the stagnant water with long poles. The still air and stifling heat was oppressive as the hollowed-out log boats glided slowly across the surface.

There was little light from above—occasionally a single ray of sunshine penetrated the gloom as the men made their way to Diablo Island.

"How's he doing?" asked Pantera.

Grasshopper poured water on a handkerchief from a canteen and applied it to Crank's forehead, and then his neck. "I don't know. He's been out for a long time now."

"When's the last time you gave him any antibiotics?"

"I managed to get some tetracycline down him before we got on the damn boats."

A bright stream of light washed over them. Crank mumbled something then sat up bolt upright and shouted, "Conserve your ammo...keep moving..."

Pantera placed his hands on his chest and gently pushed him down. He looked at the men in the other boats. *He's delirious. Looks like I'm in charge now.*

The channel began to narrow even more as the thick foliage brushed against the boats as they passed. The dense cover began to descend as well and the natives polling the crafts often had to bend over to avoid low branches and vines.

Grasshopper peeled back the bandage on Crank's calf. The smell of rotting flesh was strong. The maggots were not keeping up with the infection. "Shit," he said softly before laying the blood-soaked cloth back over the wound.

"Give me the phones Crank collected," Pantera ordered.

The varied shades of green mingled with the black and gray of the tree trunks and vines. They were deep in the bowels of the jungle of lost souls.

MARK'S TEAM

The sound of the grenades set by Ido at the native village echoed through the forest. Everyone slipped to the side of the narrow trail and squatted or kneeled.

"Cheyenne?" Mark called out softly.

"A mile...maybe a little more."

"We're closing in bro. What's the plan?" asked Rhino.

"Not sure. The 130 should be getting close," Mark replied. "Everyone off trail...ten yards." He motioned the direction he wanted them to take and slipped into the tangled undergrowth.

Zorro dialed his phone. Chikako moved to him. She took a drink from her CamelBak after downing a pair of hydrocodone pain pills.

Getting no answer on his first call, he dialed another number. He looked back at his shadow. "How you holding up?"

"I'm good to go."

"Zorro...I need your coordinates," Hans answered the call.

"I'll text them. Any word on Buck and Ken?"

"In the air. I picked up the images of a trio of explosions a few moments ago. Zoomed in and I could make out what looks like a small village. Also, the thermal images of a force I suspect is the rebels keeps popping in and out."

"We're close," Mark relayed. "Any chance you can alert Buck? If he's making the Angola play he could reduce the odds for us."

"I'll do that. You aware Crank is wounded?"

"No."

"Shot in the calf. It's been more than thirty-six hours now. That sort of wound needs medical attention, especially where you all are."

"Yeah...yeah it does. He's a former corpsman. Have to believe he's doing all he can."

"Hal is calling. I have to go."

Zorro lowered his head for a moment and closed his eyes. He let out a long slow breath before looking back up.

"What is it?"

"Nothing we can do anything about. Move down the line. Tell everyone to rally on me."

She slipped off silently and disappeared.

Mark slammed his fist on the ground. *When is this gonna turn?*

NORTINO'S REBELS

The smoke cleared to reveal eleven bodies and another dozen were injured by the booby trap. The rebel leader walked past the dead and wounded without looking down into the clearing and surveyed the cluster of huts.

"Clear the houses. Bring me anyone you find."

Twenty men moved past him to follow his orders. They advanced cautiously after the surprise that greeted them on the trail.

A half dozen village dogs spied the new visitors and ran into the jungle with tails between their legs. One remained and barked in defiance. A rebel shot him causing the animal to whelp once before falling.

McCAMBELL'S C-130

Buck responded to his phone vibrating. "You have the aircraft," he said to Jerry.

"Roger that, I have the aircraft," he said as he took hold of the yoke.

"Shoehorn."

"Hans here. I just picked up some thermal images you should be aware of and I spoke to Zorro."

"What's his position?"

"Sending you his coordinates. Said he hopes you can even the odds."

"Oh, we'll even the odds all right."

Buck loaded the coordinates as a way point in the FMS. "That's our new destination, my friend. Head there while I check on the progress in the back."

"Can do. Can you bring me another water?"

"You bet." Buck unstrapped and worked his way aft. He entered the cargo bay to find Ken, Sloan and Mantle finalizing preparations to drop the ordnance. Forty of the 250 pounders with daisy cutter extensions were lined up and strapped to the D rings inset in the cargo floor.

Tarzan looked at Buck and gave a thumbs-up. "We're ready, big guy. When are we going to deliver some pain?"

"Ten minutes. I'm calling Zorro now to give him a heads-up," he replied as he dialed.

"Zorro."

"Hans gave me the location of the rebel force. We're about to drop a world of hurt on 'em. Suggest you dig a hole."

"What about the Nic army on our ass?"

"I'll get back to you on that. Have to let Hal make the call on starting a dirty war down here."

"As far as digging a hole? You're a funny man, Shoehorn."

"Figure of speech. Just hunker down, get low...make like a lizard. You know, dazzle me with all that Marine sniper crap."

McCAMBELL'S JET

Hal had a topographical map of Nicaragua laid out on the small table studying the area known as Cerro Wasashan. The vast expanse of low central mountains, forest, jungle and swamp covered over 600,000 hectares. Much of the area had never been seen by any human—at least one who had survived to tell of it.

The biodiversity of the region was based purely on speculation since modern man had little real knowledge of the region. The indigenous people tended to avoid human interaction as much as the animals of the region.

Zorro wasn't kidding. This'll be worse than looking for a needle in a haystack.

Hal recognized the ring tone and answered, "Go ahead."

"We're five from dropping some of our load on the area we think the rebels are in."

"Some?"

"What do you want to do about the Nicaraguan Army on Zorro's six?"

"Damn. We can't go bombing another countries military, Shoehorn. Bonehead will have to dig himself out of that one."

"Then we'll dump all ordnance on the rebels and make a run for the border."

"You can't go back to Honduras. Some bastard named El Rata blew up the fuel dump and the infirmary since you took off."

"Who the hell is El Rata?"

"Based on the intel I received a half hour ago, he's a dead bomb maker. You'll have to land in Costa Rica. I'll send some documents ahead to cover your ass."

"Mighty nice of you, considering we're flying an illegal bombing mission to cover your boys on the ground."

"I had Maggie call the medical operatives in San Jose and alert them we will have incoming. I'll have her text you the phone numbers to contact. Need you to set up a transport from the airport to the hospital for the wounded."

"That'll be the easiest part of the whole damn charade. I gotta go…we're on approach now for bombs over Nicaragua."

Hal leaned back in his chair and closed his eyes. *I have to get out of this business. Just don't love it like I use to.*

MARK'S TEAM

The men and women were well hidden from the trail below, but in an exposed position if any bombs landed near them. Mark climbed up on a moss covered boulder and scanned the terrain.

Can't see a damn thing in this shit. Tangled mass of trees, vines and brush too fucking dense to see any good place to hide.

He turned to the rest. "We need to move off this high ground. Follow me."

Without a question they fell in behind as he started down the side of the hill.

"This is some sick shit right here," said Malakhi.

"Ag man, worst I've seen since Angola," Rhino replied. "Haven't seen any water that's not brak since we roped in either."

"I have some 07 if you need any," Chikako offered.

Rhino glanced over at her. "You're a lot more than a choty goty, you are."

"Choty goty?"

"Beautiful girl," Malakhi translated. "Rhino has his own weird South African lingo. Takes a bit of getting use to."

Bianca—bringing up the rear of the team—called forward. "Shut the fuck up. If I can hear you, the Nics can hear you."

Rhino and Malakhi exchanged a look.

Malakhi spoke softly, "Zorro has the makings of an Amazon warrior team going on here."

"Ja, I'd expect nothing less."

MCCAMBELL'S C-130

The ship's altimeter read 5,000 feet as Buck leveled out from the descent. He adjusted the throttles to maintain exactly 250 knots. "Well hell, this ain't exactly like doin' in the Thud. Besides, it's been a week or two…"

His copilot looked at him slightly askance. "Thud? You flew the 105?"

"You bet. A long time ago in a land far, far away."

"You ever dropped bombs from a Herc?"

"Nah. Dropped some out of a Gooney Bird in Angola once...that count?" He grinned and then laughed. "Hell of lot of fun, as long as you're on this end on the deal."

Buck picked up a heading ninety degrees off the line from Mark and the others to the target. He rolled out of the turn and checked the wind direction on the INS display. *Not bad only fifteen knots of left cross.*

"When will you know when to drop?"

"TLAR."

"TLAR? What the hell does that mean?"

"Jerry, my boy, all this gray hair comes from decades of aviation experience...Stands for 'That Looks About Right'...Don't you know nothin'?"

"Whatever...How much time we got?"

"'Bout a minute...give or take." He reached for the PA microphone. "Hey, Tarzan. Sixty seconds."

Ken handed Sloan and Mantle a set of body harnesses. "Shit! Put these on and get your dumb asses attached to the airframe with a line so you don't fall out."

The two men scrambled to get into the nylon webbing as Farmer hit the green button and started the cargo door opening.

Buck's voice came over the speakers—barely audible over the roar of the engines and wind noise that filled the cargo bay. "Twenty seconds."

"Get the arming wires in those first four bombs...Then unbuckle the tie downs," Ken yelled.

Mike and Roger quickly removed the safety pins and inserted the arming wires before releasing the tie-down straps. Ken stood close by and took the wires in a gloved left hand.

"5-4-3-2-1. Let 'er rip!"

Sloan and Mantle kicked the four bombs loose. As they slipped over the edge of the ramp, they reached the end of the arming wire—the propellers on the fuses began to spin once the ordnance hit the slipstream.

Ken moved to the end of the ramp, holding on the safety strap connected to the fuselage. He smiled as he watched the bombs all the way to impact.

NORTINO'S REBELS

The simple comforts of the abandoned village were a welcome respite for the men and women. They had rekindled the fire pits and were cooking a pair of Baird's tapirs on spits as well as pots of rice and beans. Three other men entered with a couple of water opossum and began to skin them in preparation of adding them to the feast.

Nortino lay in a hammock in front of the Chief's hut gazing at the sky. *Let them eat. Tomorrow we build rafts and find the mercenaries.*

No one took note of the C-130 almost a mile above them initially. It was just another aircraft moving above in the clear blue sky. The village clearing did allow for visibility, but in return provided good target identification if someone were looking for the rebels.

A shrill whistle was the first warning—not enough to offer any time to find cover, though. The first bombs landed on target with devastating effect.

The extension on the fuses made the Mark 81's high explosive detonate immediately above the surface—sending interlocking rings of lethal shrapnel in all directions. Those not immediately killed or severely wounded ran into the jungle like rats abandoning a sinking ship. No one paused to assist the wounded.

"Run!" Nortino yelled as he grabbed his rifle and sprinted back down the path back towards the mine. Tall trees prevented the rebels from seeing the flat gray-painted Hercules as it banked steeply for another pass.

McCAMBELLS'S C-130

"How did we do on the first run?" Buck asked on the interphone.

"Looked good. Maybe a tad long on the last one," Ken said into the mic.

"Many thanks. See if you guys can get five or six this time." He rolled out of the forty-five degree banked turn and headed in for a second drop. "One minute out," he transmitted as the wings came level.

"We ain't got all day, ladies," Ken yelled motioning at the bombs. "And get your damn leash line on, Mantle."

Working quickly Mike and Roger had the next ones ready.

On Buck's command they began rolling them to the ramp. The tail fin of the last bomb caught on Roger Mantle's pants leg and jerked him off his feet. As the steel 250 pounder rolled aft, it pulled the former Secret Service agent with it.

"Ahh, shit," he screamed.

Mike on the other side of the cargo bay, lunged to help his partner, but hit the end of his safety strap when his hand was only inches away. Ken was too smart to get tangled up with the tragedy as it played out—both men watched as Blaster fell out the back of the plane and disappeared.

They stood in stunned silence for a moment.

"Cowboy up, kid," Ken yelled as he moved to remove the safety pins in the next row of bombs. "Get the arming wires in place."

Sloan snapped out of his daze and fell in as Tarzan had ordered. *Damn glad that wasn't me. Hell of a way to go.*

Ken tapped the former Ranger on the shoulder. "He's gone. We ain't...Focus, dammit."

NOTRINO'S REBELS

Two minutes passed without any further exploding bombs falling on the village. Many of the rebels began to filter back in and attempt to help their fallen comrades. The scene was utter chaos.

The second wave of iron bombs landed in a rapid fire string. The sequence of death and destruction was immediate and panic renewed.

Nortino did not reenter the village, but stood on the trail where he could see what was going on. A bomb landed within ten feet of him. The daisy cutter extension did what it was designed to do.

***

CHAPTER EIGHTEEN

MARK'S TEAM

Well away from the drop zone, the six operatives lay in the tangled jungle—the ground shook beneath them.

"Wouldn't want to be where they are," Malakhi said after the fourth run.

"Yeah…on the other hand…fuck them," Bianca said.

Five minutes after the last bomb exploded, Mark stood up. "Let's go. Any survivors will be on the trail making tracks for home…We need to finish 'em."

They fell in behind him as he pushed through the jungle toward the trail.

Chikako managed to fall in last. *Can't let them know I'm going lame. Can't.*

CAPTAIN ROJAS SPECIAL FORCES

Captain Rojas called a halt when he heard the first series of explosions. He motioned his men off the trail, and then for his radio man to come forward.

"General Sacasa, come in."

"Go ahead, Captain Rojas."

"Are you attacking the rebels, over?"

"No. I received intel that another rebel force, suspected to be lead by Collins, has attacked a base to the north. I have diverted to catch him."

"Someone is attacking, sir. We just heard a series of explosions."

"You are on your own, Captain. Do your duty. When I am finished with Collins I will come to support you."

The Captain sat dazed by the turn of events. Deep in the jungle he had consoled himself with the thought that reinforcements were on the way.

"Yes, sir. I will continue forward, sir."

He handed the unit back to the radio man and stepped out on the trail. "Get up. We go."

The remaining men emerged onto the trail and fell into formation. The captain motioned them to advance.

The team moved east at a slower rate than before, knowing another force must be out there. How else would the explosions occur? How many were there?

Every tree, every tangled stand of brush became a hiding place for the unknown enemy.

CRANK'S TEAM

The sounds of the explosions drifted in, but the distance between them and the villagers caused them to be muffled.

"Who do you think that was?" asked Grasshopper.

"Don't know," Pantera answered.

Santiago walked up. "Let me take my men and do a scout. I'll get the chief to send one of his with us to handle the canoe."

"Do it. And fire a flare from the clearing where the villagers set up camp. If that's Hal's 130 we need to let them know where we are," Pantera replied.

"What if it's the Nicaraguans?" asked Grasshopper.

"Then they will know," Pantera replied.

McCAMBELL'S C-130

Buck had turned the aircraft around one last time to take a visual on the carnage below. He came in lower and banked the craft for a better view.

As the Herc swept over the destroyed village, Ken placed a stream of lead from a pair of M-240s across the terrain.

"Dance, muthfuckers...dance," he shouted with glee.

Sloan watched with a satisfied smile. *Glad I'm on his side.*

Santiago's flare flew skyward just as Shoehorn started to climb.

"Down there…See that?" he asked Jerry.

"I see it. Who is it?"

"Has to be Crank. Get a fix. Need to inform Hal and Zorro." He turned the aircraft to line up with the flare.

MARK'S TEAM

"We let them into the killing field…as many as we can before we open up. Rhino, you will be at the far end. You take the first man when he is right in front of you then work your way back down the line."

"Got it, boss." He prepared his gear.

"When Rhino opens up, the rest of us eliminate as many as we can in our zone. Cheyenne, want you on the other end of the line."

"Grenades?" asked Malakhi.

"No. We'll be too close…Could get caught in the overage. Use what ever ammo you have to but keep in mind there's a Nic patrol on our six and we ain't got any resupply…"

"Free the dead of whatever they carry," Bianca said as she pulled her K-bar from its sheath and twirled it with practiced ease.

"Damn straight," Mark replied.

"What if there are too many to catch in our zone?" asked Cheyenne.

"You seal 'em off 'til we join up," Zorro said as he flipped a skeletonized drum to the Indian. "As soon as we have suppressed their fire, move…Make sure everyone is dead. Then hustle to Cheyenne…We'll advance 'til the bastards are finished."

"Strength?"

"No idea. Let's hope Buck and Ken did some serious damage and we're just the mop up crew. Okay, Cheyenne, you set up here. The rest of you, on me."

Mark turned and started down the trail indicating where he wanted each of the team to find a hide.

Once everyone was set, Mark walked back down the trail checking each person's position. When he reached Chikako he paused. "Stay covered. Don't step out…"

"I got this…No heroics."

"None. You and I are going on a trip around the world when this is over."

"Promises, promises."

Assured the team was positioned to his satisfaction, he took his place in the middle of the formation. He laid out a fifty round drum beside him, dropped his pack and loosened the tie straps that secured his battle ax. Looking around, he selected a tree trunk and drove the two-headed weapon in at shoulder level.

The birds begin to sing a few moments after the team settled—the jungle became their ally.

KILL ZONE

The jungle went silent as the first two rebels passed Cheyenne's position at a trot followed shortly by the others…

McCAMBELL'S GULFSTREAM

The old Scotsman had finally fallen asleep and tossed fitfully in his seat. The cell phone vibrating on his chest woke him.

"Hal, here."

"We dumped the load. On our last pass I spotted a flare coming up about three miles from the drop zone. I think it's your boy Crank," Buck said.

"Okay…" Hal answered as he sat up. "What is the long/lat?"

"Texting them to you. I circled once. Looked like a small clearing. Maybe big enough for you to get your chopper guy in."

"On it. Get your ass to Costa Rica and organize the transport of wounded to the hospital."

"Ten-four."

Hal studied the map before calling Watts. He wanted to make sure the run would be on target knowing a squadron of Nicaraguan helicopters were roaming around.

He dialed for Hans and waited—his eyes closed and his head resting on his left hand.

"I am here."

"I have coordinates for a possible location on Crank and his team. I just texted them to you before I called. Can you get a visual on the satellite feed?"

"Give me a moment."

Hal pulled a cigar from his coat pocket and removed the wrapper before starting to chew on it.

"I'm on the location now. There's nothing but green down there now. Let me back up the feed."

"I have one shot to get a chopper in there and pick the boys up, Hans. Make it fast."

"I have a flare. Yeah, it's definitely a flare. It has to be your men. That area is so damn dense no one else could be there."

"Except Zorro and his team."

"Yeah, that's true. But his last message indicates he would be several miles from there. No way he could get there in such a short time. I'm going back to live feed…"

"Do you see the C-130?"

"Yes, they will be back over the border into Costa Rica in two minutes. Why?"

"I need you to manufacture some flight details and get them to our man in San Jose immediately. Buck doesn't have any clearance to land."

"Consider it done."

KILL ZONE

The sound of Rhino's unsupressed .308 shattered the erie silence.

The sounds of Mark, Chikako, and Bianca's suppressed weapons were but whispers in comparison. Cheyenne's M-16 spewed death with its characteristic signature ripping through the jungle. Malakhi's 12 gauge sounded like a chainsaw.

Rhino rolled onto the trail in the prone position and fired directly down the narrow path. He kept his aim low, knowing the enemy would drop to the ground. With one fluid motion he rolled to the other side while changing out his magazine and slamming another one into the well.

Cheyenne shot two men and a woman in front of him, and then began to lay fire into the trail behind them. If there were any stragglers, he wanted to include them in the warm welcome.

Malakhi fired off short bursts with his full auto shotgun. One rebel was cut in half when two *Macho Gaucho* rounds struck him in the gut. Another had his left arm blown off before one caught him in the head—spraying the tangled jungle with a red and gray mist.

Bianca pumped round after round through her 870 with well practiced efficiency and dispatched three men before they could react and fire a shot.

With the team spaced out at ten yard intervals, the fire control was devastating. Vines, branches, leaves, twigs and bark exploded all around the rebels. Even so, a few men managed to dive off the trail and return erratic fire in self-defense.

A round impacted Mark dead center on his armor plate by nothing more than random chance. From less than twenty feet the round knocked him back and caused him to lose his breath for a moment.

"Ah, shit," he gasped as he tried to breathe.

A second round sliced through a cargo pocket—tearing a two inch wound on the outside of his left thigh.

"Damn," he exclaimed as he emptied the fifty rounder into the brush, killing both men there. When the last two rounds—both tracers—exited the barrel, he fluidly dropped the empty and replace it with another.

Two more men dove into the bush directly in front of Chikako—seemed like a good idea at the time. She dispatched both with two quick bursts. *Oh, I love this brace. Feels like the weapon is an extension of my arm, it does.*

A woman ran back from Rhino's position and the Yakuza killed her with another short burst. She fell forward and tumbled like a sack of grain before coming to a halt on her knees face down. *That has to be the strangest position I've ever seen anyone die in...other than a Samurai.*

Malakhi battled with a man who had taken cover and avoided the initial fusillade. The rebel leapt up and tried to run only to be cut down by a round fired by Rhino. It impacted his knee and blew his lower leg off.

The wounded man screamed in pain and horror as he tried to reach for the detached limb. Malakhi stood up beside the tree he was using for cover and sent a round into the dying man's throat. The forty steel cores tumbled on impact acting like little lawnmower blades. His head exploded in a pink mist. The body trembled in a death spasm and collapsed to the muddy ground like a wet newspaper.

A rebel laying on the trail had avoided being killed. Catching Malakhi's move, he turned his AK on him and ripped off half a mag. One round chipped off some bark that caught the Israeli in the left side of the face. Another struck him in the left arm and spun him before knocking him to the ground. Thinking he had killed his adversary, the insurgent rushed toward him to get out of the killing zone—it was the last bad decision he ever made.

As he entered the bush, Malakhi drew his Desert Eagle from his thigh holster and shot the man once in the chest—he was dead before he hit the ground.

As abruptly as the firefight started, it ended…

CAPTAIN ROJAS SPECIAL FORCES

Captain Rojas and his men knelt hearing the firefight ahead of them.

After the gunfire ended Rojas stood up and motioned his men to move forward. His point team waited for him to arrive.

Once the main body was with the three man team, the captain motioned the soldiers to halt and move off the trail.

"Capitan, we are close. What are your orders?" the team leader asked softly.

"We move. There is only one way our enemy can go…It's on this trail."

"Who would the rebels be fighting? Are they attacking each other?"

"I have no idea. We will know when we close with them. Until then…be vigilant. Now go."

"Yes, my Capitan."

Rojas felt a cold chill run up his spine despite the hot humid air around him. *Who indeed is fighting ahead of us? Did Nortino's men catch the survivors from the mine? Are they fighting amongst themselves?*

His men—well-trained and armed—begin to move past him. They assumed they were capable of handling any rebel force. Unfortunately—as Captain Rojas and his men would learn—Mark and his team were not rag-tag rebels…

CRANK'S TEAM

Isolated on Devil Island resolved the rebel threat, but time was running out for Crank.

"I bring more maggots," the chief said as he approached.

"*Gracias*," Grasshopper replied. "I don't think he's going to make it."

Pantera peeled back the bandage to find the flesh below the knee was now completely blue with some turning black. Dark streaks ran up the leg above the knee. "Boil me some more water and give me the last of the antibiotics."

"We used the last of it this morning."

The two men shared a look. Ido and Adom joined them.

"If the leg does not come off he will be dead by this time tomorrow," Ido said.

"If we cut it off he could die from the shock," Pantera replied. "Fucked either way."

"I cut off my cousins leg in Nigera. He lived," Adom added. "I prepare my knife. I will need the sharpest blade we have for the flesh."

"Prepare your knife?" The tech geek was starting to look green around the gills at the thought of the field procedure.

"Yes. I make some notches with rocks…to saw the bone."

"Saw the bone? We don't have any anesthesia. How will he survive the shock." Grasshopper looked at Adom.

"He will pass out from the pain. We hold him down until he does. You go find me the sharpest knife. I will need hot water, any antiseptic we have and some clean bandages." Adom walked away.

The geek turned to Pantera. "You really going to let him do this?"

"It's a long shot…a really long shot, but it's the only chance we got. Go get the water boiling and find a knife." He lifted Crank's head and offered him a sip of water. "Find Santiago. Tell him we need him here…now."

One of the satellite phones rang. Grasshopper picked it up. "Hello."

"Who's in charge down there?" Sundance asked.

The geek handed the phone to Pantera. "Someone wants you."

"Pantera here. Who is this?"

"Name's Sundance. If you set off a flare not long ago I'm closing on your position."

"Holy shit, man. Are those chopper blades I hear?"

"Yes. I have some detcord. When you hear me overhead fire another flare. My man will drop the cord to you. Clear a landing zone."

"I'm on it. How many of us can you lift off?"

"A dozen at most. How many are there?"

"Nine."

"Send the flare, let's rodeo."

Adom walked up with his notched blade in hand just as Ido returned with boiling water and some bandaging materials.

"There's a helicopter coming in. Get the last flare and get to the little opening where the villagers are camped. When you hear the chopper fire it off," Pantera ordered.

KILL ZONE

Rhino, Malakhi and Bianca walked among the dead and wounded, dispatching those still alive with their knives. Mark had joined Cheyenne and stood watch on the trail leading to the village. Chikako stood vigil on the back trail watching for the Nicaraguan Army.

"Did you see anyone get out?" Mark asked softly.

"No, but there could still be stragglers."

"Roger that. Malakhi...with me."

Once he joined them, Mark ordered a cautious advance—acting as point for the move to the village.

Rhino and Bianca slipped up behind Mark and knelt.

"Go back and bring Chikako up here." Mark nodded at Rhino.

The big man moved off with surprising speed for someone his size. Bianca reloaded her shotgun while they waited.

Looking back, Mark saw Rhino and Chikako approaching. His heart sunk when he saw her limp. *Yeah, you're good to go, girl...about as far as we can carry you.*

"No sign of the Nics yet," she said as she reached the others.

"Rhino, you up for some extra baggage?" Mark asked.

"Jabo. What you need humped?"

"Carry Chikako for twenty, then she walks for ten..."

"I don't need anyone to..." she spat defiantly

"Shut the fuck up...I run this show. You come up lame and we all pay."

They locked eyes. For a moment it was unclear who would blink first.

"Come on coty goty...I got you," Rhino said as he stood up and grabbed her by the arm.

Reluctantly, she stood. Rhino turned his back to her and squatted down. "Wrap your arms around my neck."

"Bianca you take our six. Keep a close eye on the backdoor." Mark turned and moved down the trail.

"If you want to argue with Zorro, this would not be the time," Rhino said waiting for Chikako to climb on his back.

She let out a breath, slung her rifle to her back and accepted her fate. Once settled—no small task with his pack and magazine pouches—they started off.

Well, I didn't see this coming, Bianca mused. With a quick look behind, she fell in ten yards behind the team and followed—constantly checking their back trail.

CRANK'S TEAM

Sundance had landed in the clearing created by the det cord. The members of the team carried Crank on an improvised stretcher and boarded quickly.

Santiago, Pantera and the village chief stood close exchanging good byes.

"Tell him we leave all this." Pantera waved his hand at the stack of rifles, ammo and assorted military gear. "Also, we offer our gratitude for his help."

The chief smiled and nodded. "It is good."

As they walked to the chopper, Santiago looked back. "That's a whole lotta firepower we're leaving behind."

"Hey…we kept our pistols. We'd look pretty suspicious showing up in San Jose armed to the teeth, don't you think?"

"Oh, I'm not complaining. Just making an observation. The next outsider that runs across that tribe is in for a serious surprise."

"Well it won't be me. I'm never coming back to this third-world shit hole." Pantera climbed in the chopper.

***

CHAPTER NINETEEN

SAN JOSE, COSTA RICA
CIA Safe House

Alan Matthews walked in circles as he fumed about the disappearance of Mark. *Where the hell did that bastard go now?*

His cell rang. The man detailed to watch the airport was calling to report.

"What have you got?"

"McCambell's plane landed. Four men were met by one of Hal's employees here in Costa Rica. They left in a..."

"Left? You mean you didn't follow them?"

"You didn't tell me to follow them...You said to..."

"Damn it, man! How stupid can you be?" Matthews blurted out.

There was a long pause.

"Are you still there?"

"Yes, sir. I'm right where you told me to be. I have the license plate number of the van."

"Give it to me. Get you ass back to the house."

Alan wrote the plate number down and immediately called a contact with the vehicles registration department. *Working with these central American monkeys is driving me bat shit crazy.*

CIMA HOSPITAL
Escazu, Costa Rica

Built by CIMA Centralized Services—head quartered in Dallas, Texas—the facility was the best in Costa Rica. Hal had a golf round with the CEO every other week. This biweekly paring insured McCambell operatives had first rate care wherever a CIMA hospital was located.

"Wow, this looks just like a hospital in Dallas," Sloan said.

"That's because it's the same blueprint, kid," Ken replied.

"Really?"

"No. I'm making it up for grins and giggles."

The Toyota SUV turned into the parking lot and stopped at a side entrance.

"Find a parking place, then come find us," Buck ordered the ICC. "Wait...have you arranged any transpo from the airport to this hospital?"

"Yes, sir. I have three private ambulance companies standing by."

"Well done. Park and find us…Let's go boys. Need to make sure the docs are standing by for the troops."

McCAMBELL'S LEAR JET
Nicaragua

The old Scotsman talked with Chuck Watts while his jet was being refueled.

"How many wounded?"

"Three. Crank's the worst. His leg is in really bad shape."

"I'm ready to go as soon as you get here."

"Another half hour. Any word on the Nicaraguan helicopters?" The stress of knowing attack choppers were in the air could be plainly heard in Chuck's voice.

"Last time I had word they were north of your position."

"I'm thinking I may need a lift out of Nicaragua when you take off."

"I'll have room. Get here. I already have a wire transfer ready to go for your outstanding work."

MARK'S TEAM

Arriving at the village, the team spread out at the edge of the clearing—hiding the undergrowth. The Buck and Ken bombing runs had really shredded the area. Bodies were scattered and lay in positions only the dead could assume. Several of the dogs had already returned and were making a meal of the carnage.

Mark gave a low whistle and stepped into the clearing, his weapon at the ready. The others did as well and waited for him to signal advance.

Motioning to Bianca and Rhino to move to the left flank he indicated a sweeping move. He pointed at two others and repeated the signal for Malakhi and Cheyenne—only to move to the right.

"You stay with me," he said without looking to Chikako. They started forward into the center of the destruction.

Ten minutes later the sweep was complete. They gathered at the communal firepit and knelt in a defensive position.

"Chikako, get the BioStove out of my pack and get it going. I need to recharge the sat phone."

"Whew…those bodies are already starting to stink," Rhino said as he wiped his face with the end of a towel hanging around his neck.

"You guys bring any claymores?"

"Two each," Cheyenne replied.

"Grenades?"

"Four willie petes and four frags each." Rhino poured water from his canteen on the end of his towel and wiped his neck.

"There has to be something still usable among the dead. I'll check it out." Bianca moved off and began the search.

"Malakhi, go twenty-five yards back trail…keep a watch. Rhino, Cheyenne…help Bianca."

The three moved off leaving Mark and Chikako alone.

"Once the charger's ready, hook this baby up," he said tossing his sat phone to her. Let me know when it' a hundred percent."

"I'm moving over there," she answered indicating a hut that still had a partial roof. "You should let me look at that wound. We don't want you going one legged on us," she said with a smile.

"Right. We already have one gimp."

"Up yours. I didn't need to be carried…"

"Yeah, you did. Besides, Rhino needed the workout."

The team joined Mark as Chikako was finishing a field dressing on his leg.

"Best I can do with what we have."

Thanks. Work your magic on Malakhi's arm next."

"We found four AKs that are still functional and maybe a hundred rounds apiece. Three frags. The rest of their gear is as fucked up as they are." Rhino glanced back at the bodies.

"You want me to set a trap on the trail?" asked Cheyenne.

"No. We're going to let 'em in. Set up a two-pronged killing field."

"Bro, you think it's wise to divide our force?"

"We put all the suppressed weapons on one side. You guys take the AKs and open up first. Lob grenades…then hit the deck. When the Nics fall back from your fire…we'll cut them down from behind real quiet like."

"What about the clays?"

"We'll set them in front of our two positions. If they try to make an assault we use 'em and grenades to repel them.

"That's going to take some timing," Bianca said.

"Again, use the Aks then grenades. Empty a magazine then hit the deck. Keep your weapons in reserve," Zorro said as he tested his leg. "Ugg... shit...this sumbitch will be stiff soon if I don't keep moving."

"Batteries are charged."

"You guys dig in over there." He said pointed at the south side of the village. "I need to call Hal."

"On it boss."

"Bianca, you and gimp here set us up over there." He pointed to the north. "I'm in the middle."

Mark dialed and walked in slow circles while he waited.

An anxious Hal answered. "'Bout damn time you called. Where the hell are you?"

"We're in the village the Buck and Ken show landed on. Damn fine job."

"I'll have Crank and his team in the air soon..."

"How's that?"

"I flew down in the Lear. Gonna to take the boys to San Jose and get medical treatment for the wounded."

"How's Crank's leg?"

"Let you know when I see for myself. Pantera said they were about to do a field amputation when the chopper showed up."

Mark's face clouded at that unwelcome news. He and Crank went way back and each had saved one another more than a half dozen times. "Damn."

"Hell, Zorro, he'll be surfing in a year. They have some amazing prosthetics these days."

"What's the plan to extract us?"

"You tell me. The chopper pilot is going to fly out with me. Thinks he's burned his welcome."

"First things first. We have the Nic army about to land on us. I'll get back to you on ideas for extraction."

Mark hung up and surveyed the team preparing for another firefight. *If this ain't hell...it's the gates to it.*

CAPTAIN ROJAS SPECIAL FORCES

One of the point team trotted up to the Captain. "There are a couple dozen bodies up ahead. Looks like someone wiped out a number of rebels in an ambush."

"Move on."

"Yes, my Capitan."

McCAMBELL'S GULFSTREAM

Hal stood on the tarmac, in the blazing sun, watching for Chuck Watt to arrive. His phone vibrated with a text message.

Three minutes to landing.

The Scotsman turned to the executive aircraft and made a circling motion with an up stretched arm.

The pilot acknowledge his signal and began the start up procedure for the jet. By the time Sundance and Crank's team landed, the aircraft was ready to taxi.

As the helicopter touched down, the sliding side door opened and the first of the team jumped out. Santiago and Striker turned back and grabbed the makeshift stretcher and started pulling it out. Ido and Adom leapt to the ground in time to take the back end of the litter. As soon as they had Crank out, the men ran to the jet.

"Let's go!" Hal yelled.

Chuck exited the chopper last and sprinted to the waiting transport pausing only long enough to say, "Chuck Watts, sir. Damn happy to meet you."

"Get aboard. We'll deal with the howdy-dos in the air," Hal replied.

SAN JOSE, COSTA RICA
CIA Safe House

Matthews tipped a glass and drained the last of the Jamaican rum. He picked up an empty pack of Marlboro cigarettes and realizing there was nothing inside, crumpled it and tossed it in the general direction of the trash can.

His cell rang.

"Matthews."

"A contact in Nicaragua just called. Hal McCambell's jet just lifted off. The flight plan calls for arrival in San Jose."

"Is Zorro with him?"

"No, but a beat-up team of operatives landed in a chopper, loaded up and flew out with him."

"All right. Keep looking for the bastard. He has to turn up sooner or later," Alan said as he fumbled through his travel bag searching for another pack of smokes. *Beat up team. Time to check the hospitals.*

MARK'S TEAM

Waiting was never easy and even worse when oppressive heat and humidity laid a heavy blanket on those who did. The sounds of the jungle went silent. Someone was approaching.

Mark gave a hand signal to the men across the clearing, then one to each of the women on either side of him. He rolled to a prone position and rested his rifle on the down tree trunk in front of him. Out of habit he reached over and placed his left hand on the spare drum, then the Willy Pete grenades.

A three man point team entered the village cautiously. They showed good training and continually swept the area with their weapons as they advanced.

Reaching the banks of the river they paused and gave a signal to their comrades. They main body of the Special Forces unit advanced equally as cautiously.

Rhino identified the leader, Captain Rojas, and took aim on his chest. The AK round sliced through the man's right arm above the elbow before severing his spine.

Malakhi and Cheyenne let loose a blistering fusillade of automatic fire.

The soldiers wheeled and returned fire as they backed away from the attack—directly towards the waiting Mark and women. As men fell, one would grab him and drag the wounded as they retreated.

Showing some good training there, boys Mark mused as he waited.

As planned Rhino and his team stopped firing, tossed grenades and hugged the ground. Mark's team opened up and with deadly accuracy laid suppressed rounds into the men.

To further disorientate the soldiers Zorro yelled, "Grenades."

All three lobbed a frag into the now disorientated and frantic men. It was the final blow. Those who were still alive dropped their weapons and raised their hands screaming in Spanish, "We surrender."

Mark's team ceased firing. The jungle became silent except for the sounds of the wounded and dying.

"Drop you side arms! Gather your wounded and get the hell out of here," Mark commanded in Spanish.

As the men followed his orders, he called out once more to his team, "Hold your postions."

The team kept a bead on the last of the soldiers until they disappeared down the trail. Only then did Mark stand up and advance into the clearing. With a hand signal, he instructed Cheyenne and Bianca to follow the retreating soldiers.

He and the others moved to insure those left behind were truly dead.

"Bro, you just broke rule number one," Rhino said.

"They're soldiers. They followed their orders and fought well. No longer a threat."

"What if they lead reinforcements back here?" Malakhi asked as he kicked an AK away from a dead man.

"We'll be gone by then."

"Where the hell are we going to go?" Chikako asked.

"With them," Mark said nodding his head at the natives on the river.

The chief and his warriors were positioned only close enough to see their village. Behind them were other canoes with the women and children.

Mark walked to the waters edge, laid down his rifle and held up his right hand palm open. The chief returned the greeting and motioned the canoes with the warriors to advance.

****

TIMBER CREEK PRESS

PREVIEW

of the Next Exciting

MARK INGRAM Novel

EL ZORRO PLATA

GUAVIARE RIVER BASIN
Colombia

One minute, the chorus of night creatures was wafting through the jungle—then quiet. Mark knelt, as did his friend, Captain Tomas Lopez.

The members of the Colombian DEA platoon followed suit, but the army unit ahead continued forward.

"Make small," Mark whispered.

Lopez hand-signaled his men to spread out and get down.

Seconds after they complied with his order, the eerie silence was shattered with the sound of small arms fire and explosions from grenades.

"Fall back," Lopez yelled.

The unit withdrew with tactical precision as the massacre ahead of them continued. At a hundred meters, the men set up a defensive position.

"Looks like Major Contesa found El Cobra," Mark growled.

"We are next, I fear."

"There's a rocky rise about two hundred yards behind us. If we can make it…we might have a chance."

Lopez stood and turned to lead his men. A fullsaide of small arms fire ripped through the jungle. One round caught him in the chest, sending him spinning to the ground.

"Cover fire!" Mark rushed to his fallen friend—rolled him up onto his shoulder and ran.

"Fall back in fives," Sergeant Hernandez called out.

The men withdrew in good form. As a group finished a magazine, they rushed to the rear. The next five offered cover until empty—then repeated.

The running gun fight continued in the moonlight. Mark left the trail and climbed a rocky incline to his right. The others followed pouring suppressive fire into the enemy.

Mark laid Tomas down gently in a trio of large boulders, and then joined the firefight.

In the distance, the larger battle ceased. Only an occasional shot was heard—as the rebels dispatched a wounded soldier.

The jungle went silent once again.

"How is our Captain?" Hernandez dropped a magazine and slammed another into the well.

"Ain't good." Mark leaned his M14 against one of the boulders and pulled his headlamp from a cargo pocket.

He adjusted the lamp to its red lens and immediately applied a compression bandage to the Tomas' front and back—securing them with Vetrap.

"Get on the radio. Let your command know…"

"Corporal Gonzales was killed. He carried the comm."

"Well, fuck a damn duck." Mark looked to the sergeant.

"Six others were also killed…There are only nine of us now."

"Position everyone as best you can. Inventory our munitions…Tend to the wounded. They'll be coming…"

From below, a voice called in the darkness, "Tomas…My brother…we met again."

"El Cobra," Hernandez whispered to no one in particular.

"How are you doing? How is your family?" the rebel leader taunted.

"Pass the word. No talking. He's trying to mark our positions," Mark said softly. "Move it. Set the defense."

"Oh...don't be like that. Tell me...how is our mother? And your wife. That Marta...she is a beautiful woman. Too bad she will be a widow soon."

Mark fit a suppressor to Betsy, moved to his left and picked a boulder with a tree trunk leaning on it. He eased the barrel through an opening, rapidly fired 'til his magazine was empty—dropped it and reloaded.

A scream pierced the darkness—one of the rounds had found a target.

"Very clever...You use a silencer. Very clever indeed. Mother always said you were the clever one."

Sergent Hernandez returned and offered a drink of water to Tomas. He glanced over at Zorro. "He will not last long if we stay here."

"None of us will. Send a man over the ridge. Find a back trail."

"This little mountain...very good you choose it. I would have myself as well...Only one problem. The river...It is behind you...And the cliff is very high."

Mark moved back to his friend and checked his pulse.

Tomas opened his eyes. "You must go..."

"Ain't leaving you, amigo."

He gripped Zorro's arm. "You must go...protect my family."

They shared a long look.

"I will give Marta your regards when I see her…and your children," El Cobra continued taunting.

"I am dying, Zorro. Promise me you will…" He coughed up blood. "…you will protect…protect my family."

"We'll get out of here. You can…" He realized his friend was dead.

"I will make Marta my whore…"

"Big talk for one with the dick of a flea!" Mark shouted back.

A long moment passed.

"Zorro? Is that you?"

"I'm coming for you, Cobra. No hole is too deep. I will find you and when I do…I'll castrate you with a dull knife."

"Ha ha ha…you are funny man, Zorro. I am here now. Why not come and cut me now?"

Only silence answered Cobra's question.

"What? You have no words for me?"

Seven grenades fell among the rebels—three of them were Willie Petes. The explosions shook the ground—the noise faded and the smoke slowly cleared.

Cobra called out again, "You missed me."

There was no answer.

"Let us end this. You cannot escape. I will show you mercy. One quick bullet to the head."

Silence.

"The sun will be up soon…I want to see you clearly when I kill you anyway…I wonder…what is Marta doing now?"